[handwritten inscription] T... your support. Hope you enjoy! JE

A NORTHERN GENTLEMAN

A novel by
L. E. Everett

Senior Prospect Productions
New York

ISBN: 0996397701
ISBN 13: 9780996397704
Library of Congress Control Number: 2015910310
Senior Prospect Publishing Co.
New York New York

To those not with us anymore, or yet.

"A good story has five elements: religion, family, sex, money, and mystery."
—Garrison Keillor

I. ATLANTA

CHAPTER ONE

There's a photograph that's kept upstairs in the same wooden box that holds the invitation to Grandmother's wedding and some yellowing stationery that is all but illegible, and an election-year button that used to be blue and bears a name that used to be important. The photograph is black-and-white and there's an inscription on the back of it, in looping longhand, in dark ink. Five words, each character tied together by a dragging pen as their author noted what the photo captured: *Atlanta Southern National Bank, 1890.*

The picture is a portrait, though there's no one in the photograph. There's a desk, but no one sits behind it. There's a window, but no one looks through it. Instead, what must have been the golden light of a low and setting sun streams through the window onto the lonely desk. And somehow, though the sloping curves of human flesh are absent, and in their place only the severe angles of lifeless wood appear, the photograph becomes a portrait none-theless. A portrait that, even without eyes or lips or teeth, captures the stilted smile of capitalism begging the question of the hour: Isn't there something more than *this?*

The desk didn't always sit unmanned, and to glimpse this particular photograph is to witness a ship without its captain. With a broad body of dark wood, the desk was itself both ocean liner and iceberg. It was a vessel on which one could have enjoyed a comfortable cruise up the corporate ladder; yet, simultaneously, it formed a ruinous blockade against all that stood beyond the door. And though its home in the office of the vice president of Atlanta Southern National Bank should have made it a vehicle of transport to the highest ranks of economy and society, to its owner it was a slave ship.

When the desk belonged to Atlanta Southern National Bank's vice president, Drucker May, the desk sat squarely in the middle of an office that was regal in its décor. A green rug lay underfoot, gold cresting marked the line where wall ended and ceiling began, and a garish bronze sculpture of a tufted eagle perched above a second doorway.

In an office quite remarkable for its ornamentation, that second door was perhaps the most notable sign of prosperity. Though the door itself was unembellished, confederate in its colorlessness, its value was inflated greatly by a single fact: it led directly to the bank president's adjoining office, which was twice the depth, thrice the length, and many multiples as lavish as its neighbor. The desk there was no dowdy brunette, but rather a brilliant blonde, painted in gold leaf, and more like a banquet table than a workstation. Next to it, Drucker's mahogany steamship was reduced to tugboat. It was as if the bank's own vault had been emptied and its content melted and molded into the shape of a desk, behind which sat the bank's president, a king on his throne, presiding over business.

Daily, the door that joined the offices would swing open, and the booming voice of the bank's president would rouse Drucker from his daydreams. The accuracy of a clock could be measured against the precisely timed roar that each day at half past one prompted a dozen bankers to rush to the threshold of the ornamented office. Drucker was among the crowd, though he was never the first to arrive, which the president was pained to notice every time.

This daily assembly was brief and usually followed by a demand that some item or other that the president had misplaced be found before the hour was up, inevitably prompting a scramble.

The lengthier congress would follow each day at three. One financier would read aloud from the newspaper. Another would recite notes from a pad—covered in his own scribbles—on the availability of silver or the latest blustering of William Jennings Bryan, at which all in attendance would groan in unison. No matter how little there was to say, the meeting would always manage to drag on for an hour.

For Drucker, the afternoon assembly was a prime opportunity for him to do what he was best at: daydream that he was somewhere else. As his eyes wandered to the windows, his thoughts drifting in the same direction, he would lose himself in a world where the memories he had mingled with the ones he had not yet made, where he could be anyone, do anything, live anyplace. Though he was careful to keep a straight face so as to appear engaged, in his mind he was running, arms flailing, through a meadow of tall grasses, never looking back as the banality of a life spent behind that wooden desk grew smaller and smaller in the distance behind him.

Outside the boardroom's window, the sun shone brightly over Atlanta's verdant Peachtree Street. There was one tree in particular that had the same branch structure as the one Drucker used to climb as a boy, when Atlanta was nursing its burn wounds and the talk of rebuilding, like the lemonade he would gulp on blistering afternoons, was endless. These days it seemed that the only thing *endless* was the daily midafternoon summit, and so Drucker allowed himself to drift back into the comfortable memory of what it felt like to perch in the highest branches of the tree.

⇌⇋

"Drucker!" The voice was sweet but sharp, the last syllable pronounced fully, unlike when his mother called his name, dropping the final 'r'.

"I brought you a glass," called Lucy.

"Just one?" asked Drucker, looking down through a leafy web of foliage below him.

"Yes. And a peach."

"Throw it up here," instructed Drucker. "The peach, not the glass," he added slyly, "I'll have the lemonade when I come down."

Even through layers of leaves and branches he could see her frowning. "Ten minutes," she sighed. "Or I'll climb up there and get you. Your mother wants you to know that dinner is at six, and if you're late, you won't be served."

Drucker reached out his hands, beckoning for her to toss up the peach. Lucy was more than a governess to Drucker. She was an ally and a friend, and he had no doubt that his mother had instructed her not to give him the peach, but she had snuck it to him anyway. "Toss it," he urged. "C'mon, toss it up here."

Toss she did, but the arch of the fruit's trajectory was short of where Drucker could reach, and Lucy threw up her arms, waving him off from the catch. "No, no! You'll fall!" she called up to him as the peach thumped back into her outstretched palms.

"Aw, Lucy," he teased, "I thought you could have thrown it better than that!"

"You *know* I could have thrown better than that."

"Or forgot that you couldn't throw it better than that," he taunted from a dozen feet off the ground.

The playful exchange delighted nine-year-old Drucker, who prided himself on keeping pace with the twenty-six-year-old blonde who had lived upstairs for as long as he could remember. Drucker considered her a best friend, and it had never occurred to him that she felt any different than he, or that the fact that she was paid to look after him was the reason they spent their days together. Though to his mother she was one among a crew of employees who flitted about the property, gardening and cooking and generally serving as directed, to Drucker she more than took the place of the sisters and brothers his parents never gave him, and she lavished on him the attention and affection his parents similarly failed to provide.

A slap on the table ceremoniously ended the meeting. The men rose to their feet and shuffled papers and murmured to one another, their voices blending into a single sustained note. It was not unlike the drone of the meeting itself, which was little more to Drucker than a continuous low-pitched whine.

Back at his desk, Drucker eased into his chair, reclining for a few moments before hearing footsteps approaching his door and, on cue, straightening his spine. He glued his eyes to the front page of the newspaper that lay across his desk. Not a sentence was familiar, though the meeting had been dedicated to hashing through each and every headline.

"Hello, Drucker. I'm sorry to interrupt."

Drucker looked up from his display of feigned diligence. The interruption was, in fact, not an interruption at all, as the scene in which Drucker was consumed by work was no more than a show, performed for the benefit of his one-man audience.

"I just spoke with Hank," continued the bank's president before Drucker could get a word in, "and I'm more than a bit concerned.

Another five accounts have moved over to Georgia Consolidated Bank, and Hank expects the Langdons will move most of their assets by the end of the year. That damn bank hasn't been operating six months, and already we've lost a dozen of Atlanta Southern's…" he hesitated, grasping for the right word.

"Richest sons of—" Drucker tried to offer.

"Beloved patrons," the bank's president cut him off, giving Drucker a stern glance.

Drucker smirked but returned to the question at hand. "Five more accounts," he mused.

"Since March, no less. At this rate we'll be sucked dry in a matter of months," the president replied, gravely.

"Well," said Drucker, feeling apathetic, "I'd say it sounds as if this calls for a detailed discussion in tomorrow's afternoon meeting."

Sarcasm was always lost on the bank's president. "Forget the meeting," said the president, waving a dismissive hand. "This is a project for you."

He looked down at Drucker's desk, which was artfully staged to look like the station of a diligent worker. "You're very busy, I know, but we'll just have to find someone else to take the rest of this." He motioned toward the stacks of financial records and yellowing newspapers on Drucker's desk, all of which had been carefully arranged to look worn out from frequent and heavy use.

Drucker admired the scene he had crafted. "It *is* tiring," he said. This was the truth. He couldn't fight the sedative effect that all things banking had on him, even the relatively exciting prospect of the bank's demise.

"Good then, it's settled," said the president. "You'll be in charge," he added, gaining momentum, "of making sure that Atlanta Southern doesn't see the—suffer from the—well, that we don't…" Momentum halted. He stammered through a long sentence that ultimately went unfinished.

"To be clear," said Drucker, "you're telling me that you'll give all my work to someone else in exchange for me coming up with a plan to stop our accounts from moving to our competitor?" It suddenly occurred to him that this was a disadvantageous trade. He had made a practice of doing practically nothing all day, and suddenly here he was being asked to barter it away for a nearly impossible task.

The president nodded. "Precisely. This will look quite good for the board review, too." It was widely known that the president intended to step down by year's end, and the board would soon be appointing his replacement. Despite Drucker's lackluster performance at every element of his job, the president threw the full weight of his portly existence behind the naming of Drucker as his successor.

"Or, I suppose, it could look quite bad for the board review. That is, if Georgia Consolidated continues to steal our customers," Drucker replied evenly.

The president cringed deeply. "It could, yes, if you fail. But if you fail, I suppose we all shall. And if there is no bank for me to preside over, there will be no bank for you to preside over."

A glum thought, but for some reason it delighted Drucker. "Well, when you put it that way," said Drucker, "you give me no choice."

Another glum thought, but for some reason it delighted the president. "Good, then it's settled. I'll tell Hank. I'll tell him I've put you in charge, and that Atlanta Southern is in good hands." He paused to consider his last statement and then added without humor, "It's sink or swim now, Drucker, but you'll keep us afloat. Won't you?"

"Yes," said Drucker quietly. "Of course, I will, Father."

CHAPTER TWO

Silence filled the room much like the president had filled the threshold to Drucker's office. Completely and ominously the noiselessness stretched from one side of the room to the other.

"Drucker May," whispered Drucker to himself, his words piercing the quiet. "Why yes, I *did* save Atlanta Southern from going under." He shook his head. It didn't sound right.

He tried again. "Drucker May, *president* of Atlanta Southern National Bank. Pleasure to meet you." He extended his hand, though no one was there to shake it. His shoulders slumped. It didn't fit.

"Drucker May." He paused. That much was right. But what came next? If not *banker*, what? For all his doodling mindlessly in meetings, he was no artist, and if the director of the church choir was any judge of talent, he was no vocalist, either. "Drucker May, Fulton County sheriff. Drucker May, newspaperman. Hello, I'm Drucker May, I own Harper's Saloon down on Mulberry Street."

He repeated his name until it lost all meaning, each time casting himself as a new character, each identity linked to the one that preceded it, and to himself, only by name. By the time that he ran out of breath, he had exhausted not only himself but also a list of professions that ran the gambit from sailor to sorcerer.

Drucker found something titillating in the quick succession of identities, though. The fluid, ludicrous introductions were so full of possibilities that he couldn't help but feel as if he was bursting with potential until he was hit by another thought. A rush of sadness coursed through him when he considered the disappointing reality that he could never be all of those things and most likely would never be any of them.

On the third day after the inglorious coronation of Drucker as strategist in chief, father returned to ominously fill the doorway of son's office once again.

"Hello, Drucker."

It was the usual greeting, but Drucker didn't match it with his routine display of surprise and forged diligence, his showmanship crumpling under the weight of the crown.

"Have you been able to put anything down on paper?"

"I have," said Drucker, glancing down at a pageful of scribbles that fortunately was angled out of his visitor's view. For as long as he could remember he had been unable to lie, and in this instance it was the truth to say that he had put *something* down on paper.

Hank, a wiry, bespectacled banker, stood dutifully behind the president, his thin frame all but blocked completely from Drucker's sight by the sheer size of the bank's president, who plugged up the doorway like a cork.

"So you'll be ready to present to the board tomorrow?" asked Hank, eager to expose what he assumed was a grand lie on Drucker's part. A smile snaked across his face.

"No," said the president, craning his neck to address Hank, who was cast as his evening shadow, long and thin behind him. "Tomorrow's the Fourth of July. We'll be out for the holiday."

Drucker couldn't tell if his father was trying to save him or draw out his misery.

"He'll present to us a week from tomorrow at the quarterly review," the president declared without consulting Drucker, who nodded in agreement as if this were the plan that had long been agreed on.

"Oh," said Hank, masking his disappointment in pleasure, "that's wonderful. Drucker, I look forward to hearing what you've come up with. I'm sure it's"—he paused for effect—"quite clever." The combination of spittle and grimace punctuating his sentence made it clear that the only thing Hank considered clever was the elaborate hoax he believed Drucker had dreamed up in pursuit of the adjoining office.

Drucker pursed his lips and looked down, deciding it was time to reprise his celebrated role as Drucker-hard-at-work. Without further conversation, the two men disappeared down the hall, leaving Drucker alone with nothing but a pageful of scribbles and eight days to turn them into something brilliant. *If only I had been charged instead with the relatively simple task of turning water into wine,* he lamented.

The midsummer holiday came and went, the hours of freedom escaping out from underneath Drucker. He wished desperately to stop time, to control the flow of seconds and minutes, to slow their passing in the idle hours of Fourth of July picnics, pleasure. There was more to his desire to slow the ticking of the clock than the pursuit of amusement, though. If he could halt time, as Drucker found himself trying to, he could delay the inevitable moment when he would stand in front of the bank's board and admit failure.

No matter how hard he wished, though, Drucker found that the holiday passed all too quickly, and before he knew it he was back at his desk with just a few days standing between him and the fateful board meeting. Because he couldn't stop time, instead he wasted it, fruitlessly scribbling and sketching his way through the week, feeling time slip away as uncontrollably as a river current, carrying him along with it.

Four days after his last visit, Hank once again appeared in the doorway to Drucker's office. This time he was alone. "Hard at work?" He sneered. "Or hardly working?"

"I could ask the same of you, Hank. I've seen you walk past here at least six times today. Either you've forgotten where your desk is, or you intended to ask me that half a dozen times and lost your nerve each one of them."

Hank was unmoved by the affront. "Hardly working it is." He laughed without smiling, a feat he had perfected in the years he had spent working alongside the spoiled son of the bank's president, who occupied a seat that, though repellant to Drucker, was enviable to everyone but him.

"Frankly, I don't see why you even bother pretending," continued Hank. "You could hand in one of your pathetic little sketches, and *he*"—he cocked his head, gesturing toward the president's office—"would frame it and hang it on his wall."

Drucker winced, flushing pink with self-consciousness. No one had ever said anything about his distraction at the office. That is, at least not to his face.

What they said behind his back, on the other hand, Drucker could only guess. Ever since he had begun working at the bank seven years earlier at the age of eighteen, Drucker had always been aware of the gentle undertow of jealousies nipping at his ankles. Recently, though, it seemed that ill will had intensified, and the bank's stale air was starting to stink of resentment toward the indifferent heir to the president's office.

Yet it wasn't the envy or bitterness or even the hostility that bothered Drucker. It was the fact that everyone seemed to be noticing his apathy except for the one person that it should actually offend. If it was so obvious that Drucker had mentally resigned, why couldn't his father seem to notice? What more would it take to be fired or, at the very least, not promoted to president? Looking toward the doorway, seeing the tall, thin watchtower of a man who stood menacingly on the threshold, Drucker felt certain that if anyone had an answer, it would be Hank.

Hank leaned against the doorframe, his eyes fixed on Drucker. His neatly clipped mustache was—much like the rest of his body— narrow, dark, serpentine.

"I'm not sure if that's a critique of *my* artistic skills or *his* judgment for artistic talent," replied Drucker.

"His judgment of talent," countered Hank without missing a beat. "Artistic and otherwise."

Their eyes locked, and for a moment neither spoke. It was a stalemate, since Hank had the rhetorical skill, but Drucker, thanks to a lucky lineage, would always have the upper hand.

"Yes, well," said Drucker, shuffling through the stack of papers in front of him, "I suppose I should get back to it." He added quickly, "The planning, not the sketching." He gave a wink, but not a smile.

"Of course," said Hank, who could always be counted on to sidle up to, but not cross, certain boundaries. He would not enter Drucker's office without invitation but would perch smugly on the threshold of it. In the same vein, when asked to leave, he would do so obligingly, even if his arrival in the first place was unwelcomed.

As Hank turned to go, he hesitated, stalled by an afterthought. "You do know that you're wasting your time though, don't you, Drucker?"

"I know that *you're* wasting my time," Drucker said softly, without looking up.

Hank heard it and turned back to face Drucker. "Really," he said, lowering his voice. He looked over each shoulder. "That board meeting makes no difference. Your father will convince them to vote you in whether you present them with the plan of the century or show up in blackface quoting Lincoln."

"That's what *you* think, but it's not true," protested Drucker, wondering if it might actually be.

"It is, though," insisted Hank. "It's a waiting game now, that's all. By the time the year is out, your father will have installed you comfortably in his throne, and you'll have everything you've ever wanted."

The hard stop on the word *wanted* surprised Drucker, as if Hank had hit the wrong note in a familiar song. The discordant melody of Hank's argument reminded Drucker of a fact he often forgot: everyone around him envied the fate he was about to be handed, and they all assumed he wanted it, too. After all, who would refuse an easy ascent to the highest post in the bank and what was practically the guarantee of a lifetime of wealth and status to rival, if not far surpass, that which his father had known?

Only someone who's bored out of his skull, thought Drucker miserably. And even then, he acknowledged, most people would gladly take mind-numbing tedium if it came with the salary associated with the top post. For anyone who had ever lived without the privileges of wealth, a chance at it surely would be enough to compensate for lack of interest in the work. But Drucker was different; Drucker had never known any other way.

All his life, Drucker had been the beneficiary of his father's tenure in the president's office at Atlanta Southern. As a child, the comforts of his father's station were too complex for him to comprehend completely, but they could be translated into a boy's language: toys the other children didn't own, rooms his friends' homes didn't have. Even his friends who lived in the big plantation estates, who a generation earlier would have had every luxury in the world at their disposal, were aware of the things that Drucker had that they did not. Like his mother's kitchen, always full of food and servants, even in the years when the South's economy slumped after its backbone of slave labor had been crushed.

Then, of course, there were the lavish dinner parties his parents threw, when the house would be filled with harp music, ladies in colorful, full-skirted dresses, and the smell of quail roasting to golden-brown perfection.

"I like the pink dress best," said Lucy, crouching next to Drucker, both of them peering down from the second-story landing. Below them waltzed a dozen couples, spinning in perfect harmony with the bouncy rhythm produced by a handsome string quartet.

"You always like the pink dresses best," noted Drucker, dressed in his uniform for party-night spying sessions: blue cotton pajamas.

Lucy always let him stay up well past his eight o'clock bedtime on nights when the house was filled with dancing. Drucker had initially thought that perhaps this was his mother's wish—a way to include him in the evening's festivities—but the more he grew to know his mother, the more he suspected Lucy just wanted someone to watch with.

Lucy sighed. "It's true. They're all so beautiful, though. Look at that one." She pointed down at a vibrant-green dress. "I never saw parties like this in Boston. They're so thoroughly..." She paused to find the right word, a word Drucker would understand.

"Southern," she finally came up with and then added, "it's like going back in time."

"Back in time?" asked Drucker. "To when?"

"Before the war."

"Oh," said Drucker. "I wasn't even born yet."

Lucy smiled and put an arm around his shoulder. "I know that." She conferred a prolonged and tender smile on Drucker, who felt warm and safe in its glow. "You were born in 1865, the year the war ended."

"November twenty-fifth," said Drucker proudly.

"Yes, and that was the year that I came here to Atlanta."

"To live with us and look after me," said Drucker, again proudly.

"Well, yes," said Lucy, running her fingers fondly, maternally, through Drucker's blond curls, "but first I was a teacher. I've told you that before, haven't I?"

Drucker ignored the question, already busy formulating his own. "They don't have schools in Boston, Luce?"

Lucy looked at him blankly. "Of course they do."

"So why did you move to Atlanta, then? If there were schools in Boston, I mean."

Below them, the song drew to a close, and the muffled sound of polite applause signaled a break between dances.

"Well," she said slowly, still twisting his curls. "After the war ended, a man started coming to our church every Sunday. He used to stand right outside the doors to the church, handing out these little books and talking about how the South had been destroyed by the war—horribly destroyed. He kept saying that if we ever wanted the United States to be whole again, we'd have to mend where it was broken. Most Sundays I just passed him right by, never took a book from him, or even looked him in the eye. But then one day as I was filing out of the chapel with my sisters"—Lucy grabbed Drucker's arm, reenacting the scene—"he took my arm, sort of hard, like this, and he looked me straight in the eye and whispered in my ear, 'Be odd.'"

"Be odd?" repeated Drucker.

"You know, be different, don't just file out of here like the rest of them. So I took a book. And I told myself I wouldn't read it, I'd just put it away, and he'd leave me alone, but that night—I don't know why, but I opened it up, and I started reading, and before I knew it I'd stayed up all night without ever putting it down. There was a story about this little girl, who lived alone with her mama after her daddy died in the war, and her school was burned down, and most of the teachers in the whole county left town after the fires, and I just—I wanted to help her. To help rebuild the whole South, but not just put the buildings back the way they were, but build the cities back to what they used to be like." Her fingers moved from his hair to his cheek, which was beginning to flush with drowsiness. "Except better," she added, quietly.

Drucker considered the images for a moment. "Were you a teacher when you lived in Boston?"

"No. That's another reason I left," said Lucy softly. "I worked in a factory, sewing fabrics. You know, cloth." Lucy's fingers lightly touched the cotton pajamas, a royal shade of blue. "We would sew all day and sometimes most of the night, cramped together in these dark little rooms." Lucy paused to assess Drucker's expression, to judge if her words were too harsh for the nine-year-old. "My family needed the money, so I didn't have much of a choice, you see. That book, though, that little book said that in the South they needed so many teachers and nurses and..." She looked off into the distance, letting her voice trail off for a moment before finishing. "I knew that if I went south I would never have to work in a factory like that again."

"No wonder you moved to Atlanta," said Drucker. "It's nothing like that here. I've been to Father's office, and it's never dark or cramped or cold at all. His office is as big as"—he gestured over

the railing at the expansive gallery turned dance floor below—
"all that." He expected Lucy to nod in agreement, but instead she
cringed, and her smile dimmed.

She patted his smooth, youthful cheek. "Drucker, darling, most
people in Atlanta don't have a life like this." She motioned upward
to the high ceilings with their intricately carved moldings and down
to the floor below where the dancing had started up again. "That
big office of your father's is in a bank, not a mill, and because he's
the president there, your life isn't like most other people's."

Drucker looked down at the twirling ladies. Were they who
Lucy meant by "other people"?

"Most people," Lucy continued, her tone soft but serious, "work
all day long just to make enough money to have food for their
families. And sometimes the conditions are so bad that they end
up just getting sick or worked to death. So they're working just to
live, but really they're working just to die. Do you understand what
I'm saying, Drucker?" Drucker nodded slowly, eyes growing heavy
with sleep.

As she had tucked him into his bed that night, Lucy had kissed
his forehead and whispered, "Things will always be different for
you, Drucker. Because of your daddy, things will always be different for you."

And it was that very turn of phrase that had echoed over and
over again throughout Drucker's life. First on the lips of Lucy, then
later, in his teenage years, his classmates had picked up on the
sentiment, phrasing it in their own, harsher way. Now here stood
Hank, spouting what to any other man would have sounded like
nothing more than the sour song of jealousy. To Drucker, though,
it sounded like that same refrain he had heard all of his life. As he
looked up at Hank standing in his doorway, singing that same old
song, Drucker realized how sick he was of hearing it.

That was when it dawned on him that perhaps it was finally *his*
turn to "be odd."

CHAPTER THREE

Halfway through the week that he had been given to think of a way to save Atlanta Southern National Bank from a swift and ugly collapse, Drucker found himself with nothing to show for his efforts but a pageful of scribbles and a pounding headache.

In those moments when he wasn't battling the throbbing at his temples, he did his best not to yield to Hank's menacing voice in his head: *Frankly, I don't see why you even bother pretending…That board meeting makes no difference…Your father will convince them to vote you in.*

Every time Drucker felt himself getting close to coming up with some sort of plan for the bank, those words would begin to ring in his ears, distracting him. He heard them again as he stood next to his desk, gazing out at the sunny summer afternoon on the other side of the window, feeling guilty that his efforts thus far had been fruitless but also wondering if perhaps there wasn't a part of him that *wanted* to fail at this task he had been given.

After all, if he were to be struck by a miraculous idea, he could save face in front of the board. But then what? A good showing in that meeting would only add fuel to the fire of his father's already heated desire to install Drucker in his post. On the other hand, if Drucker were to show up at the board meeting empty-handed and unprepared, he would certainly embarrass both himself and his father. But might a mediocre performance in front of the board actually be to his advantage? It would certainly tarnish his image. Perhaps in just the right way.

A disappointing show at the board meeting could heap a little extra dirt onto his already soiled reputation, and it could be just enough to prevent the board from endorsing the president's proposal of Drucker as his successor.

The thought intrigued him, but Drucker couldn't bring himself to give up entirely just yet. The family name was among a small and dwindling list of things that he and his father shared. To sully his own name would be to drag his father's down in the dirt, too, and he couldn't bring himself to do that to his father.

He couldn't deny that a part of him very much wanted to, though, and the guilt of knowing it gave Drucker a suffocating itch in his lungs. He felt the desperate need for fresh air, and so very quietly, to avoid catching anyone's attention, he snuck out of the building.

The July day was warm and drier than usual, with a light breeze that smelled alive compared to the musty air inside the bank. Drucker walked to the base of the tree that he had so often gazed at through the window. He reached out and touched the bark and was surprised to find that it was rough, that it was real.

In his mind, the tree had become a symbol of all that was outside the bank, and therefore, off-limits to him. He'd spent hours, days even, staring out the window at the tree, thinking of how that thin pane of glass made the tree seem so far away. Plucking a leaf from a low-hanging branch, Drucker considered that it wasn't the fact that the tree was real that was so remarkable, but rather how easy it had been to touch. All he had done was get up from his desk, walk outside, and there it was, waiting for him.

Drucker lowered himself to the ground, where he sat leaning against the tree, careful to shield himself with its wide trunk so that no one inside the building could see him. It felt right, to be outside in the fresh air, with his back facing the bank. A lifetime—a life—could be sucked away in that office, and his *would be* if he didn't walk away.

If he wasn't fired after the board meeting, Drucker decided, he would have to quit. But why stop there? If he could leave Atlanta Southern, he might as well leave Atlanta altogether. He could go north, perhaps to Boston. He had been fifteen when Lucy's mother died; she had moved back to Boston to be with her sisters. Fifteen was too old for a governess, his mother had declared, and so Lucy had been replaced neither in Drucker's home nor in his heart.

For the first time in quite a while, Drucker felt a rush of excitement course through his veins. In Atlanta, everyone knew him even before they met him. Whether he worked at Atlanta Southern National Bank or not, he would be known as his father's son.

If he were to go to Boston, though, there he could be anybody. He could be the son of a banker as easily as he could be the son of a farmer—if they had farmers in Boston. He'd have to check. Maybe he would say that his father had died on a whaling ship and left Drucker and his mother with nothing. Or maybe he would say that he was a descendant of one of those men who had poured tea into the harbor or signed the Constitution.

Yes, Boston would be the perfect place. He even had the accent down perfectly after years of spending so much time with Lucy. As a child he'd taken special notice of the way words tripped off her tongue a little faster, the way she hit consonants a little harder than the native-born Southern ladies he knew. Often during their long afternoons together he would switch into his Northern accent, changing the pace and style of his speech, as if he were speaking another language. At first Lucy had laughed, but then she became like the teacher she once had been, gently correcting him when he lapsed for a moment.

"We say 'get', not 'git,'" she'd say. "Rhymes with 'bet.'" And Drucker would repeat after her, quickly picking up on the distinctly Northern vernacular.

⟞⟝⟞⟝

The happy yelps of children chasing one another down Peachtree Street snapped Drucker back to the present moment. *Two hours must have passed*, he thought as he pushed off the ground and rose to his feet. He walked back toward the bank, which looked different somehow, now that he was taking it in with the eyes of a man who knew he would soon be leaving it.

As he paced slowly down the hallway back to his office, he felt the sturdy clap of a hand on his shoulder. Drucker turned to see his father, with Hank trailing behind him like a faithful Labrador.

"There you are," said the bank's president. "I've been looking for you, but you weren't in your office."

"I stepped outside," said Drucker.

"Oh?" asked the president, a bit surprised. "And what were you doing out there?"

"I was just doing some thinking," answered Drucker, not untruthfully.

The president brightened. "That's my boy!" He beamed. "My best business ideas always congeal when I'm taking a walk. So you've come up with a plan, then?"

"There are still some details to attend to," said Drucker, thinking of his recently hatched plan to leave Atlanta.

"By all means, attend to the details!" roared the president with excitement. He took a step closer to Drucker, his nose twitching as he examined his son's face. "By God, you're close, Drucker. I can sense it. I can always smell a good idea and"—he turned his head and sniffed the air—"it sure does smell like you've got something juicy cooking!"

Drucker smiled meekly. "I do think I may be on to something," he said, again not untruthfully.

The president, smiling heartily, patted Drucker on the back. "You remind me of myself, Drucker," he said happily, eyeing Drucker's well-kempt blond hair and manly jaw. "Though more handsome than I ever was, I must admit." He cleared his throat and averted his eyes from his son's charming dimples. "At any rate, if anyone can get us out of this, you can, Drucker."

Drucker tried to protest, but the president was already waddling proudly down the hall, forgetting about Hank, who hung back with Drucker.

"So what were you really doing out there?" asked Hank, nudging Drucker in the ribs as soon as the president was out of earshot.

"Thinking," repeated Drucker earnestly.

"About?" Hank sneered.

"Trees," said Drucker. "I was thinking about what happens to them when they die."

"Fascinating," scoffed Hank. "Not exactly the stuff plans to save a bank are made of, though." He raised his right eyebrow high with skepticism. "Come to any groundbreaking conclusions?"

"Yes," said Drucker. "They become desks."

CHAPTER FOUR

Six men greeted Drucker with handshakes and hellos when he entered the boardroom, and Drucker smiled as he returned their greetings. Though he had given up on trying to think of a plan that could save Atlanta Southern from going under, he had done so in good spirits. Rather than pushing the task away in despair, after his trip to the tree trunk he had simply released it, allowing it to float away from him like a bubble. In its place he took hold of and clung to the happy thought that soon the drudgery of life at the bank, including this particularly arduous task, would all just be a distant memory.

Instead of slaving to complete his assignment, Drucker had managed to spend the better part of his last week at the bank in a state of relaxation, interrupted only when he would pick up his pencil, massage his forehead, and put on a show of great mental exertion when the occasional audience appeared at his door.

Unfortunately, that state of blissful repose had only lasted until noon on the day before the board meeting, when a hazy cloud of guilt had descended over Drucker. Then he began to picture himself in the board meeting, standing there with nothing to offer but a shrug of the shoulders.

How disappointed his father would be then, how flushed and contorted his father's face would grow. Just to think of it knotted Drucker's stomach. Yes, he had wished his father would notice his apathy, but not because he wanted to hurt him. It wasn't proof of his father's pain that he was after. He just wanted some acknowledgment from his father, some recognition of Drucker's unhappiness at the bank. Something to show that father realized son wanted to be somewhere else, should be somewhere else, could be somewhere else.

But there never had been and never would be any such indication, and Drucker knew that his father would be crushed if he showed up at the board meeting completely unprepared. Yes, his father was the reason for his employment in the bank and therefore the cause of Drucker's misery, but he was also the provider of Drucker's twenty-five years of undeniably privileged life. What gratitude for that life of great comfort and security would it show if Drucker marched into a meeting of his father's colleagues and confessed to being a fraud and a failure, and a lazy one, at that?

No, Drucker couldn't stand to hurt his father so brazenly. For his father's sake, he would have to impress the board just enough to save face.

Though just *how* exactly, he didn't know.

Drucker shook the six pale-skinned hands extended to him and took his seat at one end of a long mahogany office table that was too big for the party of seven that surrounded it. Three men sat on each side of the table's far end, leaving eight seats on each side between Drucker and the board members seated closest to him. At the opposite end of the table from Drucker, the chair at the head of the table sat empty.

Feeling his skin turn to gooseflesh under his collar, Drucker told himself that in the hour and a half that was about to unfold, he had no choice but to give the greatest performance of his life. All those displays of feigned engagement in his work that he had perfected over the years—they were backwoods theater compared to the momentous performance that this afternoon would require.

Drucker surveyed the six members of his audience. Each had unwittingly gained admission to what Drucker was already imagining would someday be remembered as quite possibly one of the most magnificent, if improvised, acts of theater in modern memory.

His eyes darted from one man to the next. They looked nearly identical, each of them impeccably dressed in a three-piece suit that was some shade of gray or brown wool, an unfortunate uniform on a July day, but one that was nevertheless worn dutifully and rarely complained about. Five of them were crowned with perfectly coiffed heads of silvery hair, which made them all, save for the one bald head in the bunch, look quite stately to Drucker's eye.

At that moment, a second door to the boardroom opened, and through it lumbered the bank's president. The board members stood to greet him, and Drucker, not wanting to appear rude, mimicked the gesture, though a moment too late, arriving on his feet just as the others returned to their seats.

The president sidled up to his chair at the far end of the table and smiled at Drucker, the only man left standing. Drucker smiled weakly in return. There was pride and excitement in his father's eyes. It was a look, Drucker had come to understand, that was usually reserved for moments when father looked at son as a man into a mirror, preening and pleased with the reflection.

"Please be seated, Drucker," said the president. Failing to gently position his own ample rear end into his seat, he landed forcefully with a loud thump.

"Thank you," said Drucker, and then to himself silently added, *And the curtain rises.* He nodded at his father, who in turn gave him a wink. There was so much more separating them than a too-long mahogany table, a fact his father had tried for so many years to overlook.

"Gentlemen," said the president, "thank you for joining me at the quarterly assembly of the board of trustees of the Atlanta Southern National Bank on this"—he consulted his notes—"the eleventh day of July, in the year eighteen hundred and ninety."

Drucker winced at the formality of the language, a custom that he knew his father relished.

"We will begin today's meeting with a discussion of what can be done to bolster the health and well-being of our esteemed financial institution. To lead this discussion we have Vice President Drucker May who is, of course, a relation of mine, but nevertheless quite an intelligent, hardworking—not to mention good-looking—young man."

The president, grinning, paused for effect, and the members of the board supplied the polite chuckles he expected of them. "And after that we will review the financial statements from the second quarter." He squinted down at his own handwriting in front of him, trying to make out a hastily scrawled word. "After that we will discuss the upcoming nominations for my successor. And after that we'll open the discussion to any other miscellaneous orders of business."

"And *after that* I'll need a stiff drink!" declared one of the silver-haired board members, inciting another round of chuckles.

The president looked unamused. "Gentlemen," he chided, "let's focus our attentions now and welcome Drucker to our meeting. Drucker has assured me that he has come up with quite the plan to strengthen Atlanta Southern against the"—he grasped for the right turn of phrase—"pressures exerted upon us by the competition. And I assure *you*, that when Drucker assures *me* that he has come up with something, well, I'm sure you all are as intrigued as I am to hear the plan he has come up with."

The president stopped just short of assuring anything in particular to anyone in particular, leaving the board members to exchange puzzled glances and Drucker to wonder when in the past he had ever assured his father that he had come up with anything.

Smiling proudly at his son, the president concluded, "I now turn this meeting over to Drucker."

With that, Drucker could feel all eyes turn toward him. *How to begin?* His mind raced around in circles, trying to remember if he'd thought up an opening line. He was just about to open his mouth when the words "So, Drucker, won't you begin by outlining for us the basics of your plan?" came out of somebody else's.

Drucker looked up at the panel of inquisitors. At the other end of the table, his father could hardly contain his foolish pride. He was so pleased to see Drucker finally taking his place in the front of the boardroom that his mouth was pulled tight by a smile as oversized as the table in front of him.

In contrast to his father's giddy joy, the three men on Drucker's left were staring in silence, and two of the men on his right were staring similarly, pencils gripped firmly. The third man on his right, the one who had asked the question, looked poised to ask another, prompting Drucker to speak quickly lest the next question be more specific.

"I'd be happy to," said Drucker. "First of all, thank you so much for allowing me to join your distinguished group today." Drucker had always considered flattery an effective way to kill time. He wondered if he could somehow drag out this one obsequious sentence for an hour and half. "As an employee of this bank I have always admired the guidance that you have provided for Atlanta Southern, and…"

His father was motioning to him, raising his palms in subtle jerks toward the ceiling. *Stand up, stand up,* he was mouthing with a flicker of excitement in his eyes, and though he had not attracted the attention of any of the other six men, Drucker felt the warm flush of embarrassment rushing to his cheeks, as if his father had shown up uninvited to conduct him at one of his childhood piano recitals.

"And," continued Drucker, rolling his eyes but rising to his feet, "I hope that the plan that I have prepared"—*ha*—"for you today does not"—*embarrass that poor grinning idiot of a father I have/ make you all want to kill me/fail to materialize in the next thirty seconds*— "disappoint you."

"I'll second that," cut in one of the silver-haired board members.

"Here, here!" chimed another merrily.

The audience appeared to be in better spirits than Drucker had expected. *Perhaps this won't be as ugly as I had dreaded,* he thought for a moment. Then again, Drucker remembered, he was only ten seconds away from proposing an idea that he had not yet thought of.

Drucker opened his mouth to speak but before he could get a word out another man cut in. "Let's have it, Drucker."

The interruption bought Drucker a mere two seconds, but he used them to their full advantage by looking quickly to his father, who was gazing dreamily at the wall, where the portraits of the bank's first three presidents hung in order of their succession. In another few months, his own likeness would be added to the collection. By the wistful look on his fleshy pink face, it was quite obvious that the president was pleasantly lost in a daydream of what that framed work would look like, and how Drucker's portrait, which would someday hang to the right of it, would offset it nicely.

No, thought Drucker, *my picture will not hang there. Not at the expense of wasting my life here.* Though he hated to disappoint his father, Drucker knew that in order to spend eternity hanging on the wall of Atlanta Southern, he would have to suffer what would feel like an eternity trapped inside the walls of Atlanta Southern.

Drucker raised his arms toward the men as if to thank them for their contributions, but to coax them back to silence. "Esteemed members of the board, the plan that I bring to you today is," began Drucker, glancing once more at his father, who was still admiring the trio of portraits, "three pronged."

All seven attendees smiled with approval as Drucker realized that he had quickly made the leap from needing one plan to needing three plans, all while having zero plans. A disadvantageous equation, certainly.

"The boy's an overachiever," whispered the bank's president, loudly and to no one in particular. The men around him responded with murmurs of assent.

"A three-pronged plan? How interesting!" exclaimed the man to the president's left, Edgar Jameson.

"Yes, well, a plan in three parts," said Drucker, thinking that perhaps breaking it up could at least spread around the ugly truth that he had no plan, the way spreading a clump of uneaten vegetables around one's plate made them look attended to, even if they were not eaten. "Part one," Drucker announced, "addresses the competition."

"Georgia Consolidated," offered the man to the president's right, William Hatch.

"That's right," said Drucker. "We mustn't ignore them. Instead, we must counteract their aggressive plays."

This assertion surprised Drucker as he heard himself say it, and it made him wish he could recall what those aggressive plays were. He would need some help remembering, but he had an idea where to get it.

"We know our customers are moving their accounts to Georgia Consolidated. And why are they doing so?" continued Drucker, careful to state the question to sound rhetorical, since nothing could incite a know-it-all to speak quite like a question he is not invited to answer.

As if on cue, William Hatch piped up again. "Why, they're offering fifteen percent returns on assets! Unheard of rates, like no other bank in the country is offering. Frankly, I'm tempted to move my money there myself."

The rest of the group glared at Hatch, but Drucker was delighted. Not only had Hatch provided Drucker with the answer, he had given him an idea.

"Precisely," said Drucker. "I couldn't have put it better myself."

William Hatch looked pleased, and Drucker continued. "So we must offer returns that are even higher still. Twenty percent. We'll have all of Atlanta clamoring to sign up for an account, and Georgia Consolidated will never be able to beat our rates because…"

"But how?" cut in Archibald Sanford, a thin man with thick shocks of silvery hair covering both head and lip. "How can we ever offer twenty percent? Today we offer three and a quarter, and it's nearly breaking our backs to offer *that*. Anything additional would—"

"You make an excellent point, Mr. Sanford, but you haven't let me finish," said Drucker. "You see, today we are able to offer returns to our customers based on the returns on our own investments in the stock markets, the railroads, our real estate ventures, and so on. But what I am suggesting is that we, shall we say, experiment with a new method of procuring dividends."

Drucker took a deep breath. He couldn't be sure how the idea he had churning would be received. "All we have to do is pay out the monthly accrual on the older accounts with the investments we get from our newer clients, rather than the profits from our investments. It will be as if we are investing in, well, our own bank, and the more we advertise our twenty percent interest rates, the more accounts we'll attract, and the more we can pay the customers who came before them."

"That's—" started Archibald Sanford.

"Neither moral nor legal," stated William Hatch flatly.

"Interesting!" exclaimed Edgar Jameson at exactly the same moment.

"Not possible," Hatch cut in again, shaking his head.

"Let him finish," urged the president. "Go on, Drucker."

"I'm not suggesting that we lie about anything," said Drucker, picking up momentum. "We don't need to tell our customers what we are investing in, and I'll be damned if it ever occurs to them to ask. Who, after all, would question twenty percent return rates on their assets? Did the Israelites, seeing manna falling from the heavens, question why it was falling, and how?"

This time, no one attempted to offer an answer, and Drucker didn't need one.

"Of course they didn't." He mimed the frantic collection of food falling from above. "They put out their arms and feasted."

There was a long pause then, and Drucker looked from one man to the next, trying to assess their degree of horror at what he knew full well was, as William Hatch had stated, if not entirely illegal, certainly immoral. But to Drucker's great surprise, the faces in front of him were not contorted in revulsion but rather were expressing a sort of careful curiosity.

"I'll say it again," Edgar Jameson offered, after a prolonged silence. "I think it's interesting."

"It's something to think about," said Archibald Sanford. "That is, if we can be sure that we have enough cash on hand to pay out." Sanford went on, and the others joined him, listing the details that would need to be taken care of, scribbling down notes excitedly. Their words faded into background noise for Drucker. What a relief that somehow, miraculously, he had not only come up with something to say, but he had found words that fit together, that made sense, that convinced and excited the others. And in just a few hours he would be on that train to Boston, finally free.

As the men continued to hash out the details, Drucker, still standing at the front of the boardroom, felt transported completely. He pictured himself on the train to Boston, alone with a copy of that newest Mark Twain book—the one about the Connecticut Yankee who meets King Arthur—that he'd been wanting to read. He could picture how he would walk down the aisle of the passenger car and find an unoccupied seat next to a lovely young lady who would blush when he asked, "Is this seat taken?" and blush even deeper when, now sitting beside her, he asked the young beauty her name.

Drucker had never before been quite so excited by the thought of a tomorrow. Then again, a tomorrow had never before promised to be a day when he and a Connecticut Yankee and a charming young lady could ride off into infinite tomorrows, their whole lives laid out ahead of them like a hundred miles of railroad track.

"Drucker, are you all right?" asked his father from across the room.

Drucker snapped back to the reality of the boardroom, where he saw that the men had composed themselves and were waiting quietly, like eager schoolchildren whose teacher was about to declare the school day finished.

"Yes, of course," said Drucker. "I'm perfectly fine." He tried to shake off the daydream but felt still entranced by it.

"Well then, please, by all means, proceed," said his father.

"Proceed?" Drucker repeated, not sure where in the conversation he had left them and boarded that train.

"With part two. Of the plan. There are three parts," his father reminded him, "of which you've presented one."

Damn, thought Drucker. *Did I say three parts? Damn, Damn. Damn.*

Struggling to free himself from the glossy pleasure of his daydream, Drucker made an effort to remember where he had left off, but he was consumed by a hazy vision of railroad ties, the sweet scent of a stranger's perfume and the rhythmic chug of the iron horse's mighty engine.

"Ah, of course. Part two," said Drucker. "Part two has to do with…" He groped, but he could latch onto no words, no ideas, no financial wizardry. There was only the vision of the train *chugga-chugging* through his head. He could feel the seconds passing as he tried to will the thought to leave, but it wouldn't. It had stalled.

"Part two has to do with…" Archibald Sanford repeated, growing impatient.

There was no choice but to answer now. A full minute had elapsed. If he waited any longer they would begin to suspect there was no part two, that there never had been. He needed to say something, but his heart was pounding with the rhythm of the train's chugging, and all he could see was miles and miles of track.

"The railroads," said Drucker, because he could think of nothing else. "Part two is about the railroads."

"We already invest in the railroads," Archibald Sanford said flatly. "We practically own half of the Atlanta and Florida line."

"Why, if we invest any more money in that godforsaken industry, we'll have to rename ourselves Atlanta Southern National Railroad," said William Hatch, shaking his head.

"I heard the government has approved a loan to the Cleveland and Pittsburgh," offered the mousy Melville Kratch, speaking for the first time. "That scoundrel Jay Gould must be paying off half the Congress."

"I'm not surprised," replied William Hatch, glad to engage in his favorite subject, the identification of all things below himself in the grand hierarchy of moral standing. "Everyone knows he's a crook."

"Men, please, we're veering off point," urged the president, hushing the men and unwittingly affording Drucker just the time he needed to regain composure.

"Gentlemen, you're right as always, but once again, you haven't let me finish," said Drucker. "As you've just said, if we invest another dollar in them, we'll cease to be a bank so much as a railroad holding company. But I'm not suggesting that we invest any more in the railroads. In fact, I'm saying just the opposite. The railroads are old news, gentlemen, a thing of the past, an investment straight out of the seventies, a symbol of yesterday." As he spoke each word he heard himself betraying that glorious image in his mind, which was for him very much a symbol of tomorrow. "No, I'm not saying that we pour more money into the railroads, those"—*lovely, wonderful, freeing*—"dreadful, old, corrupt railroads. I say we pull our money out and put it somewhere else. I've thought long and hard about the railroads—that is, about this part of the plan—over the last week, and if I've ever known anything to be true, it's this…"

That I must get out while I still can, thought Drucker.

"That we must get out while we still can," said Drucker.

There was a moment of stunned silence. Finally, Archibald Sanford spoke cautiously, as if Drucker's suggestion was incomprehensible. "I don't understand. You're saying that we should—"

"Divest. From the railroads," said Drucker matter-of-factly.

"But why?" asked Archibald Sanford, sounding more suspicious than curious.

"For the very reasons just discussed. We're heavily invested in that industry already," said Drucker, silently thanking the group for providing him with that fact. "And why should our business be tied to the fate of an industry that, as Mr. Hatch so eloquently stated, is populated by a bunch of—"

"Rat bastards," grumbled William Hatch.

"We could be exposing Atlanta Southern to financial distress if, for example, the Atlanta and Florida line were to run into any trouble," continued Drucker.

"But it won't run into trouble," Sanford retorted.

"Why not? The Savannah and North Alabama did just last month," Melville Kratch pointed out. "Look at them, forty-five years in business, and they've gone belly up." His tiny gray head bobbed excitedly, making him look like a scurrying mouse in the hot pursuit of a crumb of cheese.

"The whole idea is preposterous," said Archibald Sanford. "The railroad industry is the backbone of the American economy. Strong as ever. And more to the point, our biggest returns came from our railroad investments for the last two quarters. That business is as sturdy as an ox."

"Sanford's right," said Edgar Jameson. "I find it interesting that you would suggest that we pull out of our most rewarding venture, Drucker, quite interesting indeed."

"Edgar, you're being too polite. What you call interesting, I call ludicrous," Archibald Sanford snapped. "The American railroad industry is healthy as a horse, and if you think we should take our money out of the one place we've actually been enjoying any success lately, then I must say that you, Drucker May, are nuttier than slice of pecan pie."

Drucker stood quietly. Although he couldn't prove beyond a reasonable doubt that the railroads would collapse or even falter in the near future, Sanford had no guarantee that they wouldn't. *Best to stand my ground*, Drucker thought. After all, a little pushback from Archibald Sanford was nothing compared to the acrimony he had expected from this meeting. Actually, his presentation was going quite well, save for the fact that he still needed to think of a third plan in the next minute or so. Of course, there was also the fact that so far he had presented one plan that was popular but mostly illegal, and one plan that was legal but highly unpopular.

"Now, Archie," said the president, "there's no use in name calling. I think we can all agree that—"

"It's a bad idea," said Sanford, interrupting the president.

"Now I wouldn't say that just yet," said Edgar Jameson. "I'd say it's interesting, and I'm interested to hear more about—"

"Oh, Edgar, for the love of Christmas morning, you're *interested* in everything!" exploded Sanford, his face flushing purple with anger. The man to his left leaned away as if trying to avoid sharing Sanford's noxious air, and across the table from him, Melville Kratch wriggled nervously in his seat.

Only Drucker was smiling. Despite his heated expression of it, Sanford did have a point, and it gave Drucker an idea.

Edgar Jameson turned to Drucker. "Let's move on. I'm interested to hear the third part of the plan. Please continue."

"Of course," said Drucker, pleased with the idea he was forming. "I'd be happy to."

Thirty minutes later, Drucker found himself on the tail end of a surprisingly uninterrupted monologue. Atlanta Southern, he had explained over the course of half an hour, could strike a deal with customers whereby the bank would initially pay for their purchases of goods or services. The customer would simply give the merchant his account number, and Atlanta Southern would pay the debt, noting the name and number of the account and how much would need to be paid back. The customer would then have a month to pay Atlanta Southern back in full, plus *interest*, an idea sparked by Edgar Jameson's incessant use of the word. The longer the customer took to pay back Atlanta Southern, the more interest would accrue, allowing Atlanta Southern to make a profit from the inevitable passing of time. Drucker himself was impressed by the plan. Though he doubted it could ever work in practice, he felt certain that it could hold in theory. His audience, however, was not equally convinced.

"You mean a loan?" Archibald Sanford asked incredulously.

"This sounds like a mortgage," said Melville Kratch. "What's new about a mortgage? We already offer them."

"Not a mortgage," corrected Drucker. "Atlanta Southern wouldn't own the purchased goods. We would just stand to profit if the customers are late on their payments to us."

Archibald Sanford, ever the skeptic, cut in again. "And what would stand in the way of someone, anyone, let's say Kratch over there"—he jabbed an open palm in mousy Melville Kratch's direction—"racking up a load of debt beyond what he could ever repay and sticking it on us to foot the bill?" Melville Kratch flinched nervously, but joined the others in looking to Drucker for an answer.

"Well, I suppose there's no absolute guarantees," Drucker said after a moment of thought, "but at Atlanta Southern we know our customers, and Atlanta isn't so big a town that a person could hide out for very long before someone found him. A man would have to pick up and leave town completely to escape this bank." Drucker smiled at the dual meaning only he could recognize.

There was another prolonged quiet, punctuated by the occasional head nod or thoughtful glance between men. Then, just as Drucker thought he had made it into the clear, Archibald Sanford began shaking his head.

Sanford looked up at Drucker. "But why would anyone ever sign up for this?" he asked. "My wife already has a tab at the market and the tailor and the cobbler and the milliner's shop. Why would I sign up my family for all the convenience of the tab we already have, but with the added bonus of the possibility of owing twice as much if we pay up a little late?"

Drucker nodded. "I understand, but wouldn't it be easier if you had one account that could be used at all of those places? Rather than have to make good on all of them separately, you could just pay up with us."

Sanford squinted in Drucker's direction. "Sounds like a lot of malarkey to me," he grumbled, and Drucker didn't bother trying to piece together a rebuttal. *Sanford's right,* he thought. Beyond its clever origins, this last idea held little promise. *What kind of man would ever use credit issued to him on the premise that the later his payment, the steeper the interest rate? No customer of Atlanta Southern, probably no one in all of Atlanta.*

Drucker sighed and the rest of the room seemed to share the sentiment. The hubbub from the board members started up again, one man elaborating on how improbable the idea was, another declaring that he himself would never sign up for such a disadvantageous bank account and couldn't imagine the halfwit who would.

As the discussion propelled itself forward without him, Drucker derided himself silently, *A system of credit where interest rates rise the longer it takes to pay back the loan? Ridiculous.*

"I suppose it makes more sense on paper," said Drucker, feeling the attention of all fourteen eyes returning to him.

"Well, I count three," said the president hurriedly, trying to force an end to discussion on the topic.

"Yes," said Drucker, with a sigh of relief. "I'm done here." He meant it.

"Well, it's obvious you put a lot of work into this presentation, Drucker. We all thank you for that," said his father, looking from one man to the next with an expression that said, *Don't we, gentlemen?* All of the men smiled and nodded, and Drucker waved off their displays of gratitude, mirroring their head nods and smiles as he exited.

"I think that first idea has some potential," offered Melville Kratch after Drucker had left the room, and two of the other men quickly joined in, concurring that yes, the first of the ideas had some real potential. They would not divest from the railroads, the men decided unanimously, until any evidence could be exhibited that the industry was not as strong and viable as ever, if also morally decrepit, as William Hatch insisted on until the group agreed. As for the third plan, it was largely ignored in the discussion that followed Drucker's exit. It went without saying that such an idea held little benefit for the customer, the merchant, or the bank itself. It certainly would never catch on among the American people at large and certainly not the discerning citizens of Atlanta.

Meanwhile, Drucker sat for what he recognized as his last time behind that wide wooden desk in the vice president's office. His stomach churned with a cocktail of great relief mixed with mild embarrassment, and he tingled with what he took at first to be elation. Then, as the tingling spread from his toes, up his legs, through his stomach and arms, Drucker realized that it was not the joy of knowing that this was his last day at the bank that was pumping through his veins, but rather the terror of having to tell his father as much.

Drucker stretched out his neck, letting his head fall backward and forward, side to side. That improvisation in the boardroom, the act that was supposed to be the best performance of his life, Drucker realized, was nothing but a warm-up act for the real show that—Drucker counted out the remaining hours on his fingers— would be playing just one time and would be opening that very night.

CHAPTER FIVE

The tinkle of a handheld crystal bell signaled that the dinner hour had arrived and, as he did every night, Drucker joined his parents in the formal dining room, where the table was set with blue-and-white china, as it was on all nights except for Sundays, when the rose-colored set was used. Drucker sat on one of the table's long sides, his father at the head of the table, his mother at the foot. Occasionally, when guests would join them, Drucker would be given his mother's usual seat and his mother would sit facing the door to the kitchen so that she could get the first look at the trays as they were carried in. That way, with a wince of her eyes or a subtle shake of her head, she could silently veto an item before it caught the others' attention. Over the years, Drucker had deciphered that his mother's double blink meant, *That looks undercooked*, while a right-eyed wink meant, *We're not ready for the next course yet, turn around and go right back in that kitchen, Mary Alice.*

When Drucker arrived in the dining room, both his father and mother had taken their seats, and a bowl of chilled cucumber soup waited for him.

"I'm sorry I'm late," said Drucker. "I have trouble hearing that new bell."

"Yes," said his mother coolly, "that's apparent." Without taking her eyes away from the arch of her spoon from bowl to mouth, she motioned for Drucker to take his seat. It was she who had insisted on the switch to the crystal bell. The old silver one gave her a headache, she said, and besides, with the so-called silverites causing a stir across the country championing the "other metal," Drucker's mother had declared using silver to be uncouth.

Drucker sat down and began ladling the cool consommé. It was creamy and rich, delicious as all meals in this dining room had always been for as long as he could remember. He wondered what the food in Boston would be like. He wondered if they served chilled cucumber soup, and if they didn't, if he would miss it.

"The soup is delicious tonight," he said.

"A bit salty, I'd say," said his mother, again without looking up. Her thin fingers, beginning to wrinkle with age, were wrapped tightly around the spoon, which was engraved with a delicate, swooping M that looked like a W from Drucker's angle.

Drucker's father let his own spoon clink down into his empty bowl. "Drucker was very good today," he announced.

"How lovely," replied Drucker's mother, crinkling her nose at the soup. "Too salty for me to stand." She set down her spoon and looked to Mary Alice who stood silently by the door to the kitchen. "Take this away," she said, to which Mary Alice replied, "Of course, Madam," while scurrying to retrieve the unwanted bowl.

"I think the board was quite impressed by him," continued Drucker's father, as Mary Alice picked up his bowl and carried both off into the kitchen.

"But Father, they hated my ideas," protested Drucker.

"Now, that's not true at all," corrected his father. "We all thought the first one in particular had great potential. I'm going to tell Hank to look into getting that started as soon as possible."

"But, Father—" started Drucker.

"Of course," cut in his father, "I know you'll want to be involved greatly. And you will be. It was *your* genius mind, after all, that came up with the thing. But I thought we'd bring Hank in on it so that you don't get bogged down with the details. When you're president, you know, you don't want to get stuck knee-deep in a sludge pool of minutiae. You have to clear your mind so that you can see the big picture. And judging by how well you did today, Drucker, I must say I think it will be just a few months before—"

Now it was Drucker's turn to cut in. "Father, there's something I have to tell you." *Better to make it quick, just spit it out,* Drucker told himself.

At just that moment, though, the door to the kitchen swung open, and Mary Alice, followed by Clive and Louisa, paraded through, each carrying an armload of fragrant goodies. Mary Alice placed a silver tray of sugar-cured ham hock, pink and juicy, in the center of the table, and the others surrounded it with plates of seasoned potatoes, greens, pickled beets, and gravy biscuits.

"I heard the youngest Harper girl is being courted quite seriously," said Drucker's mother apropos of nothing. It was unclear whether she had heard her husband and son's conversation and was trying to change the subject, or she had not heard it because she didn't care to. "I feel just terrible for Mrs. Harper," she added, shaking her head sadly. "Five daughters, and none of them pretty."

"Father, I—" Drucker tried again, but his mother wasn't finished.

"I've been thinking it's time we invest in some new dishes," she said. "This pattern is so awfully boring, and we've had it for ages." This was true, the china had been a May family heirloom passed down through the generations since General Thomas Winfield May, a decorated veteran of the Revolutionary War, had bought it for his wife when they left Connecticut to move south. Both father and son ignored the comment, which Drucker's mother seemed to expect and not to mind.

"As I was saying," said Drucker's father, "I think you left quite the impression on the board today, and I would be surprised if anyone put up a scuttle against your nomination to be my successor."

"Father, I don't want to be president of the bank."

The words came out quickly, but they echoed under the dining room's vaulted ceilings. When his father said nothing, Drucker added, summoning all his bravery, "I'm not going to be president of Atlanta Southern, Father. I'm not even going to work there."

From the kitchen came a gasp and then a muffled tittering, followed by a stern hush.

"Don't be ridiculous, Drucker. You did well in that meeting. The board thought very highly of you. Sure, your idea for that idiotic new credit system was a little farfetched, and no one believes the railroads will falter anytime soon, but I'm telling you, that first idea of yours, the higher returns, that may just do the trick."

"No, Father, it has nothing to do with the board meeting. It's... it's not about that."

"Then don't be silly, Drucker. You'll go back to work tomorrow and—"

"I can't. I won't," said Drucker, firmly. "I'm not going back to the bank tomorrow."

His father speared a beet on the prong of his engraved silver fork. "Oh?" His jaw had tightened, and his face had flushed deep red to match the beet.

"I actually thought I'd go north," said Drucker, trying to keep his voice steady, but light.

"North? To Charleston?" asked his mother, finally looking up and joining the conversation.

"To Boston," said Drucker.

"Boston?" his father and mother repeated in unison, creating a chorus of astonishment.

"Yes," said Drucker. "I thought I might try to go find Lucy."
He paused. His mother was looking down once again, watching
her knife as it tore through the pork's juicy flesh and screeched
against the patterned surface of the century-old china.

"Fine," said his father. "Go. Go for a month. Take a little time
off, if that's what you need."

"I don't need a month," said Drucker.

"Good," said his father, misunderstanding.

"No, I need many, many months. I need years. I need to get out
of Atlanta and find a job that doesn't make me want to quit every
day. If I stay at the bank, I'll spend a lifetime trying to fit into your
shoes, into your chair, when just the thought of spending my life
in *any* chair makes me feel sick. I need to be my own man, and I
need you to hear that, to know that. To appreciate that would be
too much to ask, but if you can't find it in your heart to bless what
I'm doing, or maybe not bless, but recognize why I—"

"Go then," his father cut in with a growl. "Get out."

Drucker hesitated, trying to gauge his father's anger.

"Did you not hear me?" his father asked, his voice louder than
before, his eyes meeting Drucker's. "I said get out."

Drucker shifted in his chair. His natural urge to stay and ap-
pease was met by a new and very intense urge to run.

Another beat passed before his father roared, "Get out!"

Drucker jumped to his feet.

"Now!" boomed his father. "Get out of my sight!"

"I'm sorry," said Drucker, turning to leave.

He wondered if there was protocol one followed when leaving
one's family abruptly and on such poor terms. Did one say good-
bye to the gardener or thank the kitchen staff? Does one push in
one's chair during a dramatic final dining-room departure? Given
that his dinner had been cut short, would it be in bad taste to take
a gravy biscuit to go?

Forsaking the biscuit but pushing in his chair and nodding politely at Mary Alice, whose face had drained of all color as she manned her post by the kitchen door, Drucker left the dining room without another word.

As he climbed the stairs to his room, he could hear his father's voice. It rose and fell, growing loud and then softer before growing loud again, varying in volume but remaining consistent in the richness of its rage.

Predictably, the only response from his mother was the screech of her knife as it scratched against the blue-and-white china plate.

Though the rest of the May estate was undeniably lavish, Drucker had always eschewed the ostentation of his mother's style and chose to keep his bedroom sparsely adorned. It was to this modest refuge that he retreated after his announcement and there that he lay on his narrow bed, the mattress firm and outfitted with a single gray top sheet, standard fare for bedclothes during an Atlanta July.

Because wearing shoes on the bed was a practice that Drucker's mother had always detested and never allowed, over the years it had become habit for him to remove his shoes even if only sitting on his bed for a moment to straighten his tie. Now, however, as he lay on his bed, listening to his father's roar echoing up from the dining room, he kept his shoes on, laced up tight, wondering if years later he would remember this act as his first as a new man, perhaps the way an old woman remembers fondly the musky way her first beau smelled the first time she was kissed.

Even with the door to his room shut tightly, Drucker could hear his father's booming voice. For a few minutes he listened closely, feeling both privileged and pained to be overhearing the harsh words that his father didn't realize—or didn't care—that Drucker could hear. As he stared up at the ceiling, Drucker took note of the phrases that were repeated most often. *No longer my son,* came with frequency, and *not welcome in my house* repeated like a chorus.

At times Drucker felt a surge of anger or the desire to respond and defend himself, but mostly he was overcome by the irony of it all. This night, this moment, these words his father was spewing in the dining room, these were exactly what Drucker had wished for all these years, because this was the night, the moment, the recognition that set him free. It had finally arrived. And in just a few hours he would be on a train to Boston, unshackled from his life at the bank. Drucker pulled out his pocket watch and glanced at it. He couldn't wait to be on that train.

Though the plan called for Drucker to leave first thing in the morning, given his status as an unwelcome guest in his father's house, Drucker wondered if an evening departure might be in order. Sooner or later the yelling would die down, and his parents would adjourn to their chambers, and he could sneak out the back and sleep at the train station if he had to, Drucker decided.

But instead, as the waves of his father's echoing voice washed over him, Drucker fell into the deep and vital sleep of a man with a long journey ahead of him.

———

Six clangs issuing forth from the grandfather clock in the hall roused Drucker from his dreams. For several moments he lay still, eyes closed, listening for the cries from the dining room that he had fallen asleep to, but save for the echoes reverberating from the clock, the house was silent, his father's tirade concluded—at least for the night. *Maybe some rest will calm Father,* thought Drucker, though at the same time he realized that his own sleep had changed nothing for him. He knew what he had to do, and even after a good night's sleep, he still wanted to do it.

When he opened his eyes, he saw the first light of dawn beginning to creep up over the horizon, illuminating his bedroom just enough so that he could scavenge around without the help of an oil lamp. From his closet he pulled a brown leather valise that was just large enough to hold a few pairs of pants and several shirts, all that he would need until he got to Boston, he reasoned, before thinking better of it and squeezing three books, a hat, two neckties, and a three-piece suit into the case.

When he had stuffed it to the seams and zipped shut his luggage, Drucker stopped to survey the room, trying to separate the necessary from that to which he merely hated to bid good-bye. He knew he couldn't take everything he wanted, but he managed to fit into his pocket a few small items that he couldn't bear to part with, like the silver metal sheriff's badge that he had won off Jimmy Mathers in a primary school bet over who could run a faster mile. Drucker had won the race easily, and his opponent, though claiming a leg cramp, had made good on his promise to give up the five-pointed pendant that Drucker had admired up until that day and considered lucky ever since. He couldn't bear to leave it behind.

Nor could he leave the gold pocket watch his father had given him for his sixteenth birthday as a welcome to the world of manhood. At the time, the idea of being an adult had held so much promise and excitement: independence, self-reliance, all the fun of making up the rules. Not since that birthday had he so wholeheartedly looked forward to—and felt on the cusp of—attaining those things. Until that moment.

Even at daybreak the air was warm and humid and growing more so as the sun broke free from the horizon. The sticky air made Drucker remember what Lucy had often said about Atlanta's climate being so much warmer than Boston's, and he wondered what exactly people wore in the frigid Boston winters. Or in their North Atlantic summers? He would have to buy something when he got there, he decided. That would be his first order of business when he got to Boston. Something warm for himself, and something fashionable for Lucy. And maybe something for her sisters, too, if she was living with them and—

Drucker stopped himself in midthought. He mustn't get carried away buying gifts for everyone in sight if he wanted his savings to last, he reminded himself. Not that he was short on funds. Thinking of the reserves of cash he had packed, he tallied practically enough to buy winter coats for half of Boston.

While there had been certain disadvantages to living in his parents' house all these years, it was undeniable that the arrangement had afforded him the considerable benefit of never having to pay for food or shelter. As a result, Drucker had saved enough so that he could already, at the age of twenty-five, nearly afford to buy a respectable place of his own. Before his final departure from Atlanta Southern he had closed out his account there, and his life savings in its entirety now lined the bottom of his valise.

After a final glance around the room, Drucker turned his bedchamber's gold-plated doorknob. "Good-bye, room," Drucker said aloud, raising a hand as if in salute. "Thank you. For everything."

He fought the urge to get sentimental with the bare white walls and austere gray bed that had been his refuge for a quarter century. Still, he took one final look—at each corner, each wall, and through the window once more—before he turned back to the door, finally feeling ready to leave.

Just as he was about to close the door behind him, though, Drucker stopped short at the sight of a white envelope lying on the floor by his feet.

It must have been slipped under the door while I slept, he thought as he picked it up and turned it over, examining it front and back. A fat D was the only marking on the envelope, and though it was no more than a single character, Drucker could tell that it was his father's handwriting. The envelope was heavy, stuffed full of something.

Money, thought Drucker, feeling offended. *He thinks I can't make it on my own, that I need his handouts, his bank, his life.*

Drucker was about to throw the envelope back to the ground when he thought better of it. *In case of emergency only*, he told himself, giving the envelope a shake. He knelt to slip it into the hidden pocket of his fully stuffed valise, promising himself that he would never touch the money unless it should be a matter of life or death, sustenance or starvation, sin or salvation.

Then Drucker snuck out the back door of the mansion and didn't look back.

CHAPTER SIX

The first thing that Drucker noticed when he arrived at Atlanta's Union Station was the giant clock that hung high from the rounded arch of the depot's lofted ceilings. He stood mesmerized by the minute hand, thick and black and as long as he was tall. He watched as it crawled slowly down the enormous white face of the clock, and he thought of how fitting it was that a clock should be so prominently on display in the railroad station.

He could remember the day, not yet seven years earlier, when time itself had been handed over to the railroads. The "day of two noons," the papers had called it, the day that the time zones were reshaped to facilitate and adhere to the railroad schedules.

Until then the very notion of time had always existed as a local concern, which had hardly posed a problem when the time it took to cross a time zone was measured on a calendar, not a clock. By the time a person had marched, galloped, sailed, or wagoneered across a time zone, the difference of a minute or two hardly mattered.

As travel increased, though, both in popularity and speed, and as the railroads developed into an institution, the move from sun time to standard time grew ever more important. Without it, a cross-country traveler would have to reset his watch twenty times between the coasts, a small burden compared to the one borne by the railroad companies that observed more than one hundred time zones. That is, until that November day in 1883, when every clock in America was changed to match railroad time.

On that day, it was as if time died and was reincarnated a moment later as *railroad time*, its rebirth a declaration that the railroads, in function and spirit, had been officially declared to be as important as time itself and —

The collision of an elbow and his lower back woke Drucker from his reverie.

"Excuse me, sir," said a young boy in a floppy cap and overalls. "I didn't mean to bump you. I was pushed."

Drucker turned to look at his small assailant and saw that in the minutes that he had spent entranced by the clock, the station around him had filled with people. The morning calm had dissipated, and the once-quiet depot was now overrun by a throbbing mass of travelers.

"It's fine, son, just be—" Drucker froze in midsentence. As the sensation of pain faded, it was replaced by one of alarm when he saw that not thirty yards away was Atlanta Southern's moralistic board member, William Hatch, his silver hair glistening in the morning light. At the exact moment that Drucker recognized him, the silvery head began to crane toward Drucker. Then there was eye contact.

It couldn't have lasted more than a second, more likely a fraction thereof, but to Drucker it felt as though the instance of their locked gaze lasted for an hour. It was as if the moment had slowed to a stop, as if time had been manipulated once again by the supreme power of the railroads. In that seemingly endless moment a single thought filled Drucker's mind: *run!*

And so he did.

Drucker turned on his heel and ducked into the swarm of travelers, doing his best to dodge clusters of bodies as they moved across the platform. He ran and he ducked and he swerved, wiping the sweat from his brow and the blur of it from his eyes, until suddenly he felt the heat of someone else's flesh against his forehead and then the unforgiving sting of cement as his rear end met with it forcefully.

When he opened his eyes, Drucker saw that the collision had been worse for his victim, who had been carrying a stack of leather-bound books that had landed on top of him. From beneath the pile of splayed pages, the man was quick to understand what had happened in a way that Drucker, feeling woozy as he got to his feet, could not quite piece together.

"You ran into me, you rat!" the man, still on the ground, yelled up at Drucker.

"I...I'm sorry," said Drucker, wiping the dust from his pants and peering nervously over his shoulder to make sure that he had lost Hatch.

He had. But he had gained a bigger problem, he realized. *Bigger* because the man that he had knocked over had managed to get to his feet and must have had six inches and no less than forty pounds on Drucker.

"Well, you gon' pick up my books, or you gon' stare at 'em?" the man asked, and Drucker dropped to his knees to gather the volumes. No more than a brief glance was needed in order to understand that carrying huge stacks of heavy books was the perfect job for this man, all bulging arm and shoulder muscles and a thick neck propping up a small square head. Drucker was eager to comply with the man's demands, lest his victim turn into victimizer.

As Drucker collected the fallen inventory, the book carrier stood over him, cursing and spitting and wiping his chin repeatedly, insisting that the fall that Drucker had caused would leave a scar on his face and dents in his books and a hole in his pants and... he went on and on not stopping for breath until Drucker broke in unexpectedly.

"What—what did he say?" asked Drucker, looking up, trying to hear a nearby conductor's call through the buzz of the crowd and the rant of the man and the ringing in his ears.

"I said, ain't you gon' to stack em?" repeated the man impatiently.

"No, I mean what did the conductor say?" asked Drucker, feeling frantic. "I heard 'all aboard,' but did he say that train is going to Boston?"

"Even if he did—" started the man, but Drucker was already on his feet and running toward the train. With nothing but his single suitcase to weigh him down, he was nimble as he wove through the crowds once again.

From behind him he could hear the oaf's breathless calls. "Get back here, you rat," and variations of that sentiment, but Drucker didn't look back.

He neared the train just as the wheels began to churn. Without thinking twice, Drucker made the leap from the platform to the railcar, quite the feat since the benefit of train's slow speed was negated by the detriment of his uncontrollably shaking legs.

As the train began to pick up speed, Drucker turned to look back at the town he was leaving. He didn't know how long he would be gone, nor was he sure that he would ever be back. The train lurched from a crawl into a jog while he bade a silent farewell to Atlanta. And though it was bittersweet, Drucker couldn't deny the feeling that never before had he done anything that felt quite so right.

Inside the train, Drucker wandered from one car to the next. The only thing that he could be sure of was that this was the moment that the rest of his life began. From this point on he was no more, and no less, than the man who he himself created. Who exactly that man would be, he would have to find out, of course. But for the moment, his growling stomach and still-shaking legs reminded him that he had more immediate concerns. He needed to find sustenance and a seat and though he wasn't quite sure of the proper protocol for attaining either, he reminded himself that a little confidence and plenty of attention to his surroundings could go a long way.

All he had to do was notice how other passengers conducted themselves, and he would learn quickly. *The trick is to never look lost,* he thought. And then he made himself a promise. *When in doubt, I will observe, follow my instinct, and never tell a lie,* he pledged.

And with that, Drucker set forth down the long thin corridor of the train in search of some breakfast, a place to sit, and whatever else it was that he had been searching for all his life.

CHAPTER SEVEN

T o Drucker's great delight, not only was breakfast served on the train but it was served in a car that was populated by both men and women sitting at tables, several of whom were already forkfuls into the morning meal when Drucker wandered into the dining car.

"Biscuit with gravy, sir," said the attendant as he placed a flour puff in a brown puddle of pudding-like substance in front of Drucker, who had managed to find an unoccupied table across the aisle from the only three women in the dining car who were not accompanied by men. Though the middle-aged trio hardly amounted to the perfumed young lass from his boardroom daydream, Drucker had a penchant for conversation with older women that dated back to his childhood spent with Lucy, who was seventeen years his senior. He took the presence of these three women, so conveniently stationed within earshot of his table, as a sign that someone, perhaps a higher power, was smiling on his escape from Atlanta.

After eagerly devouring a first biscuit and then ordering another, Drucker tuned his ear to listen to the women's chatter from
across the aisle, waiting for the right moment to invite himself to
join their conversation. Unfortunately, that moment never materi-
alized. Drucker found that the chirping tones of the ladies' gossip
mingling with the effects of his rising at dawn proved a soporific
combination. Before long, he had been lulled to sleep as the train
picked up speed on its hasty exodus from Georgia.

When Drucker's eyes fluttered open, his second biscuit had appeared, but the three ladies at the adjacent table were gone. A pair
of men sat where the trio of women once had, and Drucker felt
disappointed that he had not had the opportunity to meet—and
perhaps to charm—the ladies before they left. In his experience,
men were not nearly as easy to win over. But then, nearly all of
Drucker's contact with men had been confined to the bank, where
everyone had regarded Drucker as the object of envy, scorn, or
skepticism. Except, that is, for his father who, Drucker was fairly
certain, now regarded him with distaste the likes of which made
the other men's scorn seem like affection.

But that was his *old life*, Drucker reminded himself, and it was
a new day. In fact it was the *first* day of his new life. He no longer
had to be the one that the other men loved to hate. *This is the
beauty of an identity yet unformed*, thought Drucker. The less that had
emerged, the less there was to be disliked.

Drucker sat very still, trying to catch as much as he could of
the men's conversation, which was carried on in a country drawl so
thick that even Drucker, with his Atlanta-born ears, had to struggle to discern what they were saying. Something about a horse,
Drucker thought at first. No, not a horse, a house. A house thief. A
domestic burglar?

Drucker tried to piece the fragments of softly spoken sen-
tences together, but every time an important word was about to
be uttered, another table would erupt in laughter, or the train's

whistle would suddenly sound. At least he could be sure that he heard the word "thief" batted back and forth between the two men.

More useful than the words he could hear were the sentiments he could read on the men's ruddy, freckled faces. The slow nods of recognition, the narrowing eyes of moral indignation.

Drucker noticed that both men were modestly though professionally dressed, and each kept close watch on a case that he kept near the heel of his shoe. *Traveling salesmen*, thought Drucker. *Fellow traveling souls.* Though he had only been gone for three hours and realized that perhaps it was premature to consider his soul a traveling one, he couldn't help but wonder couldn't *his* be a traveling soul from this day forth if he wanted it to be? Who was to say his soul hadn't been a traveling one all along?

Inspired by this notion, Drucker summoned the courage to address the duo. "Excuse me, gentlemen, but do you know how long it will be until we reach Boston?" Drucker asked, feeling confident that he had chosen the right moment to cut in.

For a moment neither man spoke. Both simply stared at Drucker.

"You a Northerner?" one man asked suspiciously.

Drucker was taken aback. He had not even drawn on his ability to mimic the Boston inflection. "No, sir. I come from Atlanta," answered Drucker, but the men just squinted at him as if he had affirmed their foregone conclusion. Evidently, whatever backwoods post these two hailed from, it was so deep in the low country that it made Atlanta seem like the great metropolis of the North. Both men continued to stare at Drucker, as if awaiting, though not a-welcoming, his next comment.

"My apologies for the interruption," said Drucker, tipping his hat as he stood to leave. Neither man spoke as Drucker scuttled from the dining car.

When he had made it as far as three cars back, Drucker decided that he had put ample room between himself and the couple of surly souls to whom, he had also decided, his soul was not akin. Drucker had just slouched into an empty seat when a ticket-taking conductor approached.

"Ticket," said the man flatly with no discernable emotion in his voice or expression on his face.

"I'd like to buy one," said Drucker, trying to sound confident. This being his inaugural train ride, he wasn't entirely sure how one went about obtaining a ticket and how quickly one could be thrown off the train for having failed to procure one.

"To?" asked the conductor. It was a question, but because he didn't seem on the verge of kicking Drucker off the train, it was also an answer.

"Boston," said Drucker, more confidently than before.

The conductor looked blankly at Drucker, but as blank stares seemed to be status quo thus far, Drucker was undeterred.

Drucker fished in his pants pocket for the proper funds. "How much will it be?" he asked.

"To?" asked the man again as if he had not heard Drucker the first time.

"Boston," replied Drucker, hearing a note of irritation creep into his own voice.

"Boston." This time the response was neither a question nor an answer from the ticket taker.

"Yes, Boston," repeated Drucker. "How much will it be?"

"That depends on how you plan on getting there."

"Well, I was hoping to get there on this train," said Drucker, marveling at how very dense the population of this vehicle was proving to be.

"Well, you'll need to start hoping a good bit harder than that," countered the ticket taker flatly.

"And why is that?"

"Because this train's headed for Austin."

First one beat passed. *Austin?* Then another.

"Austin what?" asked Drucker, a fleeting instant of confusion giving way to a rush of dismay as he realized the answer to his own question.

At that moment, Drucker and the ticket taker, who up until that point had been conversing as if speaking two different languages, suddenly found their voices united in a single word, spoken in unison: *Texas.*

Slumping deep into his seat, Drucker's mind raced like the train as it rushed through the cotton-bearing countryside. He had paid the eighteen-dollar fare to Austin in full, a sum that hardly dented his savings, yet amounted to a heavy price to pay for a trip he had not intended to take.

Drucker fought the urge to mourn the death of his well-laid plan. After all, he reminded himself, it was neither particularly well laid, nor—he told himself consolingly—completely dead. He could get off at the next town and catch a train headed north or perhaps take a train back to Atlanta and realign himself onto the correct route, having lost no more than a few hours.

Still, the realization that he was riding a speeding bullet west, not north, was disarming. It forced Drucker to question if this train wasn't taking him in the wrong direction in more than just the geographic sense.

In the six hours since he had left his home, he had managed to run *away* from his family and directly *into* an imposing man who looked like he could carry a grudge as skillfully as a stack of books; he had missed the chance to make friends with three women yet managed to disgruntle two men; and just when he had succeeded at securing a one way ticket out of Atlanta, here he was, being told that he could ride this train, but it wouldn't take him to Boston. Not even close. Drucker had to wonder if the fare he had paid was just the least of the price he would pay for leaving Atlanta under such circumstances.

As Drucker berated himself for his hasty decision, he suddenly became aware that though the chiding voice in his head was loud and persistent, it was neither as loud nor as persistent as the chirping voices rising up from the seats behind him and across the aisle. When Drucker craned his neck he saw that the voices belonged to the women from the dining car, still tittering gaily.

"Could it be a coincidence, Maude?" one woman asked, her voice quivering with intrigue.

"Impossible," said another—Maude, apparently. Drucker could see the women out of the corner of his eye without much more than a slight turn of his head, a position that allowed him hear the women without difficulty, though they did not become aware of him, just as they had failed to notice him in the dining car.

"Two could be a coincidence. Three or four, perhaps. But twenty-five horses? That's not called a coincidence, Mary Ellen, that's called a crime spree." Maude's voice shook with vibrato on the word crime, drawing out the single syllable until it became song.

"Well, imagine that," continued Mary Ellen. She turned to the third woman. "Do you remember the last time we were there, Ida? And those boys shattered the front window of that little store on Main Street by throwing stones? Oh, what was the name of that store? And that nice man who ran the place?"

"McKinstry," Ida remembered.

"That's right! McKinstry's. Why, everyone in town was talking for weeks as if they'd tar and feather the boys that done it. I can't imagine what a thing like this must do to the place. Horse thieves in peaceful little Clayton, Arkansas!"

The words wove their way into Drucker's imagination and set something aflame. Though had never heard of Clayton before, as he gazed out the window at the cotton fields rustling in the clumsy July winds, Drucker wanted nothing more than to save peaceful little Clayton from the crime spree that afflicted it. No doubt it was the same rash of thievery that the men from the dining car had been discussing earlier.

Not house thieves, horse *thieves. And it must be big news,* thought Drucker, *for the story to be carried on the lips of traveling salesmen.*

"He says the whole town is up in arms," said Maude, scanning the letter she held in front of her.

"Oh, you know how William exaggerates," Ida protested, but warmly. She was the oldest-looking of the three, her hair graying at the temples and forehead. She addressed the other two, "You remember Mother's nickname for him?"

"Iggy," started Mary Ellen.

"Short for ignore," added Maude cheerfully without lifting her eyes from the page, her finger tracing the lines left to right as she read. "Listen to this! He says the sheriff has sent for the Pinkerton National Detective Agency, asking for help in solving the case. Says the town doesn't have the resources to solve a crime the likes of this, Clayton, of course, being the peaceful little hamlet that it is."

"They've sent for detectives?" Ida asked breathlessly, as if she'd never heard anything so quite so intriguing.

Maude nodded, still reading.

Mary Ellen sighed. "Oh my, and I was so hoping for a quiet little visit with our dear baby brother. I suppose the whole town will be just crawling with Pinkertons now, making everyone...making everyone—"

"Safe?" tried one sister.

"Gossip?" tried the other.

"Perfectly titillated," cried Mary Ellen, causing her sisters to laugh and forcing Drucker to conceal his own amusement at such an unexpected word coming from such a prim little lady.

As he sat there listening to the women, though he was still slumped in self-pity, Drucker realized that he had also begun to enjoy himself a bit. He found something comforting about this trio of sisters. He felt an instant connection to them, as if he had known them for much longer than the time that had elapsed since his path had first crossed with theirs in the dining car that morning. He wondered if he would be brave enough to introduce himself to them. It even crossed his mind briefly to wonder if he would miss them when they eventually disembarked.

Drucker found the answer to this last question several hours later, when the whistle blew, and the conductor called out, "Last call for Clayton." The three ladies stepped off the train but Drucker wasn't sad to see them go.

Because he was right behind them.

II. CLAYTON

CHAPTER EIGHT

From the moment that he stepped off the train in Clayton, Drucker could tell that he had indeed arrived in a sleepy, little town that was totally unprepared to defend itself against a horse thief, or any other kind of crime spree for that matter.

To avoid being noticed by the trio of sisters that he had followed off the train, Drucker forced himself to take an extra beat between steps as he walked towards the town's main thoroughfare. Luckily, he didn't have far to go. Though the depot itself was an unimpressive affair of architecture abutting a lone pair of tracks, it stood just a stone's throw away from what Drucker could see was clearly the drowsy hamlet's main street.

The air was cloudy with the low-hanging dust kicked up by horses as they pulled wagons through the streets, and the late-evening sun cast a red glow as it reflected off the flaky-clay terrain, parched dry from the heat. The strangeness of his surroundings enchanted him, though. Even the arid landscape was welcome respite from Atlanta's swampy summer climate.

As he walked, Drucker found himself thinking that there was something lovely and alive about the little town, which though so ordinary in many ways was also so *extraordinary* for the fact that it was someplace completely foreign to him. He delighted in not recognizing anyone as he doffed his cap in passing. Everyone was a perfect stranger to him, and at that moment in his life, nothing could have been more perfect than that.

Drucker smiled to himself as he strolled down Main Street, watching merchants unload their wagons and shopkeepers sweep balls of dust back out onto the streets from which they came. He meandered past a butcher shop with a pink pig's carcass dangling in the window, past a shingle advertising the services of a seamstress, then past that of a milliner, the sign above the window promising hats for "Ladies, Gents, and Everyone in Between." A saloon flanked the opposite side of the street, and Drucker stopped to watch a slow stream of patrons meander in, then one stagger out.

As the sun dropped lower in its haze of pink sky, though, Drucker realized that he had not yet seen the one type of structure he would need to find. Absent a boardinghouse, he would be spending the night on the dusty streets, forced to wait until morning to board the next train.

When a sign identifying the Clayton General Store appeared in front of him, Drucker quickly stepped inside to inquire about a place to spend the night. The very moment that he set foot in the store, Drucker heard a man's low drawl addressing him.

"'Lo there," came a voice so plodding that it made Drucker imagine its speaker had slowly chewed and swallowed the first syllable of the greeting.

"Hello," Drucker replied. He turned to face a thin man, gray of temple and ruddy of cheek. The man stepped out from behind a counter lined with brown-glass bottles.

"Something you lookin' for?" the man asked, eyeing Drucker. He wiped the sweat from his forehead and deposited his moistened fingers into the front pocket of his green apron, which hung loosely in front of him, untied at the back.

"Why yes," said Drucker. "A place to stay, actually. For the night. You see I'm new in town and—"

"I see," cut in the man, his tone exposing the native suspicion of a man who hadn't met many strangers and hadn't a reason to like the few that he had.

"Perhaps there's a boardinghouse in town?" tried Drucker.

"Perhaps there is, perhaps there ain't," countered the man. "What brings you to Clayton?"

The answer to this, Drucker could tell, would mean the difference between a night of shelter and supper and a night spent sitting upright against the wall of the train depot, counting down the minutes until the next train passed through.

As he tried to piece together a response, Drucker became suddenly and acutely aware that *I followed three women off the train* was not only an unacceptable explanation but also quite a shortsighted choice. He had no time to waste second-guessing himself, though. Not in the face of his more pressing concern of how to talk his way into the good graces of this gruff, apron-wearing store keep.

"Horses," Drucker heard himself say.

"Horses?"

"Yes," said Drucker, resorting to God's honest truth, just as he'd promised himself that he would whenever in doubt. "There was a letter. About horses."

The man kept his eyes trained on Drucker, searching his face as if preparing to ask another question, but one that had not yet come to him. The silence gave Drucker the feeling that there would be no boardinghouse for him. Suddenly, the hope that there could be seemed foolish, and his escape from Atlanta reckless and ill-fated: first boarding the wrong train, then impulsively getting off at what was quickly proving to be the wrong town.

Drucker began to fish in his pocket for a few loose coins with which to buy enough food to make the merchant happy and keep his own stomach full through the night on the floor of the depot that seemed inevitable.

"Look," said Drucker softly. "I don't mean to bother you. I'll take two of these," he said, moving two yellow loaves from a platter labeled "Corn Cakes" onto the counter that stood between the two men. The cakes hit the counter with the dull thud of stale cornmeal. "Make it three," he said, grabbing for a third with one hand, removing the other hand from his pocket to produce a few coins.

Ignoring the cakes on the counter between them, the storekeeper motioned to the floor. "You drop something?"

Drucker looked down.

"Ah, indeed I did." He stooped to retrieve the scuffed silver badge that he had won as a child and stuffed in his pocket before leaving Atlanta, unable to stomach the thought of leaving it behind. He picked it up and dropped it on the counter, letting it fall with a clank against the handful of coins he had placed there. "How much will it be, then? The cakes. The three cakes," asked Drucker, turning his attention back to the transaction at hand.

The shopkeeper had no interest in the cakes, though, and when Drucker looked up he saw that something had changed in the man's face. A light not previously there sparkled behind his eyes, and the frostiness of his manner seemed to be melting away right in front of Drucker, as if a spring thaw was now reaching the snowcapped crags of the man's temples.

"I thought it was you," the man said conspiratorially, his voice still slow but his tone now soft, hushed.

"You had me fooled," replied Drucker in an equally hushed voice.

"Couldn't be sure till I saw the badge."

"Then it's good that I dropped it," said Drucker, as much to himself as to his companion.

"The horses. The letter. The badge," continued the shopkeeper. "It was my brother that sent you that letter, you know?"

"I didn't," said Drucker, taking a leap of faith, thinking back to the conversation that he had overheard between the three sisters on the train. "All I know is that when I heard this town was looking for a Pinkerton detective, I had to come." It was nothing less than the truth.

Drucker was rewarded with the continued thawing of the once-icy demeanor of the storekeeper, who confirmed Drucker's suspicion that he had been mistaken for the Pinkerton detective for whom the mayor had sent. With the mistaken identity confirmed, names were exchanged, hands were shaken, and Drucker's confidence that a night on the streets could be avoided was restored.

"About that boardinghouse," Drucker tried once more. "Now that we've cleared up this misunderstanding, perhaps there *is* one?"

"Not for you," said the shopkeeper. His words were harsh but his tone was light, leaving Drucker confused but undeterred.

"Well, my friend," said Drucker, smiling and laying a hand on the other man's shoulder, "I'm afraid I'm not so skilled a detective that I can close this case before sunset. At least not without a hot meal down the hatch." He winked.

"'Course not," replied the man, returning the wink, "but a fine detective like yourself don't need to be shackin' up in a boardin' house. Anna'll take you home."

"Anna?" repeated back Drucker.

"Anna—my niece. The mayor's daughter. You'll stay with them. They got plenty a room."

"Oh," said Drucker, worried that the case of mistaken identity that had a moment ago been his meal ticket would surely unravel if he were to actually meet the author of the letter that Drucker had not actually received. "I couldn't impose."

"You won't," said the shopkeeper matter-of-factly as he straightened a row of bottles on the counter in front of him.

"It's very hospitable of you, really it is. It's just that I wouldn't want to be"—*found out, tarred and feathered, run out of town*—"a burden to anyone. Suppose the investigation takes weeks. I wouldn't want to put upon the mayor. Surely he's a very busy—"

"Oh, don't you go on worryin' about him," assured the shop keep. "Clayton's a small town. There ain't so much to occupy that man's time that he can't make room in his home for the man who's come down south to little old Clayton on account a our horse thief. Besides, I reckon you'll be busier than he is."

"With the case?"

"Yes, sir, that's right. This rash a horse thievery been darn close to all there is to talk 'bout 'round here for months. This town ain't never seen nothin' like it."

The two men locked eyes. "That's why we need you, Detective Drucker."

That entreaty, there it was again. That desperate plea, ringing eerily similar to the one his father had made in Drucker's last week at Atlanta Southern. This time, though, unlike at the bank, the call to action lit a fire within him. Something inside of him had changed, as if a new hand had been dealt him, the ante upped.

He wasn't at the bank any longer, and Clayton was not Atlanta. If he had saved the bank from collapsing, his reward would have been to inherit a life he didn't want. But this—this new challenge in a new town—held so much more potential. Here in Clayton he could be anyone he wanted to be. If he could find the horse thief, he would be the man who solved the greatest crime this county had ever fathomed. Stepping up now would mean writing his own destiny. And why had he left Atlanta, if not to do exactly that?

"Very well then," said Drucker. "I'll wait here while you send word for Anna."

"Oh, no need to wait, Detective," said the shopkeeper, looking pleased. "She's right here." He turned and hollered his niece's name in the direction of the back of the store.

A few beats passed with no sign of her. The shopkeeper shook his head. "Now where has that girl run off to this time?" He sighed. "Wait here. I'll git 'er." And with that, the man disappeared through a doorway hung with a curtain that flapped as loosely as his untied green apron.

Drucker's mind began to race the moment he was left alone. He was a detective now, with a crime to solve and a new town in which to solve it. He wanted to solve it, too, and not just for the excitement of it, but to make good by this little town called Clayton for which he was already beginning to feel an affinity. Not only was it the site of intrigue, but it was also the birthplace of new beginnings.

And if Drucker was honest with himself, most endearing of all at that moment was the prospect that Clayton might provide him with some female company. *Anna.*

He let the name roll around silently on his tongue. His heartbeat quickened at the thought of the alluring young damsel who would at any moment emerge from behind that fluttering curtain. *What striking beauty will I meet?* Drucker wondered, immediately losing himself in a daydream starred in by the lovely Anna who, like a beloved actress returning to the stage after a performance, was met in his mind by bouquets of roses, whistles, and applause.

Drucker barely had a chance to indulge the daydream for long, though, for at that moment the shopkeeper burst through the curtain. "Found her!"

And then there she was, materializing from behind her uncle, but so completely unlike the image that Drucker had quickly conjured that he almost said aloud, *Found who?*

This Anna who stood before him bore no resemblance to the Anna he had hoped to meet. Her hair, the color of thirsty straw, hung lifelessly just past her chin. Her eyes, rather sunken, were the color of dishwater and barely contrasted with her skin which, while unblemished, was sallow and a little damp despite the dry weather. A mouth, the third in her trio of washed-out elements, was anchored by corners that drew tiny arrows toward her strong jaw, which looked out of place on an otherwise weak-featured face.

"Hello," said Anna, looking down as she addressed Drucker, as if this sad chore of inspiring disappointment was a well-worn routine.

Drucker tipped his cap. "Hello. Anna is it?" How very hard he hoped that now it was he who had an identity mistaken.

"That's right," she said, still looking down.

"Anna," said her uncle, "your daddy done sent all the way to New York City for this man standing here. He's the detective who's come to find the thief that's been runnin' off with the horses."

"Oh," said Anna, pulling her head up, unable to hide her excitement, "how wonderful."

"Pleased to make your acquaintance, Miss Anna." Removing his hat, he bowed slightly and said, "Drucker May, detective for hire."

It may not have been his identity for very long, but at that moment it was as good as the truth, and in his whole life no introduction had ever felt so right.

"Charmed," said Anna. Her smile gave Drucker pause. Disappointing, yes, but ugly she was not. She was plain, very plain, but Drucker had to admit that when she smiled, her eyes glittered a little. Not enough to make her pretty, but enough to make it clear that the life behind her eyes was done an injustice by her washed-out palette. *A little color dabbed in the right places could go a long way,* Drucker thought, and even without it there was something likable about her: her humility, her easy excitement, that subtle sparkle like a diamond in the dishwater.

Besides, he would certainly have his hands full trying to find the horse thief that was confounding Clayton. That task alone would give him more than enough to occupy his time and his mind.

"Anna, take this man home now. He must be exhausted," said the shopkeeper. Turning to Drucker, he smiled and added, "She'll take good care of you."

Drucker smiled and nodded in return. *It's better this way,* he told himself, *the last thing I need right now is to be distracted by a beautiful woman.*

He quickly convinced himself of this and jogged a few steps to catch up to Anna, who was already headed for the door. For a moment they walked side by side in silence until Drucker fell a few steps behind when he paused just short of the doorway and moved aside to allow a couple to enter. First came a man and then a woman, whose full skirt brushed against Drucker as he stood beside the store's threshold.

"Aren't you coming?" Anna called back to Drucker from several paces ahead of him.

"Of course I am," he replied hurriedly, though in fact he felt as if he could hardly move, so paralyzed was he by the unthinkable beauty of the woman who had just glided past him.

CHAPTER NINE

O n his first night in Clayton, Drucker found himself seated in
front of a warm pork loin paired with a pile of baby potatoes
sliced into halves and still wearing their puckered purple skins,
their white centers dripping with yellow butter and sprinkled with
rosemary. He couldn't have dreamed of anything more fragrant or
delicious.

Across the table from him sat Mayor Newton, a rubber ball of
a man, short and round and wound so tightly with excitement that
he gave the impression that if you threw him against the wall, he
would keep bouncing back and forth for days.

"Very good, very good, very good," said the mayor, a tuft of
skin-colored mustache twitching as he spoke. Drucker was telling
the story of his chance meeting with the mayor's brother, and the
mayor was hanging on his every word.

The mayor's wife sat next to Drucker and while his mouth was
occupied with the savory meat, she laid a hand lightly on his fore-
arm. "Well, you're already our hero just for comin' all the way down
here to Clayton, Detective Drucker," she cooed.

Like her daughter, the mayor's wife's face and hair blended together in the colorless hue of hay, like a plant in desperate need of watering.

"Oh," said Drucker, swallowing the mouthful and blushing a bit, "not a hero, just a man trying to do a job. The moment I heard about your horse thief I knew I had to come. It was like a magnetic force was pulling me here."

"A magnetic force!" repeated the mayor's wife as if she had never heard anything so delightful. "Charles, did you hear that?" She turned to her husband. "He felt a magnetic force!"

"Well, 'course he did, Penny. The man's a detective, solving crimes is in his blood. He'll solve this doozy for us, I just know it, I can just *feel* it." The mayor's whole body shook with excitement as he spoke. "I'm already picturing the day when you find these scoundrels, Drucker. Oh, the parade I'll throw! I can see it now." He turned theatrically to his wife. "Penny, can't you just picture the parade we'll have?"

"I can see it, Charles!"

"With all due respect, Mayor, I suggest that we put one foot before the other," Drucker cautioned.

"He's right, Father," said Anna, piping up for the first time since they had been seated. "Don't get ahead of yourself like you always do."

The mayor's face contorted as his daughter's reproach brought him back down to earth.

"Anna—" he started, but Drucker cut him off.

"Mayor, tell me what you know about the horse thief."

The interruption was perfectly timed to knock the mayor's momentum from one source of excitement to the other. He turned back to Drucker. "A fine question, my boy. I only wish I had something remotely resembling an answer for you. The truth is we know next to nothing. The rascal—"

"Or rascal*s*," interjected his wife.

"The rascal or rascals," repeated the mayor, "have managed to completely elude us for months now. Eldridge Harkins, the sheriff, has been investigating, of course, but the job's too big for him. A few times he's claimed to be onto someone, but then another horse will disappear, and his whole theory'll be shot to hell. It's like nothing this town has ever seen before."

"When did the first horse go missing?" asked Drucker.

"October," said the mayor's wife.

"The twenty-fifth," added Anna with precision. "From old Farmer Bell's place out on Hillsboro Road. Farmer Bell has twenty horses, so I guess the thief thought he wouldn't notice being down the one."

"But he did?" asked Drucker, spearing a purple potato wedge.

"Of course he noticed," said Anna. "You don't own twenty horses without paying attention to…well, horses. Horses are his business and in his blood. He loves them like his own children. Gives each and every one of them a name. It was Birdie Black that went first. Farmer Bell rode into town that afternoon to spread the word and alert anyone he could find about the thief. He stopped in at Uncle's store when I was working."

"How could he be sure that Birdie Black was stolen?" asked Drucker. "Surely there are animals out there that prey on horses."

"There are," agreed the mayor's wife, "but the horse was just completely gone, not a bone or bit of flesh to be found. There were no other signs of a struggle, and not so much as a scratch on any of the other horses. If it had been the mountain lions they wouldn't have been able to completely decimate the one—"

"Not without causing a stir among the others," cut in the mayor animatedly.

"Besides," added Anna demurely, "one horse, maybe, but what could hunt this many horses without leaving a trace of any of them?"

"How many have disappeared now?" Drucker asked.

"Twenty-five!" answered the other three in unison.

"You see, my boy, what you have to understand," said the mayor, becoming serious, his tone suddenly grave, "is that horses are this town's lifeblood. Ain't hardly nothin' that can get done without 'em. Most a the homes here are real spread out. To get to your neighbor's house, you need a horse, to go into town, you need a horse, to get out of town, you need a horse. We depend on 'em. Not to mention what a thing like this does to the psyche of a small town like ours. Ain't never been much crime around here. We like to keep things quiet. People ain't accustomed to livin' with a scoundrel loose among us. Makes people nervous. Why, it's a miracle anyone can sleep a wink in this town, what with a horse murderer at large."

"So a dead horse has been found?" asked Drucker.

"No, my boy, not a one."

"Then why do you think the horses have been killed?" he probed.

The mayor paused to give Drucker's question due thought. Finally, toying with his still-twitching mustache, he answered, "Well, if they're not dead, where in tarnation are they? There's two dozen gone. Who could afford to feed the damn things? Where could twenty-five horses be kept inconspicuously? It's not as if you can sell 'em. Not around here. Everyone within a hundred miles a here knows what's been goin' on in Clayton. Anyone trying to buy a horse would know it's stolen property. Why, with the size of the reward we're offering to catch this thief, a man would stand to make three times the price of the horse for turnin' in the man that tried to sell it to him. You'd have to transport them to another time zone to escape this news, the way it's been spreadin'. And how do you do that? Every conductor that passes through has been alerted not to accept any horses onto freight cars. Then what's left? There's just too damn many questions here, Drucker. That's why we need you. To piece together some answers so we can finally start to get some rest around here again."

Drucker looked at each of his dinner companions, making brief eye contact with Anna and then her mother before settling his confident gaze on Mayor Newton. "I'll get you those answers, Mayor."

"I know you will, my boy."

The men exchanged silent nods of the head. A call to duty, accepted.

"Well," said the mayor, standing and placing both hands on his round protruding belly, "I'm stuffed. Drucker, you'll stay in Anna's studio. Anna, show Drucker to his quarters, won't you?"

"Yes, Father."

"Good girl," said the mayor. He walked over to Drucker and laid his heavy paw of a hand on Drucker's shoulder from behind. "You'll start in the morning then?"

"I will," nodded Drucker.

"I want you to know," continued the mayor, "that anything you need for this investigation, you'll have. You have my full support to follow any lead, to question anyone."

"Thank you, sir."

"And you're welcome in my home for as long as it takes. But Drucker," urged the mayor, "I want you to find this scoundrel *fast* so I can string him up and throw us all a parade."

With that, the mayor clapped Drucker on the shoulder and left the room, humming and swinging his arms wildly as if conducting an invisible marching band as he backpedaled out of the dining room.

⇥ ⇤

After dinner Anna led Drucker to a cottage behind the main house. The two had walked in silence from the dining room, but as she turned the silver doorknob, Drucker asked, "Anna, why is it called your studio?"

At that moment, she pushed open the door, and the answer to his question was revealed along with hundreds of paintings that lined the walls, sat on the floor, and perched on easels.

"It looks more like a museum than a studio," said Drucker, pacing from one painting to another. "Did you paint all these?"

"It's my hobby," said Anna quietly. She walked over to an easel, one of several, and held up a black-and-white photograph that rested on its ledge. "I find photographs of places that I'd like to go. Then I paint them, and it feels as if I've actually been there."

"Anna, these are really quite stunning," said Drucker, admiring a lifelike mountain landscape. The pieces varied in size, but each was crafted to perfection. "I feel as if I could walk right into them. The colors are so"—he paused to choose the right word—"alive."

"Thank you, sir. I mean, Detective," Anna stammered.

"Please, Anna, call me Drucker."

"I will," she said, looking at the ground. "Thank you, Drucker."

"Anna, you've got a real talent."

A hint of a blush crept into Anna's cheeks as she picked up a paintbrush. "Whenever I'm not at Uncle's store, I'm in here. It's where I'm happiest," she said wistfully, but then turned to Drucker and quickly added, "Please don't worry that I'll be a nuisance, though. This is your space for as long as you need it, and I'll stay out of it while you're here. The last thing I would want to do is impede the investigation by getting in your way."

"Anna," said Drucker, "this is your studio. Please make use of it as you'd like. I should be the one promising not to get in your way."

Anna said nothing, but her smile brought out the eye sparkle he had seen at the general store. She walked over to a ladder that pointed up toward a lofted space.

"There's a bed up there."

"Very well."

"And there's a door that leads out onto the roof. It's a nice place to sit, especially at night."

"That sounds lovely. I'll try that."

"We breakfast at eight."

"Eight it is."

"And there's water, in a pitcher, up by the bed. It's fresh from the well. I brought it earlier."

"Thank you, Anna."

There was silence for a moment.

"Is there anything else you need or...want, Drucker?" She looked hopeful.

"I think I should be just fine. Thank you, Anna."

"Very well." She headed toward the door. "Good night, Drucker."

"Good night, Anna."

Anna had reached the door and Drucker the base of the ladder to the second-story loft when suddenly he turned back toward her.

"Anna, before you go..."

"Yes?" She turned back to him eagerly.

"If I may ask, how did you remember that it was the twenty-fifth?"

"The twenty-fifth?"

"Of October. When Birdie Black went missing."

"Oh," said Anna, making sense of the question. "I remember it because I wrote in my diary that day. Whenever I see something I've never seen before, I try to record it in my diary."

"And you made an entry on October twenty-fifth?"

"That's right."

"Because it was the first time you had heard of a horse being stolen?" Drucker asked.

"Because it was the first time I'd ever seen a grown man crying," Anna answered. And with those words she turned to leave, whispering as she closed the door behind her, "Sleep tight, Drucker."

CHAPTER TEN

By early afternoon on the first day of his investigation, Drucker was seated at the kitchen table of the third home that he had visited that day. There he sipped iced tea from a sweating tin cup as his hostess, the graying Mrs. Gale, bustled between cabinets, assembling a stack of ginger cookies on a plate for him.

"Please don't bother on my account," protested Drucker.

"Don't be silly, Detective, a strapping young man like you needs nutrition to keep up energy on a hunt like this. Besides, it's hot as coals out there. More iced tea?"

Drucker looked down into his cup and, seeing the bottom, held it up to be refilled. His hostess poured ice tea until it reached the brim up his cup and then lowered herself onto the chair next to his.

"Mrs. Gale," said Drucker, "you said you lost two horses. Did they go missing at the same time?"

"No, dear, about a month apart, I'd say."

Drucker took a note in the journal splayed out in front of him. "About a month apart," he repeated, quickly transcribing her answer. "And did you notice any abnormal activity near your home around that time?"

"No, dear, certainly not."

Drucker nodded in comprehension. "Have you noticed any strangers in town recently?"

"No," said Mrs. Gale. "That is, other than you, of course. You're the only stranger I've seen in town, Detective."

Drucker continued to make notes. "Since the first horse went missing, you haven't seen anyone new in town other than myself?" he asked, clarifying.

"No, dear, other than you I haven't seen anyone new in town, period. Ever." She let loose a hearty *ha* before quickly becoming serious again. "Clayton's a very small town, Detective. If a stranger came through here, we'd all take notice. More cookies?"

"No thank you, Mrs. Gale, I couldn't." This was no exaggeration, for his first two hostesses had been no less generous with offerings of food and drink. News of the arrival of a detective had spread quickly from the general store, and at each home the citizens of Clayton had thrown open their doors to him, stuffing him to the gills with their relentless hospitality.

Drucker put down his pen. "Mrs. Gale, it sounds as if you believe the horse thief is living among you here in Clayton."

"Does it?"

Drucker pointed down to his notebook and recited back to her, "'If a stranger came through here, we'd all take notice.'"

"Well, we would."

"And you haven't."

"That's right."

"What about your fellow citizens of Clayton? Has anyone been acting strangely since the horses started to go missing?"

"Strangely?"

"Yes, behaving differently than before."

Mrs. Gale hesitated. "I've never been one to point fingers, Detective."

"But there *is* someone you find suspicious?"

She hedged. "I really couldn't say with certainty…"

"Certainty is my job, Mrs. Gale," intoned Drucker with the air of a seasoned detective.

Mrs. Gale pursed her lips and shook her head. Finally she burst out, "Oh, good gracious, I might as well just say it!"

Drucker looked at her eagerly, encouragingly.

"Detective, there's something that's been weighing on my mind for months now." She leaned in very close to Drucker and whispered conspiratorially, "Mary Louise Templeton has a new hat!"

"A new hat?" repeated Drucker.

"Yes! Oh, that feels wonderful to get off my chest, Detective, it's like I can breathe again!"

"Mrs. Gale, I'm afraid I don't follow. As far as I can see, a new hat does not a horse thief make."

"Generally, I agree, Detective, but if it's paired with a new dress and new shoes on a woman that's as modest and penny-pinching as they come…then does it?"

"Perhaps her husband has come into some money?"

"My thoughts exactly," said Mrs. Gale nodding expectantly at Drucker.

"And what does Mr. Templeton do?" asked Drucker.

"That's *Pastor* Templeton to you," said Mrs. Gale, using both hands to push herself up from her chair. "I'd look in their direction, Detective, but you didn't hear it from me."

"My lips are sealed, Mrs. Gale," said Drucker.

And sealed they were, but they were also pulled upward into a smile as Drucker left Mrs. Gale's kitchen, for at least he would have *some* progress to report to the mayor that evening.

CHAPTER ELEVEN

The next morning, Drucker left the mayor's breakfast table with a stomach as full as the pages of his notebook. In all, he had collected fifteen pages of scribbled notes during his first day on the job, and while the tangled reports formed more of a web than an arrow, several pieces of information weighed heavy with potential.

On his second day of investigation, he planned to sniff around the church to see if more roads did indeed lead to the Templetons. But first he wanted to conduct interviews at a few more homes and so, notebook in hand, Drucker knocked on the door of the first home of the day.

Then he waited as a long, quiet minute passed. He knocked again, reading and rereading his notes as he waited, until finally from inside the house came a noise. Voices, raised in anger, loud enough to suggest an argument but not so loud that Drucker could make out the words. Drucker felt compelled to give a third knock. Perhaps he could interrupt whatever strife was erupting inside. But when this attempt, too, went unanswered, Drucker turned to leave.

Better to stick to the investigation and leave the domestic disturbances to another, he thought.

When he was several paces away from the house, though, he heard the door swing open.

"I'm sorry to keep you waiting." A voice, a sniffle.

Drucker turned back toward the house. "Hello, ma'am—" his words stopped suddenly.

"Can I help you?" The woman standing in the doorway was looking down, smoothing her skirt as a single teardrop crept down her flushed right cheek. When she looked up their eyes met, and Drucker's breath was sucked back so deeply into his lungs that he could feel it in his stomach, mingling with his breakfast.

"I'm sorry," said Drucker to the woman whose beauty had paralyzed him when they had crossed paths at the general store. "I don't mean to interrupt."

"Interrupt what?" she asked, averting her eyes.

"Nothing. I just meant to say—" stammered Drucker, not wanting to embarrass the most beautiful woman he had ever seen.

"You heard us fightin', didn't you?"

"Ma'am, I don't mean to—"

She sighed, waving off his attempt at courtesy with a knowing pass of her hand. "Please, you're hardly the first."

"I'm sorry," Drucker said again, meaning it. "Can I help?" He took a step toward the house.

"You in the business of teachin' old dogs new tricks?"

"No, ma'am, but I could talk to him if you'd like."

"Talkin' won't do any good. That man won't listen to anyone." Still standing in the doorway, the dark-haired beauty lifted her eyes and looked directly at Drucker, melting him. "By the way," she asked, "who are you, anyhow?"

"Drucker May, ma'am, I'm a—"

"You're the detective!"

Drucker smiled sheepishly in response.

"You're the one who's going to save this town from that damned horse thief."

"I hope to, ma'am."

There was quiet for a moment while the woman looked Drucker over. "So what brings you to my home, Detective?"

"Please, ma'am, call me Drucker. I'm conducting interviews. Some basic fact-finding, that's all." He returned her direct gaze, wondering if she was feeling the heat of it that he was. "If I could, I'd very much like to—"

But at that moment a holler rang out from inside the house, cutting off Drucker in the middle of his statement, forcing it to hang unfinished between him and the woman in front of him, all of the possible endings to it dancing in his head.

"I'm sorry, I have to go." Her words tripped quickly over one another.

"Of course."

"But I would like to speak with you. Can you come back tomorrow?"

"I can."

Another eruption echoed from inside the house.

"I'm sorry," she said again, as she closed the door. "Tomorrow, Detective Drucker."

"Tomorrow," he repeated to the closed door in front of him. It should have been his cue to leave, but rather than walking away from the house, Drucker found himself walking toward it. An urge to protect a woman he hardly knew compelled him stay. He swore to himself that he would break down the door at the first hint of commotion inside, and so he listened for it. The harder he listened for an excuse to enter, though, the longer the house remained silent. He put his ear to the door, but still there was nothing. Minutes passed, dozens of minutes, an hour of silence.

When he finally walked away, a rush of pure excitement eclipsed the disappointment of not having had an opportunity act as the hero. Drucker could feel his ears heating up with the blood pumped by his racing, ecstatic heart. The day had just begun, and already he couldn't wait for it to end so that he could experience the word still hanging on his lips: tomorrow.

That afternoon, after an informative interview with Mrs. Hill in her home and some potentially productive palavering with the butcher at his shop, Drucker approached his fourth and final stop of the day, Cumberland First Presbyterian Church, where Pastor Templeton presided.

Though his notebook was growing fat with collected facts, Drucker's mind kept drifting back to the immensity of all that he did not yet know. Since his morning encounter, his mind had been racing with questions that looped in fast-moving circles like steeds in a derby. *What motive was there to steal a horse and who had it; were the horses alive, and if so, could they ever be recovered; what was that beautiful woman's name, and why had he not asked her for it; and did her hair smell like honey blossoms, and if it did would he ever have a chance to know it, to really know it and...*

But it was time to pull himself together and set those questions aside for the moment, Drucker told himself as he approached the church and caught sight of a figure emerging from the building and walking toward him.

"Hello there," called Drucker, waving. The two men neared each other. When they were just several paces apart, Drucker politely extended his hand. "I'm Drucker May," he said and paused to gauge his companion's reaction, thinking that certainly word of a detective's arrival in town would have reached the church, since it had seemingly reached every home in the county. Whether it had or hadn't, his outstretched hand was ignored.

"Lookin' for somethin'?" asked the strained and cracking voice of a youth not yet a man but no longer a boy.

"Yes," said Drucker, withdrawing his hand. "Pastor Templeton." He looked at the youth. "Among other things."

"He ain't here," said the young man curtly.

"And Mrs. Templeton?"

"The same."

"Do you know how I might find them?" asked Drucker, trying to remain patient.

"He'll be here on Sunday," said the surly youth. "Won't you?" he asked, without an ounce of curiosity in his voice.

Drucker didn't want to wait the better part of a week to speak to the pastor, who had emerged early on as a possible suspect. "I'd like to find him before then. You see, son, I'm—"

"I know who you are, Detective. Word travels fast in this town, and we don't get many strangers 'round these parts."

"So I gather," said Drucker, sizing up his new acquaintance, all gawky limbs, with a too-long neck that looked incapable of supporting the head that ballooned from it.

"You find them horses yet, Detective?" asked the boy, with as little curiosity as his last question.

Drucker couldn't be sure it was a taunt, but it hardly mattered. It was the first hostile interaction he'd had since those first moments in the general store. Everyone who heard Drucker had come to Clayton to find the horse thief had welcomed him with open arms. Until now.

"Look, let's start again," suggested Drucker. "I'm Drucker May. And you are?" He once again extended his hand for a shake.

"Silas," said his acquaintance without mirroring the gesture.

"Silas," said Drucker, his patience with the young man beginning to wither, "it's very nice to meet you. I have *not* found the horses yet, but today is the second day of my investigation, my third day in Clayton, and I'm hoping to interview Pastor Templeton as soon as I can. There's no cause for alarm, I'm simply trying to collect as many facts as possible."

The young man moved a pace closer to Drucker, leaned in, and lowered his voice. "I have a fact for you, Detective."

"Yes, Silas?" Drucker opened his notebook.

Silas looked left and right as if to make sure no one could see them conversing. He leaned even closer to Drucker and licked his lips to wet them. "Here's your fact, Detective," said Silas, looking Drucker directly in the eyes. "The pastor ain't here." He punctuated each word with spittle. Then he reached out and closed Drucker's notebook.

This time the taunt was unmistakable.

"Very well then," said Drucker. He had to admit there was something intimidating about his lanky new acquaintance. Young he was, but he had confidence, and whether he was employed as groundskeeper or guard dog, he was certainly doing a fine job of protecting the Templetons from getting any questions.

"If you want to see the pastor," said Silas, "he'll be here Sunday."

Drucker sighed, accepting that this would be the best and only answer that he would get on the topic. "Do you think I can ask him a few questions then?" he asked.

"I've always found Sundays to be a good day to ask questions," replied Silas cryptically.

Drucker nodded briefly. "I'll be here Sunday then," he said, but Silas was already walking back toward the church.

As he watched the young man silently disappear back into the white-steepled structure, Drucker scribbled down two words.

One was Silas, the other Sunday.

CHAPTER TWELVE

W hen Drucker returned to the home of the beauty whose
path he had by then crossed twice, it was with beads of
sweat forming on his forehead. He took the steps up her front
porch slowly, savoring his excitement.

His hand was raised to give a knock when the door opened.
The raven-haired beauty appeared with her finger to her lips. She
beckoned for Drucker to enter. "Shh. Come in," she whispered,
"but be quiet. He's sleeping." She moved her finger away from her
lips and pointed toward the stairs.

Drucker followed as she led him wordlessly through the glum
confines of the front rooms to the kitchen at the back of the
house, where two large windows granted the house some desperately needed light. It was there that she stopped suddenly, and
Drucker, unable to stop in time, ran up against her, his chest
making contact with her back, his nose nestling, if for no more
than a second, against her loosely pinned up mass of shiny black
hair.

He took a step back and she a step forward, increasing the space between them by two paces.

She turned toward him and spoke first, her voice soft. "I'm sorry for—" She smiled shyly, not finishing her sentence.

"No, no. My fault," he murmured, smiling shyly back. Their exchange of smiles paralyzed Drucker. In the light of the kitchen, the woman before him looked even more radiant than he had remembered her.

A quiet moment passed before the woman broke the silence and their eye contact, turning away from Drucker. "Detective, can I offer you something to drink?"

"No thank you, ma'am."

"Lucinda."

"Ma'am?"

"Please, Detective. Call me Lucinda."

"Yes, ma'am," answered Drucker automatically, and they both laughed. "I'm sorry. Lucinda."

Their eyes locked again, and Drucker felt compelled to take a step closer to her.

She in turn did not back away. "So, Detective, you had some questions for me?"

"Questions?" repeated Drucker, clearing his throat, feeling the hot rush of blood in his cheeks and ears. Could she read his mind? Did the words *Does her hair smell like honey blossoms?* show through the eyes behind which they whirled?

"About the horses…"

"Oh yes! The horses." With great relief, Drucker quickly pulled out his notebook from his jacket's breast pocket and opened it to a fresh page. "May I?" he asked, gesturing toward a chair.

"Please," said Lucinda, taking the one next to it.

They talked for two hours. What started as question and answer soon developed into easy conversation, punctuated at times by laughter and at times by a pervasive stillness as their eyes latched onto one another.

"You really haven't noticed anyone acting out of the ordinary?" asked Drucker after one such pause.

"I really have not, Detective." Though he had told her call him Drucker several times, the truth was that he so liked the way the word *detective* sounded as it rolled off her tongue and the way her mouth moved when she said it that he had stopped correcting her and started to let himself enjoy it.

"What about Mrs. Templeton?"

"Mary Louise?" asked Lucinda with surprise. "She's a friend. What about her?"

"Have you noticed anything…different about her lately?"

"Not really."

"Not *really*?" asked Drucker, poised to take a note.

"Well, now that I stop to think of it, I suppose she hasn't been dropping by the house as frequently."

"She comes to your house often?"

"She visits me, yes. She hasn't come by as often recently, but nothing suspicious to my mind. As I said, she's a friend."

"And her husband?"

Lucinda made a face as if she'd eaten something sour. "I wouldn't know. I rarely see him."

"Pastor Templeton? You rarely see him?"

"Hardly ever." She shook her head.

"I thought the whole town turns up at his sermons on Sunday."

"Just about everyone…"

"But you rarely see the pastor?"

"…Except for me."

"You don't go to church?"

"Do you go to church, Detective?"

Drucker avoided the question. "What about your husband? Does he go?"

"Yes, he goes. I think. He says he does. How should I know? What's that phrase from the Bible, 'I am not my husband's keeper'?" She gave a little laugh.

"Something like that," said Drucker, her laugh making him unable restrain his smile.

"Maybe if I went to church more often, I would be better at quoting scripture."

"Maybe," said Drucker, now smiling hard right into her eyes. It took everything he had in him to keep his hands off of her. He gripped his pen as tightly as he could with his right hand, and slipped his left underneath his own leg, sitting on it in order to keep from reaching out and stroking her cheek.

"I must say, I've really enjoyed talking to you, Detective. It's not every day you find someone you could spend hours just..." Her voice trailed off wistfully for a moment, and Drucker felt himself growing excited at the prospect of spending hours just...anything-ing with this woman. It didn't matter the final word of that statement, he would take whatever verb he could get and do it and it alone for hours with her. That last word never came, though. In its place a roar from upstairs rang out.

"The beast awakes." Lucinda sighed, still looking into Drucker's eyes.

"Oh?" said Drucker, exposing his charming dimples. "I thought perhaps a train was passing through."

"If only," said Lucinda, smiling, but this time sadly. "I should go." She stood, and he automatically followed suit, his body magnetized toward hers.

"Of course," he said, his tone turned serious.

"It's not that I want to, it's just that—"

"You don't have to explain." He closed his notebook and with it tucked securely back into his breast pocket, he became acutely aware that both his hands were suddenly free.

"Detective," she said, their bodies inching closer as they stood chest to chest in the middle of the kitchen. "Will I see you again?"

"Yes, ma'am."

"Lucinda," she corrected in a whisper barely louder than a breath.

"Lucinda," he repeated, their bodies pressed together.

Lucinda reached out then and grabbed the lapels of Drucker's jacket, pulling him toward her as she backpedaled, towing him along until her back was up against the wall, and his hands were on her face, and their lips were indistinguishable. They went on like this, his lips moving to her neck, her hands moving to his waist, until another clap of manmade thunder rolled through from the second story, and Lucinda pushed Drucker away and darted quickly toward the doorway.

"Detective?"

"Yes?" he asked, wiping his mouth with the sleeve of his jacket.

"Come back sometime, won't you?"

"Just tell me when."

Lucinda smiled, her eyes lighting up.

"How about Sunday?"

━╪┼╫━

And then, in the blink of an eye, it was Sunday, the fifth Sunday in a row that Drucker found himself wrapped up in Lucinda like a baby in bunting. Sunday morning rendezvous had become their ritual. While the rest of the town prayed together, Drucker and Lucinda took part in a kind of communion so awe-inspiring it felt holy. While the townspeople of Clayton worshipped from the pews, Drucker worshipped at his lover's feet, kissing them, running his tongue up the inside of her legs, starting at her ankles and moving up past her knees, her thighs.

"I can't get you off my mind, Lucinda," Drucker admitted, as he lay spent, his chest still heaving with big joyful breaths. Losing himself in the intimacy of caressing her, undressing her, and entering her week after week had helped him to break the habit of calling her ma'am.

"Right back at you, Detective." Lucinda had not broken the habit of calling Drucker "Detective," but he found it endearing when she did and downright exhilarating when she yelled it out at the height of passion.

"It worries me sometimes, though. I fear it's playing tricks with my sanity," said Drucker, more seriously.

Lucinda sat up in the bed and faced Drucker, her long hair pulled back so that her bare chest and long neck were exposed. "Detective," she said, "there's nothing sane about what we're doing here. What we have between us is beyond reason. It's called passion. If you aren't goin' insane, you aren't doin' it right."

Drucker sat up so that they were eye to eye. "Lucinda, wherever I go, I see you. Or rather, I think I see you, but it's not really you."

"Like a mirage in the desert?" She seemed to understand.

"Just like that," he nodded. "Last week, in town, I saw a woman who I swore was you but when she turned around, it turned out to just be a...a *mirage*."

Lucinda cocked her head in sympathy. "You have to stop worrying so much, Detective. So you saw a woman who looked like me. Where's the harm in that? A little wishful thinkin' never hurt anyone." She tenderly cleared a lock of hair away from his eyes and kissed his eyelid.

Drucker couldn't help but worry, though, for in truth this same experience had occurred several times over. No less than five times had Drucker been sure that he had spotted Lucinda when, in fact, it was just another woman whose shapely posterior and lush mess of dark hair made her resemble his lover from behind.

But seeing the *real* Lucinda and her bare skin just inches away from him made him do his best to shake off his concerns.

"You know what I think?" he asked after a moment, his twin dimples at their deepest.

"What's that, Detective?" asked Lucinda with a suggestive grin of her own.

"I think church will be getting out soon, and time is of the essence." He lay back down, pulling her on top of him.

"Forgive me, Father, for I have sinned," she whispered very close to his ear, letting her teeth graze the lobe.

Then they were lost again in a tangle of limbs and bed linens, Drucker's fingers playing Lucinda like a piano, making her sing.

CHAPTER THIRTEEN

The sixth week of the investigation waxed and waned and while the horse thief remained at large, Clayton was no longer the place of mystery that it had once been for Drucker. Faces that had belonged to strangers not so long ago had become familiar to him, and the stiff formalities taken with outsiders had been replaced by the warmth of vigorous handshakes, questions posed through earnest grins, and words of encouragement when Drucker made mention of the investigation.

In other words, the novelty of Clayton, six weeks in, had begun to wear off, giving Drucker pause to contemplate the ephemeral nature of newness that in the late days of August, like summer itself, always seemed to come to an end all too quickly.

Routines formed, building on themselves one day at a time. Daily he woke with the sun as it streamed through the window of Anna's studio, where he slept. He spent his days interviewing the townspeople, filling up on notes and their generously supplied sweets. During the course of a day's three or four interviews, a rainbow of iced teas and warm baked goods would be passed across the kitchen tables of the good people of Clayton. Drucker turned down no offering, knowing that it was their way of showing him their appreciation and affection, and he couldn't bear to think of offending them. His sincere affection for them all was growing in return.

Drucker's days ended, more often than not, sitting on the roof of the little cottage house with Anna, talking about paintings and books and all manner of invention that revealed their common yearning to experience the world in ways neither of them believed they ever would or could.

They exchanged stories, their personal histories. Drucker found it surprisingly easy to be truthful about who he was without divulging the critical details that would cause Anna to question his identity as a detective hailing from the North. He told her about his father and the bank and their divergent views on Drucker's future there. He recounted the pain of leaving home; the fact that his home was in Atlanta mattered not, for the heartache of leaving home was a pain so universally understood that it transcended the need for details.

When Anna asked questions about what life was like in the North, Drucker borrowed from the stories Lucy had lent him when he was a child or else delicately danced around the question. Anna, dancing delicately in her own right, did not push him for more than he chose to give. Their friendship grew naturally, fueled by these nightly retreats that usually culminated in Anna telling Drucker about the painting she had worked on that day and, in turn, serving as his confidante as he reviewed the day's interviews.

Though six weeks had elapsed without closing the case, it was not for a lack of leads.

"Leads," declared Drucker to Anna one night, "are like weeds." The problem with them was that they died out as quickly as they cropped up, once the root of them was exposed.

The case against Mary Louise Templeton, for one, had popped like a balloon when she produced the will that named her the sole heir of her wealthy aunt Magda's estate, a princely sum that left her able to purchase a new hat many times over. She had also produced the hat that had called her into question as a suspect in the first place, and with Aunt Magda's name sewn neatly beneath the brim, it was a stretch to call the hat new anyway, leaving Drucker once again without a prime target on whom to focus the investigation.

Suspects were easy to come by, but finding one who had a motive, a method, or even a scrap of proof to support the accusation wasn't so simple. As he moved through his days conducting interviews, sometimes he felt as if he was navigating a web of fingers pointing in so many different directions that they created a pattern as intricate as any spider could weave. In his notebook he kept a list of names, many of which had been scratched out, some of which had been rewritten, the scratch out becoming the thing that was scratched out.

"I worry I'm disappointing the whole town by taking so long," Drucker said to Anna while sitting on the roof on the evening of the sixth Sunday that he had spent in Clayton.

Anna was quiet for a moment. When finally she spoke, it was softly. "I have a confession to make, Drucker." She was one of the only people in Clayton who called him by his given name. Despite his growing familiarity with the people of Clayton, almost everyone called him Detective, Anna and her father being the two exceptions.

"Oh, dear God, please let it be that you're the thief," said Drucker, his eyes twinkling like stars in the moonlight. "Then this investigation can finally be over." He nudged her playfully in the ribs with his elbow. "I don't know how many more baked goods I can take."

"No, I'm not," she said, a weak smile tugging at the corners of her mouth briefly. "Still, it's very bad," she continued, turning serious. "I shouldn't say it." She looked off into the dark distance, refusing to look Drucker in the eye.

"Well, Anna dear, you've said too much to turn back now. Confess away."

She inhaled deeply and turned to him. "I can't believe I am about to say this but...sometimes...sometimes I find myself wishing against your success in finding the horse thief."

"Wishing that I won't find the thief you mean?"

"Yes. Well, no. I mean wishing that you won't do so with haste because...well, because when you *do* find the thief, your business here in Clayton will be finished, and you'll go home to New York, and then I'll never see you again, Drucker, and I've enjoyed getting to know you so much, and..."

Her voice trailed off, but her chin, quivering a little, remained lifted, and Drucker could see tears forming like clouds across her gray eyes.

"I've very much enjoyed our talks as well, Anna."

"I know you've only been in Clayton a few weeks, but I feel like you know me better than anyone ever has."

"I think I may be able to say the same," said Drucker, reflecting on the things he had told her about himself that he had never found the right time or the courage to confide in anyone else.

"Drucker," said Anna, speaking slowly, long pauses seeping into the gaps between her words. "Do you...think I could...have a kiss?"

The question caught Drucker off guard, and he wasn't able to mask the chagrin of knowing that he could not give her what she wanted. While their friendship had certainly developed over time, his attraction to her had not. Anna was a wonderful conversationalist, but he saw her as a sister, and though she had many admirable qualities, there was one she lacked: she simply didn't excite romantic urges in him, and to kiss her would be to suggest otherwise—to lie.

She looked at him, her expression vulnerable, hopeful. To disappoint her would be painful. Her lips were pouted toward him, but Drucker knew he couldn't meet them with his own. Even if he did feel even a bit of romantic attraction to Anna, it would be wrong to kiss her, given his relationship with Lucinda, and on Sunday of all days, with the sweet smell of Lucinda's intoxicating aroma still fresh on his breath.

"Anna..." He searched for the right words. Suddenly, he found them. "Of course."

He took her hand and lifted it, his lips softly touching the backside of it, resting lightly for a moment on the broad space just past her knuckles.

When he released her fingers, her eyes showed delighted surprise rather than disappointment.

"Thank you, Drucker," she said. "You really are a true northern gentleman."

Drucker felt relief at her reaction but his smile faded as her words reminded him that though she knew him better than anyone else possibly could, she didn't really know him at all.

CHAPTER FOURTEEN

As Drucker's finger traced little circles around Lucinda's navel, his mind was busy looping through silent rehearsals of the question he wanted to ask her. It was the seventh Sunday that Drucker found himself in Lucinda's bed, satiated, his brow damp with sweat, and though he usually was completely consumed by the intensity of their time together, on this occasion he was distracted.

His hunt for the horse thief was beginning to feel like a race without an end, and the recent lack of forward movement had begun to take a toll on his patience as well as his psyche. He found himself toying with the idea of calling it quits. To give up, though, he would need to leave Clayton, and he wasn't ready to go—not if it meant leaving Lucinda behind.

On the other hand, if she would agree to go with him, they could free themselves of the limitations that Clayton imposed on their relationship. The question that had raced through his mind all week weighed heavy on his heart as Drucker lay in bed, gazing at Lucinda.

His finger moved from her stomach up to her cheek, tracing a line up the middle of her sinewy torso as it did.

"Lucinda," Drucker began, his voice soft, "do you ever think of running away?"

"Yes. All the time," she answered softly but without hesitation.

"All the time?" repeated Drucker, remembering how he had felt at the bank. "Then why don't you leave?"

Lucinda stared at him, her look suddenly hardened. "Why don't I leave? Detective, you make it sound so easy. Like it's nothing at all."

Drucker had not been able to confide in Lucinda the way he found himself able to do with Anna, and he had never told her about his hasty departure from his former home. To start now would be to complicate things, so instead he proceeded with caution, speaking broadly. "What if I told you that it *could* be? That it could be as easy as just...opening the door, walking outside, and... touching a tree."

Drucker thought back to the day at the bank when he had finally walked outside and touched the tree that he had a habit of watching through his window. He remembered how gratifying it had been to feel the rough bark, the real marvel being how easy it was to simply go outside and touch it.

"I'm afraid I don't follow, Detective." Lucinda's voice was high and thin, bordering on shrill. "I don't know what you think you know about running away from somewhere, but you seem to think it perfectly simple, and I cannot agree." She sat up in the bed, pulling the bed sheet close to her chest to cover her, putting up a wall between herself and Drucker that wasn't usually present.

"Besides, Detective," continued Lucinda, "it's different for a woman. It takes money to leave. Tell me where I'm supposed to find enough money to leave this place, won't you? I haven't any money of my own. He watches every dollar that passes through this house."

Drucker was about to cry out, *Run away with me, and I'll take care of you* when he was struck by a sudden curiosity that he couldn't stop himself from blurting out. "What does he do?"

"Who?"

"Your husband. We've never really talked about him."

"I wonder why!" cried Lucinda.

"Well," said Drucker, remaining calm, and feeling suddenly quite curious. "I don't even know what he does for a living."

"Oh, please, Detective," Lucinda implored, her voice now at a fever pitch. "Don't talk about my husband. Not today. Isn't it enough that I have to live my life under his thumb six days a week?"

Lucinda got to her feet and walked across the room to an armoire, her narrow body trembling as she moved. Usually after their trysts they stayed in bed together unclothed until it was time for Drucker to leave, but now Lucinda busied herself covering up, slipping into a long white dressing gown made of patterned lace. Drucker watched as she fastened the little white buttons that ran up the front of the gown, adhering to the line that his finger had traced just moments earlier.

"If you must know," said Lucinda, turning her back to Drucker, "he's a salesman. Apothecary and beauty supplies. Happy now, Detective?"

Drucker considered her answer for a moment. "No," he said, "you were right. Let's not talk about him. Come back here, won't you?"

Lucinda turned and faced Drucker, her expression still strained. "I think you should go, Detective."

Even when she was mad she looked so lovely that it was difficult for Drucker to draw his eyes away from her. He watched her as she blustered on in a verbose fit of frustration inspired by her husband but aimed at Drucker. She moved toward him, then away; she took a few steps left, then retraced them right, barely stopping to take a breath. He followed her with his gaze, trying to take in as much as he could, knowing in his heart that even if he found the courage to ask her to run away with him, it would not be enough to sway her. And if she refused to go with him, that meant that someday, some Sunday, he would be without her.

He wondered how long it would be after they parted ways before he forgot the sound of her voice. He felt certain that he would never be able to forget the scent of her skin, no matter how painful it would be to smell her but not be able to touch her.

As she spoke he let his eyes wander the room to capture all that they could of this place where their passion had erupted so many times. He noticed the things that had always been there but that he had never noticed before, like the wall behind her, an eggshell plaster; the rim of the mirror on her dressing table, hammered silver; the chest of drawers with its knob handles and smooth chest-level surface. Then Drucker noticed something else, something he was quite certain he hadn't seen before.

"Lucinda," he cut in, interrupting her rant. "What is that? Behind you, on the dresser."

Lucinda examined the surface behind her. "A bottle of perfume," she said, nonplussed by the interruption.

"No, next to it." He pointed. "What is that?"

She lifted an amorphous black mound up off the dresser with one hand, and Drucker watched as it took the shape of a cascading black waterfall as she held it in front of her. "What?" she asked, holding it up. "This?"

Drucker felt his heart beating faster than it ever had before. "Lucinda..." started Drucker, trying his best to proceed with caution.

"It's my hairpiece," said Lucinda.

"It's a horse's tail," said Drucker.

"Don't be a fool, Detective. You're just used to seeing it in my hair," she said, holding it to the back of her head, miming the clipping action that would fasten it there.

"I'm not disagreeing with you. I believe you when you say it's your hairpiece, but, Lucinda dear, that's a horse's tail if I've ever seen one."

Lucinda examined the long black handful of hair. Her eyes flicked back and forth from the hairpiece to Drucker and back again.

"Well," she said when she finally spoke, "it's the fashion. All the ladies in town are wearing one."

They stared at each other, and for a moment neither of them spoke as their minds whirred, until Lucinda leaped back onto the bed, and they met each other with a rush of words.

She explained that she, like so many other women, had bought the hairpiece from the town hairdresser, Maurice Belcamp, who made house calls to wash, curl, and coif the ladies of Clayton. In addition to pedaling hair tonics and the like, Maurice carried with him the latest fashions from the big cities of the East.

Half a year earlier, Lucinda recounted, Maurice had sold Lucinda her hairpiece, and she wasn't the only one buying. Fueled by Maurice's assurance that the hairpieces were all the rage in New York and Paris, the trend spread like wildfire in Clayton, and by spring almost every woman and girl in Clayton was pinning up a full head of lustrous locks.

Drucker listened to Lucinda with great excitement but also relief. In addition to sounding an awful lot like the break he had been waiting for, the story soothed Drucker for another reason. With so many women in Clayton wearing the identical hairpieces, Drucker could hardly be blamed for confusing them for Lucinda when he saw them from behind.

"Lucinda," Drucker was on his feet, stepping into his trousers. "Thank you for this."

"Where are you going?" asked Lucinda, perched on the side of the bed watching Drucker as he dressed.

"To find Maurice." He hurriedly slipped into one shirt sleeve and then the other.

Lucinda sat quietly, her eyebrows furrowed.

"What is it?" asked Drucker as he pulled on his jacket. He kept his eyes trained on Lucinda. "You're lost in your thoughts. Of what?"

"Detective," said Lucinda slowly. She paused, as if to weigh the effect of the words she was about to say. "Just a moment ago, you asked me what my husband does for a living."

"Yes." Fully dressed now, Drucker was suddenly very still.

"And I told you Earl sells apothecary and beauty supplies."

"Yes."

"Well," said Lucinda, her voice shaking, "Maurice is his best customer. Earl sells him all of his supplies. The tonics, the lotions, everything…" Her voice trailed off as her eyes met Drucker's.

They stared at each other for a long moment. Neither said it, but both felt it, knew that this was it, the forward movement in the case that Drucker needed, the excitement in Clayton that Lucinda craved. In light of it, everything else—her urge to fight, his instinct for flight—fell away.

Moments later, Drucker lay on the bed staring at the ceiling as Lucinda hovered over him as a nurse to her patient. Though he had been ready to run out the door to find Maurice, Lucinda's disclosure had knocked him off his feet, making his head spin so wildly that he needed to lie down.

"I need more, though," he said, staring up at the ceiling. "The hairpieces alone don't close the case."

"But surely you can prove they're made of horsehair, Detective," encouraged Lucinda.

"It won't be enough. They could have come from any horse. I've got to prove that they come from Clayton's missing horses."

"Maybe you can get Maurice to confess," she suggested weakly.

Drucker gave a single-noted laugh. "What are the chances of that?" he asked sourly. "What I need to do is find one of those poor tailless bastards."

Lucinda nodded as they looked at each other, both of them acknowledging the challenge this presented. For a moment, neither spoke. Drucker lay still, noticing the ticking of the grandfather clock in the hall for the first time, and Lucinda sat next to him, toying with the ends of her hair. It was the first time they had shared the bed without touching one another, but Drucker was too lost in thought to notice.

Suddenly, Lucinda leaped to her feet. "I just thought of something."

Drucker shifted onto his side to face her, propping himself up on his elbow.

"Earl's mother's property in Edwardsville. It's a farm with a big old barn. A haunted-looking thing that must be a hundred years old."

"Tell me this isn't some cruel joke," begged Drucker, sitting up. But he could see there was no jest in his lover's eyes.

"This is no joke," confirmed Lucinda, her voice solemn.

A beat passed as Drucker took in this new information.

"Then I have no choice but to go," said Drucker, rolling out of bed onto his feet. "Will you take me?"

Lucinda looked down at her dressing gown and bare feet. "Now?"

"What better time than while he's at church?"

"You're right," agreed Lucinda. "I'll change." Her fingers were already dancing down the column of buttons on her dressing gown, and her face was gleaming with a dewy mix of excitement and intrigue that gave her the prettiest glow Drucker had seen on her yet.

Don't ever, Drucker thought of saying, but as with the question he had wanted to ask her all morning, he bit his tongue and restrained himself.

Besides, at the moment he had more pressing concerns in the form of a horse-mane-peddling hairdresser, a new prime suspect who just happened to be married to his lover, and a haunted barn in Edwardsville to raid.

CHAPTER FIFTEEN

After they had ridden side by side in silence for five miles in the surrey that the mayor had lent Drucker for his time in Clayton, the old barn Lucinda had described came into view, and she excitedly grabbed onto Drucker's arm.

The barn looked larger and more formidable the closer they came to it. Unable to take their eyes off it, the two bounced along in quiet apprehension as the steed pulling their wagon navigated the dirt road that had grown rutted and rocky from disuse. When they reached a narrow path that ran from the road to the barn, Drucker, pulling back on the reins to slow the stallion, decided it was time to finish the approach on foot.

Without saying a word, he slowed the carriage to a stop and stepped down. He motioned for Lucinda to stay where she was, but as soon as he had turned his back to her he heard the thump of her feet hitting the ground. Though he feigned disapproval, he felt relieved that he wouldn't have to enter the ominous barn alone.

Several yards away from their wagon, Drucker and Lucinda stood side by side, sizing up the sagging structure in front of them. The paint, perhaps red in a better time, had rotted into the distinct hue of dried-blood brown, and in several places the paint had completely eroded, exposing bald patches of gray wood that looked too weak to support the slumping roof.

Drucker wondered if there could possibly be a way to extricate himself from the situation without going into the barn but also without showing his cowardice to Lucinda.

He turned to her. "Your mother-in-law certainly isn't one for upkeep."

"No," agreed Lucinda, her eyes fixed on the barn, "and it doesn't help matters that she's dead."

"Ah," said Drucker, his eyes similarly fixed straight ahead, "that explains it." Though he felt fairly certain that the barn would be in no better condition if its owner were alive.

"It's been years since I was last here," whispered Lucinda, eyes still locked on the barn as if transfixed.

"I think it's a good bet that it's been years since *anyone* has last been here," said Drucker. "The place looks like it's just waiting to crumble at a moment's notice."

He looked at her, hoping she would take the lead and turn them back toward the wagon, but instead he saw her eyes gleaming with a hungry sort of excitement that he had not seen since the first time he had kissed her.

"Detective, certainly you don't intend to turn back now after we've come all this way?"

"Don't be silly, Lucinda dear," he said, clearing his throat. "We've come this far, and I for one intend to investigate fully."

"Then investigate we shall," said Lucinda, her voice steady but her hand shaking with excitement as it latched onto Drucker's.

"On we go," said Drucker, but he didn't move. He inhaled deeply, summoning all of the courage he could muster when—

"Ladies first!" whooped Lucinda, and without waiting for a response, she trudged off through the tall grass until she reached the barn.

It was Lucinda who pushed open the heavy, creaking door and took the first step into the cavernous barn. Drucker followed a pace or two behind her, taking small, cautious steps as his eyes adjusted to the darkness.

The only light filtered in from the door through which they entered, and without his sense of sight, Drucker's other senses were heightened. Before he could see, he was struck by the fetid smell of rotten vegetables wrought from a long-ago harvest and abandoned.

In the dark, his ears were keen. He could hear the whoosh of wings flapping high in the rafters. He found himself enjoying the fact that in the darkness he could so clearly hear the sound of Lucinda's breath, heavy in the stale barn air. The rhythm of her breathing was made rapid by her excitement, and Drucker found himself on the verge of a daydream in which her breathing was equally quick when suddenly he was roused back to reality by a noise coming from somewhere in the darkness in front of him.

At first he thought he must have imagined it, but when it came again it was unmistakably the sound he had been praying to hear. A victory anthem in three verses: first a stomp, then a whinny, followed by a neigh.

Drucker rushed back to the door and used the weight of his body to draw it open as wide as it would go to let in the maximum amount of light. As the additional light filtered in, it illuminated the middle of the barn, which until that moment had been buried too deep in the darkness for Drucker make out. The new light changed that, though, casting a glow that revealed row after row of horses, lined up and tied to their stalls. Drucker counted two dozen plus one, horses of all colors and sizes, their faces obscured and their rears extended toward Drucker and Lucinda, their tailless bottoms bare as newborn babies'.

Lucinda let out a cheer and threw her arms around Drucker's neck. He lifted her off her feet, swinging her in a circle, inhaling deeply as he buried his nose in the side of her neck.

"Detective, you've done it! You've found the horses!" shrieked Lucinda with glee as he twirled her.

"You played no small role," said Drucker, pulling his face away from Lucinda's neck to look her in the eye and prepare to kiss her on the mouth. Neither of them said a word as they smiled at one another. But suddenly, just as their lips were about to meet, Drucker quickly pulled back, jerking his head a quarter turn.

"Lucinda," said Drucker, bending his knees and lowering her back down to the ground, "do you hear that?"

They stood still, hands forming open cups against their ears. The noise came again, a soft guttural grunting noise, but unlike any a horse could make. Drucker put his finger to his lips, signaling for quiet, and Lucinda drew both hands over her mouth to cover it. They stood quietly listening as the noise intensified then ebbed.

This time Drucker led the way as they moved silently through the darkness. The backs of the stalls formed a line through the center of the barn, a kind of partial wall, half as tall and half as wide as the barn itself. When Drucker and Lucinda had crept around to the other side of it, the noise they had been following intensified, pulsing rhythmically from somewhere in front of them.

By then Drucker's eyes had adjusted to the dim light, and he surveyed the back of the barn from left to right, taking in feed barrels, stacks of hay, and a collection of oversized tools including a pair of three-foot-long shears hanging on a hook fixed to the back wall.

When his eyes finally made it over to the far right corner, he caught a glimpse of something moving, rocking in time with the rhythm of the sound they had been hearing. It was at the exact moment that Drucker realized what he was seeing that he heard Lucinda cry out.

"Earl?!"

In the dark, a shadow of a man with his pants around his ankles quit his thrusting and turned to look over his shoulder. The light in the barn was just enough to expose the outline of his body, unclothed from the waist down, the interstice of his behind peeking out from beneath the tails of his wrinkled shirt.

"Lucinda?!" exclaimed the man, dropping the pair of legs he was holding up on either side of him.

"What's going on?" the owner of the legs whined, sitting upright on the bale of hay on which she had been lying horizontal. Her face peeked out from around the side of Earl's body.

"Mary Louise?!" cried Lucinda.

The face quickly disappeared again as the woman ducked out of sight, shielded by Earl's stout torso.

"I think she saw me," the woman said in a loud, clumsy whisper meant only for her partner's ears.

"Well, of course she did, you silly jezebel, she said your damn name, didn't she?"

"That's Earl!" shrieked Lucinda. "Who else would be so nasty at a moment like this?"

"Oh, stall your mug, you pagan wench," grumbled Earl, bending to pull his pants up from the pile they lay in at his feet.

"*Me* pagan? You call taking up on a haystack with the pastor's wife 'going to church,' and you call *me* pagan?"

"You're damned right about that—"

"That's enough!" cut in Drucker, his voice so authoritative neither Earl nor Lucinda dared to say another word. Both stood silently at attention, waiting for Drucker's next command, but Drucker said nothing for a moment as his mind raced.

Yes, he had found the horses, but the fact that his lover's husband was the guilty party introduced a complication, making his next move less than obvious. To turn in Earl would elevate Drucker to hero status, but it would also raise a crop of questions about why he had arrived at the mysterious barn with a married woman while the rest of the townspeople were at church. It would call into question the nature of his relationship with Lucinda, but more important, it would call into question the nature of Lucinda's relationship with him.

Drucker knew Clayton was too small a town to forgive Lucinda once aspersions had been cast on her good name. To know that he would be the one responsible for it would be the source of endless guilt, the first pangs of which he was already beginning to feel. To go to bed with Earl's woman time after time and then to interrupt him midcoitus to send him off to jail so that Drucker could be lauded as the faultless hero just didn't sit right with Drucker. It felt too cruel, too classless. Not gentlemanly at all.

On the other hand, if Drucker left the barn without his suspect, he could bet his bottom dollar those horses would be gone in the time it would take to get back to town to tell the mayor and the sheriff what he had seen. By the time he could bring anyone back to the barn, Earl would have had plenty of time to set the horses loose, causing Drucker to look the fool, and making it next to impossible for all of the horses to ever be recovered.

One thing was clear. Drucker needed to get Earl away from the evidence before he had a chance to eviscerate it.

"Look," said Drucker, trying his best to avert his eyes from Mary Louise as she pulled her dress up in the shadows. "If you two come back to town with us now, you have my word we will never tell Pastor Templeton or anyone else about what we've just witnessed."

"You swear it?" asked Mary Louise, dressed now and in the process of pinning her hair back up into a chignon.

"I do," said Drucker, holding up his hand to give his oath.

"You too, Lucinda. Swear it," insisted Mary Louise.

Drucker looked at Lucinda and saw she was crying softly, her face in her hands, her back up against the wall. "Lucinda," he said, gently coaxing her.

"I swear it," she choked out between sniffles.

"And if we don't go?" growled Earl.

Lucinda lifted her face from her hands. "Then our first stop will be Cumberland First Presbyterian," she proclaimed before Drucker had a chance to answer. "I'm sure news of what we've just seen will be of great interest to Pastor Templeton."

"And to Silas," Drucker mumbled to himself.

"And if we do go, your first stop will be Sheriff Harkin's place, no doubt," snarled Earl defiantly.

"No," said Drucker firmly. "At least not before we get her home," he nodded toward Mary Louise. "Come with us now, and as far as we're concerned, we never saw her here today."

"But you *did* see me," squeaked Mary Louise, "you saw me right over—"

"I swear to God, woman—" cut in Earl, turning to her with his palm open, raised.

"Leave her alone," Drucker said to Earl, "and we'll do the same."

"Lot of good that does me," grumbled Earl, "if I'm sitting behind bars."

"Maybe they won't arrest you," offered Drucker.

"You mean you ain't fixin' to turn me in?" asked Earl, his words slow and laden with suspicion.

"Oh, he'll turn you in all right, and if he doesn't, I will," interjected Lucinda, her tears dried, her voice hardened with anger.

"I meant what I said," said Drucker. "Maybe they won't arrest you."

"You mean they won't be able to arrest me for this?" asked Earl, motioning toward the rows of horse stalls. There was vulnerability in his voice now; it quivered like that of a little boy who knew he'd done wrong. Drucker felt a wave of pity wash over him.

"Not if you leave town first," said Drucker flatly.

Everyone was quiet for a moment.

"Fine," said Earl after mulling over Drucker's suggestion. "We'll go."

"We will?" asked Mary Louise.

"On the condition," added Earl, "that you leave us, each of us, at our own homes before you go on to do whatever it is you plan to do."

"You have yourself a deal," replied Drucker. He started toward the door.

"Oh," added Earl, standing stubbornly in place, "and she comes with me."

Drucker turned to look back toward the other three, and his heart sank when he saw Earl was nodding in the direction of his own wife.

"Absolutely not," said Drucker. Then, sensing he had answered too quickly, too emotionally, he added, "I'm not sending this woman home with a thief."

"Then I ain't goin' nowhere," barked Earl, his voice cold and hard once again.

"Earl, if we don't go, they'll tell my husband about us," whined Mary Louise.

"I ain't goin' nowhere unless I have his word that she's comin' with me," repeated Earl.

"I'll go with him," said Lucinda, surprising everyone.

Drucker stared at her. Quietly he said, "You don't have to do that."

"It's fine," Lucinda repeated. "I'll go with him."

Though his first and very strong instinct was not to allow it, Drucker had confidence that Earl would be leaving town within hours, and Drucker had every hope that Lucinda would stay behind when he did. So "As you wish," he said, "she'll go with you."

He extended his hand toward Earl, but rather than shaking hands, he latched onto the side of Earl's shirt, creating a kind of leash with his arm. He motioned for Lucinda to do the same with Mary Louise, and in pairs they maneuvered through the dark, out of the barn, and back to the surrey.

All the way back to Clayton, Drucker marveled at the fact that he was returning to town carrying in his wagon not only his lover, but also her husband, *his* lover, and the answer to the mystery that he had become a detective to solve. It filled him with pride to know that the good people of Clayton would get their horses back, thanks to him.

Never before had his cart, or his heart, been so full.

CHAPTER SIXTEEN

The following Saturday, the mayor made good on his promise to throw the grandest parade that the people of Clayton had ever seen, and he insisted that Drucker lead it with him.

Over the course of his investigation, Drucker had met the entirety of the small town's population. On the day of the parade, between those who watched and cheered and those who marched behind him, all of them were in attendance, save for one. As Drucker had expected, Earl had fled town the very night that he had been discovered in flagrante delicto inside the barn.

As they marched side by side, the mayor's arms swung as stiffly and rhythmically as a pendulum, his chest puffed out like a proud general leading his victorious troops back from battle. Through a grin he yelled his words to Drucker, his voice barely audible over the victory call of the trombones and the cheers from all sides.

"You've done a fine job, my boy, that's for certain. The only question is, what's next for you?" asked the mayor, as they led the parade past the general store, where Drucker's identity as a detective had been born.

"Pardon?" yelled Drucker, waving his hand to motion for the mayor to speak louder, though in truth it was not the noise around them, but rather in his own head, that caused him not to hear the mayor's question.

Though Drucker felt a great sense of relief at having found the horses, at this moment when he should have been reveling in glory, he was instead thinking about Lucinda. Not his usual lascivious daydreams, though, not this time. As he marched, he kept hearing the last words she had said to him ringing in his ears, ringing even louder than the blaring notes blasting from the trombone section.

With Earl gone, Drucker had imagined that his relationship with Lucinda would develop into something more, but instead she had been acting strangely distant since her husband's hasty departure. Drucker had gone to her home exactly twice since they had returned from the barn, and each time he had left feeling confused and rejected.

On Tuesday he had gone to her and given her something he wanted her to have: the entire sum of the monetary reward he had received for finding the horses. He felt it the right thing to do, as without her, after all, he would never have found out about the barn or had the courage to enter it.

Besides, he reasoned, with the savings that he had packed in Atlanta, he didn't need the money, and he remembered what Lucinda had said about living under Earl's thumb without access to money of her own. From the moment the mayor put the money in his hands, Drucker had known that he would give it to Lucinda. What he had not anticipated was her reaction to it.

She had been polite. Grateful she was, but warm she was not. She treated him decorously, and between her chirpy refrains of "Thank you, Detective," Drucker found himself thinking that polite was the worst thing a person could be when once they had been a lover.

When he left her house that day it was the only time since he had first kissed her in her kitchen that he left her home without having first adjourned with her to the bedroom.

A day later he had returned, this time with the courage to ask her to run away with him. His stay had been short. Lucinda rejected his request without ceremony, saying she had everything she needed in Clayton, and though she didn't reference it specifically, Drucker knew she meant the money.

"I said," the mayor repeated, calling out even louder than before, "what's next for you, my boy?"

"Oh," said Drucker, leaning his mouth closer to the mayor's ear but keeping his eyes fixed straight ahead, "I hadn't thought much of it."

"This town loves you, Drucker," shouted the mayor, without missing a beat. "You know that, don't you?"

Drucker's eyes scanned the crowd on either side of them. Women and children cheered his name and waved at him as he led the parade past them.

"And I've quite an affinity for this town," Drucker shouted back. He realized as he said it that it had very much become the truth.

The mayor craned his neck to look sideways at Drucker to gauge his reaction as he said, "You know, my boy, I can see a future for you here in Clayton. And I'm not the only one."

"A future?" repeated Drucker, seeing the parade's finish line materialize some fifty yards ahead.

"Yes," said the mayor, still calling out his words at top volume. "You and Anna could have a happy life here."

"Anna and I? A life here...together?"

"Naturally, my boy. I've seen the way she looks at you. And I know she's not much to look back at, but she'll make a fine wife. Loyal, devoted, all that. Besides," said the mayor, "I think it only fitting that the mayor's daughter should go on to be the next mayor's wife."

"What's that?" called out Drucker. "I don't think I heard you correctly."

"If you heard me suggesting that you are a shoo-in as the next mayor of this town, then you didn't mishear a thing. I'm an old man, Drucker. It's time for me to step down. And I can't think of anyone better to lead this town than you."

Drucker stared straight ahead, watching the parade's finish line grow closer.

"Think of it, a fine little town to call your own, a devoted wife to stand by your side. This could all be yours," said the mayor with a wide-sweeping gesture. "That is, if you want it, Drucker."

Drucker paused for a moment before asking, "And if I don't?"

"Well, of course, the choice is up to you, my boy," the mayor said as the band behind them hit the last notes of John Philip Sousa's "The Crusader" march. "But, Drucker"—the two men crossed the parade's finish line and turned toward each other—"don't 'don't.' It would break all of our hearts."

At that moment, the mayor's wife and Anna ran up to them. The mayor's wife, Penny, threw her arms around her husband's neck. "Charles, that was exhilarating!" Penny squealed.

Anna stood next to Drucker, close enough to touch, but neither reached for the other.

"You must be famished, dear. Let's go home. I've instructed Iris to have a feast of a lunch waiting for us," said the mayor's wife, latching on to her husband's arm.

"Do you want to join us for lunch, Drucker?" asked Anna, lifting her eyes to meet his with her signature hopeful gaze.

Between the clamor of the parade's finish line, the echoing of Lucinda's unexpected words of dismissal ringing in his ears, and the mayor's momentous offer weighing heavy on his heart, Drucker could hardly make out Anna's words.

"Drucker," said the mayor, turning back to him, "do you want to?"

Drucker looked at Anna, then at Mayor Newton, then back at Anna, who in her high-necked linen dress was as plain and as good as she had always been.

The mayor gave Drucker a nod and a wink, and in that moment it became clear to Drucker that if he chose to stay in Clayton, it would mean choosing a life with Anna at his side. The mayor would see to that. And if there could be no future for him in Clayton *without* Anna as his wife, that meant there could be no future for him in Clayton *with* Lucinda as his lover. He couldn't have them both; it would involve too many lies going in too many directions.

But he couldn't possibly choose Anna over Lucinda, could he? Drucker's mind raced as he stared at the trio of Newtons, who stared back at him, impatiently awaiting his response. How could he give up the woman who excited him so for the woman whom he saw as nothing more than a friend? On the other hand, though, if he chose to stay and build a life with Anna, it would be one full of companionship and conversation and—

"Lunch," repeated Anna. "Do you want it?"

The mayor's words bobbed up and down in Drucker's head like buoys that would not sink. *Don't don't. Don't don't.*

"I…do…want it, yes," said Drucker haltingly.

"That's my boy!" cheered the mayor. "Hoorah!"

With that, he pivoted on his heel and marched off, arms swinging, chest puffed once again, this time whistling the tune of Mendelssohn's "Wedding March" as he led the four-person parade back home.

With Anna at his side, Drucker followed the mayor to his house. An hour later, though, when he found himself seated in front of a celebratory feast, Drucker couldn't bring himself to eat. This meal, this life, this town, this woman seated next to him; all could be his, but he had no appetite for any of it.

When he was honest with himself, Drucker knew that being mayor of Clayton wasn't what he wanted, nor was being married to

Anna what he wanted. Nor was living out Mayor Newton's dream for his own legacy. None of that was what he really wanted. And though he was fairly certain that those things would give him a perfectly fine little life in Clayton, he knew the only thing his heart really desired there he couldn't have if he stayed.

Instead of eating, Drucker pushed the food around his plate, mulling over the choice in front of him. By the time the others had finished their meal, though his plate was still full, his mind had never been more clear.

Drucker arrived at the train depot before sunrise the next morning. He felt sure of his decision, though waves of guilt carried his thoughts to Anna.

He had kissed her cheek the night before. A more formal good-bye would have been neither possible nor desirable, he concluded. At times during the investigation it had been her hopeful optimism that had propelled him forward. He owed her more than he could offer her, which was part of the reason he could not bring himself to marry her, tethering her to himself with a lie that would last a lifetime. Drucker could only hope that she would someday understand that his departure wasn't meant to inflict on her, but rather to save her from, heartbreak.

In front of him, the shiny black body of a steam engine threw forth a whistle as it pulled into the station. A few men stepped off the train, and the conductor's first, second, and last calls rang out.

After the third and final call, Drucker stepped up onto the locomotive and took one of the many open seats. He listened to the chug of the engine as it picked up pace, and watched through the window as the bodies of the men who had gotten off in Clayton turned into tiny figurines in the distance. He couldn't help but wonder if one of them had received a letter from Mayor Newton about a horse thief.

Even if it didn't happen that day, it would eventually, Drucker knew. Someday the real Pinkerton who had received the letter would arrive in Clayton. Drucker imagined how the mayor's face would contort when, inevitably, that man with his letter would finally reach him. It would likely resemble the face that the mayor would make in about an hour, upon learning that Drucker had left them. He could only hope that the mayor would somehow understand that his decision to leave had been made with haste, but not without heartache. Drucker knew he had won the hearts of many in Clayton, and it pained him to think that his departure would break the hearts of a few.

Still, it was necessary.

Though he had succeeded in finding the horses, it wasn't horses that he had left Atlanta to find in the first place.

The mayor could see a future for Drucker in Clayton, but Drucker could sense that the future he was meant to have awaited him somewhere else entirely.

He clung dearly to that thought. It was the only thing that could ease his mind as the train moved westward into a world still dark, yet untouched by morning's first light.

III. AUSTIN

CHAPTER SEVENTEEN

When Drucker's feet next touched solid ground he was in Austin, Texas, the original destination of the train that he had mistakenly boarded the day he fled Atlanta. On that fateful day in July he had set out for Boston, but it was toward Austin that the train he had boarded sped, and it was Austin where he would have arrived months earlier, if not for his impromptu detour through a dusty little town that a horse thief tormented.

Just as Drucker had not meant to go to Austin when he had left Atlanta, neither did he plan on it when he decided to depart from Clayton. Leaving the mayor's home, sneaking out of Anna's studio before sunlight, Drucker had every intention of finally righting his course and heading north to Boston.

One glance at Clayton's skinny, single set of tracks, however, was all it took to remind Drucker that he was captive to the direction in which the railroad ties lay, and this particular set once again derailed his plans. The trains that passed through Clayton presented him with only two options: east toward Atlanta or west toward Austin. Drucker chose the latter.

There was no sense turning back, he reasoned. Not if he was leaving Clayton for the same reason that he left Atlanta. And he was.

He was still in desperate pursuit of a future that he wanted to find, of a life that it felt right to lead.

So Drucker chose to go west toward Austin.

And though westward had not been his intended direction for very long, once he made the choice to take the adventuresome route, Drucker felt quite confident in his decision. After all, he reminded himself, the unanticipated course he had taken up until that point had yielded some providential surprises. For instance, though he had not reached Lucy, he *had* found Lucinda. And though he had not yet uncovered what he was meant to do with his life, for the few weeks that he had been a detective, he'd been a damn good one.

The universe seemed to have a way of providing trade-offs.

Keeping that thought in mind, he allowed himself to be drawn farther west as he continued on in pursuit of his own manifest destiny.

⇌

Two days of travel forced Drucker to consider questions of great weight, but within an hour of arriving in Austin, a simpler one was posed to him.

"Should I getcha another, pal?"

"Please," said Drucker, standing at the bar, leaning into it with what felt like the quickly increasing weight of his legs, which seemed to grow heavier with each drink that he took.

"Remind me," said the bartender, pointing for a fleeting second to the mug in Drucker's hand.

Drucker lifted the copper colored vessel to eye level. "Something strong. Whisky I think, though it tastes like"—Drucker paused to run his tongue across his lips with muted distaste—"could it be charcoal?"

The barman smiled, revealing more gaps than teeth. "Ah, that's right! Our house blend. We call it tarantula juice. Glad'ja like it."

"'Like it' is a powerful overstatement," said Drucker, "but I will have another."

The bartender nodded knowingly. "I s'pose it ain't a matter a likin' it. All's I know is nobody drinks jus' one," he said as he poured a heavy dose of the dark liquid into Drucker's raised mug.

"Thank you, friend," said Drucker, when the pour was complete. He raised his cup in salute then touched it to his lips with force, making the syrupy liquid slide down his throat as quickly as it could.

"Here's how!" toasted the barkeep in the traditional way, nodding his head in courtesy before turning his attention toward a patron whose rowdy call for another round rang out from the far end of the bar.

"Here's..." started Drucker, his words trailing off as he watched the barman scuttle out of earshot.

Drucker raised the glass to his lips and forced down another gulp. The charcoal flavored swill made him feel warm, bleary-eyed, and alone in the crowded room. He found that it relaxed his nerves, and though it made his legs feel shaky, the more he drank, the more he felt his nerves unwind, and the less he could feel his legs at all, and so in short order he found himself taking another sip, and then another, and then another, until suddenly Drucker felt the need for a toilet come on urgently.

"Barkeep," called Drucker, leaning over the bar, but the man barely looked up from the bottles to which he was tending. "Where's your privy?"

"Out back," the man called in reply without leaving his station at the other end of the saloon. His hands were working deftly to turn three distinct liquids into one. When Drucker didn't move, the bartender called out again, this time louder, but his words still blurred as they reached Drucker's ears.

"Out back?" repeated Drucker over the din of the saloon, the urge to relieve himself growing stronger yet.

The bartender nodded, his head looking to Drucker like a bobbing buoy. "Jus' go on out the way you done come in, go all the way 'round this buildin' and…" the barkeep was still talking but Drucker was beginning to panic. *All the way around the building?* The whisky inside him was clouding his mind and bubbling in his gut, where it was turning into something else entirely.

Just as Drucker was about to make a run for the door, he felt a meaty paw clamp down on his shoulder.

"You look like you ain't got time to spare, son," said the man with a grin and a laugh that shook his rotund midsection.

"I don't believe I do," said Drucker, cringing.

"This sure is a big buildin' to go all the way 'round," continued the man.

Drucker nodded in silence, wiping a bead of sweat from his brow.

"But lucky for you, I know a shortcut. C'mon now. Follow me. I'm going that way myself." He beckoned.

The man picked up his drink and slipped away from the bar. He strode confidently to the other side of the room where he paused, looked over his shoulder, and when he was reasonably sure that the other patrons' attentions were elsewhere, rapped his knuckles on the wall. *Knock…knock…knockknockknock.*

In a moment's time the wall swung back, turning into a door, and the man stepped over the threshold and motioned for Drucker to follow suit.

With a body so wide in a hallway so narrow, the man's shirt sleeves grazed the walls as he walked down the dark corridor, leading the way for Drucker, who followed so closely behind him that twice he had to apologize for stepping on his new acquaintance's heels. Luckily, the hallway, though narrow and dark, was also short, and when they reached the end of it, the man pushed open a door that gave way to sunlight, giving Drucker a blessed view of the much-needed privy.

"How's that for a shortcut?"

Drucker nodded gratefully but wordlessly as he lunged out of the building.

"Mind if I use it first?" asked the man, causing Drucker's feet to freeze, his face to fall, and his heart to sink.

"Oh," said Drucker, "I—"

"I'm kiddin' you, boy!" roared the man, slapping Drucker on the back. "I wouldn't do that to you!"

"You wouldn't? I mean, thank you," stammered Drucker.

"Don't just look at it, boy! Get to it."

Drucker moved toward the outhouse as quickly as his wobbling legs would take him, and again the man gave a hearty laugh that made his belly rise and fall with the cadence of delight.

When Drucker arrived back at the bar, the barkeep was standing where Drucker had left his snifter.

"Ya find it in time?" asked the bartender, smiling.

"Yes," Drucker said and then added, "but not by a wide margin."

The bartended laughed. "Ready for another?" he asked, raising a clay carafe in front of him. "This one's on the house."

"That's kind of you," said Drucker, "but unnecessary."

"Balderdash," replied the bartender reaching for a fresh mug and beginning to pour. "Any friend a the AG is a friend a mine."

"The AG," repeated Drucker, trying to keep his tone steady, though it teetered between question and statement.

"You know, Jim Hogg," said the bartender, sensing Drucker's hesitation. "The attorney general. He told me to send you to him when you got back from usin' the facilities."

"Ah," said Drucker, putting the pieces together through the fog, "of course. The attorney general. He is"—Drucker searched for words that could be at once vague and accurate—"an important man."

"No doubt," said the bartender, placing the freshly filled cup in front of Drucker. "Jim Hogg's the only damn hope the state a Texas has got. It ain't so often that you come 'cross a man with a head and a heart that fit to size with...*appetites* so large." With his hands the bartender pantomimed stroking an invisible belly, and Drucker could finally be certain that the man they were discussing was none other than the one who had shared the shortcut with him.

"You say he sent for *me*?" asked Drucker. He craned his neck and looked over his shoulder to survey the barroom, but there was no sign of the man he had met minutes earlier.

"He's in the back," said the bartender, motioning toward the wall that had yielded passage to the short dark hallway. "You know the way?"

Drucker nodded. In his mind's eye he could see the man's meaty knuckles rapping out the code on the secret door.

"Good," said the bartender. "Go on, then. Wouldn't want to keep our next gov'nor waitin' on you."

So then it was Drucker's turn to knock. Reaching out to the place on the wall just below where the oversized portrait of a frontiersman hung, he made a fist.

Knock...knock...knockknockknock, he tapped with his knuckles as the corpulent man had done. A few seconds passed and then, just as it had earlier, the wall hinged open to become a doorway, and Drucker stepped through it back into the hallway, dark and narrow.

A single sconce provided just enough of a dim, flickering light that Drucker could see as far in front of him as where he planted his foot with each new step. Six strides in, he heard a voice, his first indication that he was not alone in the hallway.

"You the one the AG sent for?"

Drucker couldn't tell where the voice came from, but he answered in haste, "Yes, sir."

"Door's to your right," instructed the voice.

Drucker stopped in his tracks but kept his arms at his side, prompting the voice to add, "Go 'head. Don' be scared."

As his eyes adjusted to the darkness, Drucker could see the outline of a man in front of him standing sideways in the hallway as if to guard another door some fifteen yards away. Drucker looked to his right, and sure enough, there was the faint outline of a door.

He reached out, his fingers making cautious contact with the slick metal doorknob. First his fingers grazed it, then his hand wrapped around it slowly, wary that the guard might change his mind and charge at him. But the man in the shadows remained still, his voice quiet, saying only, "Push," which Drucker did.

Leaving the dark hallway, he stepped into a windowless room where the air hung thick with cigar smoke and the smell of gin that had been spilled and sweat out for years. Five men sat around a card table in the middle of the room, and all of them looked up when Drucker entered, each of them scowling save for one.

The AG was the exception. He grinned widely as he looked up from his hand to make eye contact with Drucker. "Well, look who we have here!" announced the AG, in his jolly way. "I hardly recognize you with the color back in your cheeks. Feelin' better?"

"Much. Thank you."

"You can thank God almighty for that, boy," said the attorney general jovially, returning his gaze to his hand of cards. "You play?"

"That depends on the game," said Drucker, stepping toward the group.

"Hey!" interjected one of the men sharply. "You plannin' to close that door?" Drucker turned back to the door and shut it quickly, but as he did he couldn't help but sense that the man would have preferred for him to shut the door from the other side of it. When Drucker turned back to face the group, the man spoke again. "I'm sorry, I cut you off. You were about to tell us—what game *don't* you play?" Several of the others smirked.

"Horace, leave the man alone," said the AG. Then he turned to the slightest man in the group, one whose modest build and youthful face made him look twenty years the junior of all the other men. "Brownie, get this man a chair."

Brownie scuttled to the corner of the room and dragged back a chair with a frame that looked as if it weighed more than he did. "Where should I—" the young man started. There was no room for the sixth chair at the table for five.

"Here," said the AG, pointing to the few inches of space between himself and the man with the smug comments. "Horace," he said, and motioned for the still scowling man to move over and make room. The other men all shifted, including Horace, who gnawed on his cigar to obscure his grumbling.

"Have a seat, boy," said the AG, patting the newly arrived open seat.

Drucker sidled over to the chair, which was lodged so tightly between the AG and Horace that Horace was forced to get up from his own chair to allow Drucker room to get seated. When Drucker was finally settled, the AG turned to him.

"You look like you could use a smoke."

Drucker waved his hand through the thick smoggy air. "I think I'm having one right now.

The AG laughed, releasing small round clouds from his parted lips. "Brownie," he instructed the thin young man who had just retaken his seat, "go get a cigar for our friend...our friend..." He turned back to Drucker. "I don't believe I've caught your name."

"Drucker, sir. Drucker May."

"Well, which is it?" grumbled Horace.

Drucker extended his hand to the AG, who bit down on his cigar, holding it between his teeth to free his own hand for a shake. "It's a pleasure to make your acquaintance, Drucker. James Stephen Hogg," said the AG, "but these fools call me Jim, and you may do the same."

"The pleasure is mine," said Drucker.

To Drucker's left, so close that their forearms touched, sat Horace, who cleared his throat pointedly to interrupt the introduction. "I'll raise—"

"Actually," cut in the AG, "I think we should start a new hand to include our new friend Drucker here. Hand me your cards, boys," he said, throwing down his own cards to start up a collection.

"Oh, for the love of Christ," grumbled Horace, throwing down his cards and snuffing out the remaining stub of his cigar by throwing it to the ground and grinding it under his boot. "You must be kidding me. Jim, what are you doing, old man?"

The AG gave Horace a long simmering glare before he spoke. "Pipe down, Horace. Where are your manners? We have a new player, and it's only right that we include him in a hand. Am I alone in moving for this show of common courtesy?"

Horace and Drucker remained quiet while a chorus of nos and of course nots rose up from the three others, including Brownie, who had slipped back through the door, wielding a fresh round of cigars for everyone.

"I didn't think so," said the AG as he locked eyes with Horace. Then he leaned in close to Drucker and, under his breath so that only Drucker could hear, the AG whispered, "Never mind that my hand was shit."

With the new hands dealt and the fresh round of cigars lit, the room was noiseless, the quiet hanging as thick and heavy in the air as the mingling clouds of smoke.

As the newcomer and the cause of the uncomfortable silence, Drucker felt compelled to break it, so as he examined the cards that he'd been dealt, he announced, "Jim, I have to thank you for

your largess in sharing that much needed shortcut with me earlier." He nodded toward the AG and brought his freshly lit cigar to
his lips.

"Did I really just hear a man thank Jim Hogg for his largeness?"
scoffed Horace, causing several of the men to snicker and Drucker
to choke midpuff.

"Large-ess. Kindness, generosity, I mean. I owe this man a debt
of gratitude," he sputtered through his coughs.

"Ah," said Horace, adding nothing further.

The AG gave Horace a stern look. "Ante up, boys," he said,
pushing a silver coin from the pile in front of him to the center of
the table. The others followed suit.

When the men had made their contributions to the pot, all
eyes fell on Drucker, who was first in line to place a wager. He
glanced down at his cards briefly then lifted his eyes to survey the
room. It was his duty, as the first to place a bet, to set the tone and
pace of the game. The amount that he chose to bet would have to
be matched or raised by each subsequent player unless they chose
to fold. With the responsibility of being first came quite a bit of
tension for a newcomer like Drucker. He didn't want to offend the
group, or come off as ostentatious, but neither did he want his
opening bid to make him look weak or miserly.

He fingered the pile of coins and bills in front of him, recalling
that as the first in line to place a bet, he also retained the option
not to place a bet at all, passing the job of pace setting on to the
next man. That would be the safe move in this case, certainly.

But safe was not a taste he'd had much of an appetite for since
he'd left Atlanta, so Drucker slid five dollars from his pile to the
middle of the table. He lifted his eyes, trying to gauge the crowd's
reaction, but whether he'd impressed or offended was unknowable
from their stoic expressions. All he could do was hope that he had
made the right move and join the other five in looking at Horace,
whose turn it was to call, raise, or fold.

"So, Drucker," Horace intoned as he slid double the amount of Drucker's opening bid into the pot. "You're new in town, I take it."

"Yes, sir," said Drucker, as the man next to Horace quietly called his bet, matching the bid. "I arrived just today, in fact."

"And what," continued Horace, enunciating his words so sharply that tiny flecks of saliva shot outward like tiny bullets, "has brought you to Austin?"

Drucker didn't miss a beat. "The train," he said, resorting to his habit, when in doubt, of relying on the literal truth.

Horace gave him a steely-eyed glare.

"I think Horace means what business brings you here," Brownie piped up weakly from across the table, his voice as puny as the rest of him, but his wager as strong as that of three men who had bet before him.

"Ah," said Drucker, "well, you see, my arrival here is more on account of the business I've just finished."

"And what business might that be?" asked Horace, his voice as cool and dry as an empty icebox.

"Well, you see, I've just wrapped up a case in Clayton, Arkansas—"

"A case?" squeaked Brownie.

"You're a lawyer?" asked Horace, raising an eyebrow.

"No, sir," said Drucker, "I'm a..." he hesitated. Could he say it? If a whole town believes you to be one, and if you solve the crime they sent away for one to solve, are you actually a..."detective."

"A detective!" boomed the AG.

Horace leaped to his feet, toppling his chair behind him but hardly noticing. "Who do you work for?" he demanded, grabbing ahold of Drucker's collar and yanking him to his feet. "Tell us right now. Who is it? Is it Flanagan? Or Gould?"

"I don't work for anyone," Drucker said, using every ounce of self-control he had in order to remain calm. "That's God's honest truth," he said, for it was. "In fact, at the moment I lack for an employer as well as employment. As I've told you, I've just finished up a case and—"

"I don't buy your horseshit for a damned second," yelled Horace, gripping Drucker's collar and shaking him, turning them both red in the face. "Who sent you here?"

"No one," Drucker answered, his words unhurried despite the assault on him. "I wasn't sent by anyone, nor do I work for anyone. It's the truth."

"Let go of him, Horace," said the AG, his voice steady.

"Jim, for the love of God, you must be out of your ever-loving mind. This boy is clearly lying. He's here to spy on us." Horace's grip remained firm on Drucker's collar.

"Let him go. He's not lying," said the AG, rising ominously to his feet, his rotund belly knocking the table as he did.

"And how in hell would you know that?" Horace demanded, releasing Drucker and pushing him aside so that Horace and the AG could stand eye to eye.

"Because I can read this man's face like a book, and I've seen the way he looks when he's panicked, and this sure as heck ain't what it looks like," said the AG.

The two men locked eyes until the AG tired of the standoff and turned away from Horace. He positioned himself above the seat of his chair before letting his hefty frame fall back onto it.

"C'mon, boys, let's play," he said, but nobody moved. The AG looked from one man to the next. "Don't make me say it twice," he warned, and moments later all seats were once again occupied.

The men took turns discarding their unwanted cards and drawing new ones to refill their hands.

"I'll reraise," said Drucker, when it was time to place his bet in the second round of play.

As he slid a handful of bills to the ever-expanding pot, he noticed one of the men giving him a confused look. "What's wrong?" asked Drucker. "Have I done something incorrectly?"

The man scrunched up his face even more, but he shook his head. "No, no, it's just that you talk...funny. Kinda Yankee-like. Where you from, anyway?"

"Yeah," tacked on another. "You say you come off a the train today, but you ain't yet said where you was coming from."

"But I did tell you," said Drucker, smiling good-naturedly. "As I said, I've just solved a case in Clayton, Arkansas—"

"*Solved* a case! Bully for you," thundered the AG, extending his cigar out in Drucker's direction, clinking it to Drucker's like a glass. "I'll toast to that!"

Drucker brushed his cigar up against the AG's before pulling it to his lips and taking a long celebratory drag. He could feel four pairs of eyes boring into him as he did. The AG's approval of Drucker was unmatched by his incredulous companions, who watched the friendship between the AG and Drucker bud through eyes that squinted with skepticism.

"I don't follow," said the first man. "What's a case in Clayton got to do with you comin' here to Austin?"

Drucker held the smoke in his mouth for a moment then let it out slowly, feeling the smoke tickle his eyes as it floated upward.

"Well, you see, when the case closed I had intended to go to Boston," said Drucker, feeling the smoke linger in this throat. He coughed. The remnants of smoke that he had not exhaled scratched his throat on the way to his lungs. He coughed again, but with all eyes on him, Drucker felt compelled to finish his explanation as quickly as possible. "But the train only went...*cough cough*...east or west, you see...*cough cough cough*...and I didn't want to go right back home."

"Brownie, water," ordered the AG, pointing toward the door, causing Brownie to leap to his feet and scurry out of the room.

"So rather than go home to Boston you came here," said the man across the table.

"I—" *cough.*

"A detective from Boston," mused the AG. "That has a ring to it. I like it."

At that moment Brownie returned with a cup of water, and Drucker sipped gratefully from it, feeling the water clear the fog from his throat. He opened his mouth to amend this misunderstood version of his story but was interrupted when the man seated next to Horace threw down his cards.

"This pot is too rich for my blood," he said, and all eyes shifted to Brownie.

Brownie looked down at his cards and was reaching out toward the pile in front of him when from beneath the table came the dull thudding sound of one boot stomping down on another. Brownie yanked back his hand and let out a high-pitched squeal. He looked up at the group, whimpering. "Sorry," he said, reaching down and grabbing at his foot. "I fold."

Brownie looked meekly at Horace, who offered blithely, "Must be a cramp." Brownie nodded in agreement before putting down his cards and limping out of the room.

"Which leaves two," said Horace, peering over his right shoulder at Drucker. "Four of a kind," he said proudly, splaying his cards to show the others that he had obtained all four aces. "Can you beat it?" He sneered. Ashes from the cigar that dangled from his mouth dusted the face of the cards that he held out to show the group.

Drucker looked at Horace's hand, then back at his own, then back at Horace's. "I believe I can," he said, tipping his cards to reveal that the flush he held ran straight with spades from five to nine.

For a moment, no one spoke.

"Beginner's luck is all," said Drucker, starting to blush as he felt all eyes on him. He gulped down the last of the water Brownie had brought him and got to his feet. "Thank you for the game, gentlemen. And for the cigar." He twiddled the stub of his in the air in front of him. When no one spoke, Drucker continued, "I must be going now. As I've said, I'm new in town, and I've yet to find myself a place to stay for the night and…"

Drucker looked from one man to the next, each face scowling back at him save for that of the amiable AG, who took to his feet and patted Drucker on the back, smiling, but saying nothing.

"Jim," said Drucker. He extended his hand, and the two men shook before Drucker took his leave, abandoning his winnings, which still sat squarely in the middle of the table.

When the door closed behind Drucker, Horace paused for only a beat before speaking. "I don't know what you see in that boy, Jim, but I'll tell you right now—I don't like him, and I don't trust him."

"Well I *do* like him, and I *do* trust him," countered the AG. "I've got a good feeling about him. In fact, I've got the feeling that fate sent that boy here for a reason."

"Well, we're in agreement about one thing," said Horace. "He's been sent here for a reason, that's for damn certain, and it's plain as day that the reason he's here is to spy on us. I'll bet my bottom dollar he's been sent here by Flanagan to sabotage our campaign."

The AG shot Horace a stern glance.

"*Your* campaign," Horace corrected himself. "He's been sent here to ruin you, Jim. If not by Flanagan, then by Gould."

The AG shook his head. "I think he can do more to help us than to hurt us."

Horace looked away in disgust.

"But how can you be sure, Boss?" asked one of the other men.

"You heard him yourself," said the AG with utter confidence. "He owes me a debt. And I can see in his eyes that he'll make good on it. I told you, I can read that boy like a goddamned gazette."

"*He owes you a debt.*" Horace sneered mockingly. "That's enough assurance for you?"

"It is," said the AG firmly as he lumbered over to the door. "You boys go on ahead and play the next hand without me."

The others watched as Jim Hogg's large body moved through the doorway and was swallowed up by the darkness of the dimly lit hallway.

Just before the door closed behind him, from the shadows he ordered, "Brownie, you deal."

CHAPTER EIGHTEEN

B ack at the bar, Drucker was nursing a freshly poured glass of tarantula juice when the AG approached him from behind, placing a heavy paw on Drucker's shoulder.

"That may have been luck, but it sure as hell wasn't beginner's."

"Jim!" exclaimed Drucker, pleasantly surprised to see that the hand on his shoulder belonged to the affable AG rather than to the prickly Horace.

"I take it poker is one of the games you *do* play?" said the AG amiably, stepping up to the bar to stand next to Drucker, extending his arm so that it rested across Drucker's shoulders.

Drucker smiled sheepishly. "Not often, though."

"That so? What's your game then?"

"Actually, I'm not much of a gambling man," said Drucker, wondering if this was true, given that the last two months of his life had been one big gamble. He added, "Not with cards anyway."

The AG removed his arm from around Drucker's shoulders and took a step back so that he could look Drucker in the eye. "Meaning what?"

"Well," said Drucker, "put it this way. I'm not a gambling man, but lately I've been making some big bets."

The AG was quiet for a moment as he assessed what he had just heard. When he finally spoke he said, "You know something, Drucker? I like you. You remind me of the man I was at your age."

"Really?" asked Drucker, feeling pleased. "How so?"

The AG raised a hand to signal to the barkeep, who wordlessly and immediately slid a glass of dark liquid down the bar to the AG. "Because, Drucker," he said, pausing to take a drink, "you may not gamble often, but when you do, you bet big, and you know how to win." He clapped his heavy hand on Drucker's back, and the two men raised their glasses, each tossing back what he had remaining.

Drucker was careful to keep a calm demeanor despite the burning of the liquor as it went down his throat, but the AG slammed his glass down on the bar and let out a dramatic post gulp *haaaaaaah.* He wiped his mouth on his sleeve and turned to Drucker. "Never been much of a gambling man myself."

"Is that so?" asked Drucker, thinking back to how perfectly the AG had fit into the scene of the smoky back room. The leader of the pack, he had shuffled and dealt with ease. Drucker had never seen someone handle cards with such aplomb, and for a moment he considered telling the AG as much, but instead he asked, "Isn't politics a form of gambling?"

The AG smiled. "That depends on if you're doing it right. If you ask my opinion," he said, lowering his voice, "politics is the greater vice." The AG sniffed the air as if he smelled the foul stench of it. "Don't have much of taste for it. Never did."

"But you're running for governor, are you not?"

"Oh, I am," said the AG. "And I'll win the damn thing, too. But it was Horace's idea, not mine. I never would have been in this race 'cept for the fact that Horace...well, he knows how to twist an arm."

In his mind's eye Drucker could see the standoff between the two men at the card table. The AG had held the upper hand, but only slightly. Horace's power was quiet, but his hunger for more was unmistakable.

So Horace had strong-armed Jim Hogg into running for governor? *Why*, wondered Drucker, *and how*? He hoped the AG would explain further, but he could see that his new friend's mind was elsewhere.

"Drucker," said the AG, turning his body to look Drucker squarely in the eye, "are you really a detective?"

Drucker gulped and offered what truth he could. "I've the entire population of Clayton, Arkansas, to attest to it."

"And you say you haven't been sent here by anyone?"

"No one."

"Not my opponent Flanagan?" asked the AG, maintaining eye contact, solemn and steady.

"No, sir," replied Drucker, equally solemn.

"And not that scoundrel Jay Gould?"

"No, not Jay Gould or anyone else. I don't work for anyone, and I wasn't sent for or by anyone. My hand to God," said Drucker, raising his right hand, revealing a smooth pink palm that he bore like a scar from the lifetime of desk work he had narrowly escaped.

The AG stood quietly for a moment, studying Drucker with his earnest, upright hand extending toward the heavens. When finally he spoke, the AG's tone was firm. "Drucker, I want you to come work for me."

"Work for you?"

"On my campaign."

"As...?"

"A campaign manager."

"Campaign manager?" repeated Drucker with a laugh. "Jim, I'm flattered, but I've never managed a political campaign before."

"And I've never run for governor before."

Drucker smiled, conceding the point, but added, "Jim, I've never worked a day in politics."

"Not important to me," said the AG resolutely. "What matters to me is that you know how to bet big, and you know how to win."

"But surely you don't want someone who has absolutely no experience with political campaigns to be the campaign manager for your—"

The AG cut off Drucker midsentence. "I didn't say *the*. I said *a*. An *additional* campaign manager."

"I see," said Drucker. "In addition to…"

"Horace."

"I see." Drucker lifted his cup but found it disappointingly empty. "Does Horace know that you intend to—"

"No. And he won't like it. But that doesn't change the fact that I want you to join this—*my*—campaign."

Drucker put down the useless cup and took his face in his hands, massaging from the temples down the smooth boyish slopes of his cheeks.

"Drucker, let me be clear with you. I'm a Democrat running for governor in the state of Texas. I'm not looking for someone who lives and breathes the ins and outs of political campaigns. Frankly, I don't need it. What I do need is someone who I can stand to be around from now until election night. Someone who can bring a fresh perspective, perhaps see something I don't. Even more than that, I need someone who can stand up to Horace and stand between us to give me some damn breathing room."

"And what makes you think that I can be that person?" asked Drucker.

"The fact that I've seen you do it already," said the AG, smiling. "Back there, in that card room. It was when you wedged yourself right in between us at the table that I got the idea in the first place."

"So you want to use me to put some space between yourself and Horace?"

The AG replied without wavering, "I want you to work for me, Drucker. Do you want to work for me?"

It may have been on account of the most recent round of tarantula juice, but the answer that kept swimming through Drucker's head was *yes*.

"Can I have the night to think on it?"

"You'll have an answer for me tomorrow?"

"I will," said Drucker.

The AG nodded. "Fine then. I'll expect to hear from you by midday tomorrow. Have you found a place to spend the night yet?"

Drucker shook his head.

"Better go across the street then, to Lucky Lyle's place. Better hurry, though," said the AG, reaching into his coat pocket and pulling out a pocket watch. He glanced at it briefly before redepositing it. "At this hour they'll be close to full, but you tell 'em Jim Hogg sent you. Short Sam should be able to get you a room. You understand me?"

"Tell Short Sam at Lucky Lyle's across the street that Jim Hogg sent me," repeated Drucker, nodding.

The AG was busy looking down at his watch. "Better get movin'," he warned.

"Of course," said Drucker. "Let me just settle up here, and I'll be on my way." Drucker lifted the cup in front of him to be sure it was as empty as he remembered it and found that it was.

"Never mind that. This round's on me," said the AG, looking up suddenly and waving him off. "You just get on over to the inn and get yourself a room before they fill up."

"That's awfully kind of you," said Drucker. "Thank you again, Jim," he called over his shoulder as he made haste toward the door of the saloon.

The AG watched the doors swing shut behind Drucker.

"Nice to see that boy use the front damn door of the place for once." The AG laughed. "Am I right, Eddie?"

"Like you always are, Jim!" replied the barkeep as he cleared away the two empty cups from in front of the AG.

CHAPTER NINETEEN

A wave of exhaustion hit Drucker as he stepped out of the saloon and into the diminishing light of day. When he looked across the street and saw a sign reading LUCKY LYLE'S FINE HOTEL AND RESTAURANT, he felt enormous relief.

That feeling became fleeting, though, when he approached the self-proclaimedly fine establishment and noticed a second sign. One that was smaller, and legible only at close range, requiring Drucker to stand close to it to see the block lettering that read, No VACANCY, and the smaller handwritten addendum below: IF YER IN NEED OF A ROOM YER OUT A LUCK.

Though Drucker felt discouraged, he told himself not to let the signs deter him. He hadn't forgotten the AG's suggestion to drop his name with Short Sam at the front desk. *If anyone could make an open room materialize, Jim Hogg could*, Drucker thought as he strode across the inn's front porch. *All I need is a little confidence*, Drucker told himself as he breezed through the entry and made a beeline to the front desk. Yes, with just a little confidence he could simply introduce himself as a friend of the governor-to-be and surely the proprietor, Short Sam as Hogg had referred to him, would find a room for him. *Easy enough,* Drucker thought, as he approached the desk.

And it would have been, if not for one glaring problem.

There was a man behind the desk, but he couldn't be accused of standing any less than six and a half feet tall. Short Sam would certainly be an ill-fitting nickname for a man of his stature. All Drucker could do was hope that this man had the same relationship with the AG that his shorter colleague had. Otherwise, Drucker would be sorely out of luck and without a room at a moment when he could not remember ever feeling more tired.

Putting on his most confident air, Drucker walked up to the desk behind which the man stood. "Hello, friend," started Drucker.

The tall man behind the counter looked bookish and graying. He wore spectacles, a sleeve garter, and a faceful of wrinkles.

"I shore as day hope you ain't lookin' for a room," grumbled the man, without returning the greeting. He didn't bother to look at Drucker as he spoke. He was busy ambling around behind the desk, stuffing papers into slots. With his slow, shuffling gait, he looked like an old, caged animal, resigned to the confines of his unnatural habitat.

Just as the man had not returned Drucker's greeting, Drucker, in turn, ignored the man's declaration. He cleared his throat. "My name is Drucker May. And you are?"

The man turned to look at Drucker as if to assess whether this young stranger could possibly be serious.

"The proprietor of a very full hotel, son. I suggest you take yer search fer a room elsewhere."

Drucker opened his mouth to launch into his friend-of-the-AG overture, but he was interrupted by a woman's voice that came ringing through an open doorway not far from where the hotel's lanky proprietor stood.

"Walter, has Mr. Clark settled his account yet?" called the voice.

"Nawt yet," the man called back, "and if he don't do it soon, I'll be tempted to send the dogs after 'im."

So this is Walter, not Sam. Damn, thought Drucker.

"Excuse me," said Drucker, forearms resting on the counter that stood between him and the beanstalk of a man in front of him. "I understand you're quite full up, but I've been sent here by a friend who said you might be able to make room for me."

The innkeeper turned to Drucker and looked at him over the rim of the spectacles that had ridden down over the bridge of his nose. Drucker had finally succeeded in rousing his attention. "Who's your friend?" he asked suspiciously.

"Jim Hogg," replied Drucker quickly, hopefully.

The man set down the stack of papers he had been preoccupied with filing. He kept his eyes on Drucker, and shifting neither face nor body, he hollered, "Margaret! Got a man here called May who says he been sent by Jim Hogg."

Just moments later a woman emerged from the back room.

"Ma'am," said Drucker, tipping his hat to her.

"Hello," she said, politely but curtly.

"This feller here says he knows Jim Hogg," repeated Walter.

Margaret nodded, looking at Drucker as if he were not the first to come through her door with such a claim, and neither would he be if that claim were false.

"You know the AG?" she asked taking a few steps toward him.

"Yes, ma'am," Drucker nodded, his confidence growing.

"He a friend a yours?"

"Yes, ma'am," he said again.

"Mmhmm," she nodded knowingly then stopped abruptly. "He tell you the password?"

Drucker hesitated. He hadn't, had he? Had Jim Hogg told him the password to use? Was it lost somewhere in Drucker's tired, fuzzy, tarantula-juice-addled mind?

"Well, no," said Drucker, quickly adding, "but I—I was just with him. Across the street." He gestured toward the door.

"I'm sure you were, sir," replied Margaret evenly, "but we haven't any vacancy tonight. I'm sorry." She didn't sound particularly apologetic.

She began walking back in the direction from which she had come, leaving Drucker alone with Walter, who was back at the mail slots, filing, shuffling.

"Wait!" called Drucker, just before Margaret disappeared into the back room.

From the doorway, she turned to him, her face impatient.

"He did tell me the password," said Drucker.

Margaret raised an eyebrow.

"It's Short Sam," he blurted.

Margaret took a few steps toward Drucker. She eyed him carefully, but her expression warmed slightly. Drucker watched as she reached into a drawer and pulled out a long metal key.

"Follow me, please," she said, making her way toward the grand staircase in the middle of the hotel's lobby. Drucker released the breath he realized he had been holding. He had never felt such relief.

As he followed Margaret up the staircase, Drucker couldn't help but think back to the day that he had met Anna at the general store and how she had led him to her home and opened up her studio to him. The thought of it made Drucker feel both grateful and guilty. But this was not Anna in front of him, he reminded himself as they reached the second-story landing, and there was no use in thinking of her now.

When he caught Margaret's eye at the top of the stairs, she gave him a hint of a girlish smile. *She's quite pretty when she smiles*, Drucker thought, returning him to the conclusion that Anna she was not.

"We'll have to put you in the little room at the end of the hall," she said, making a right and heading into the corridor.

"Anything you can spare is much appreciated," said Drucker, following a few paces behind. From that distance he could see the shape of her as she moved through the hall. She was not Anna, certainly, but neither did she have Lucinda's siren form, he concluded. Still, there was something undeniably attractive about her.

Perhaps it was her hair, he mused, the color of sweet corn, with bouncy ringlets of it falling to her shoulders. He felt the urge to reach out and tug one of them just to watch it spring back into place.

When they arrived at the end of the hall, Margaret inserted the long metal key into the door and pushed it open. She stepped aside and ushered Drucker into the small, dank room that boasted nothing more than a narrow bed with a washbasin and a pitcher of water beside it.

"It's not much to speak of, but it's all we have open."

"It'll do just fine," said Drucker, setting down his valise and placing his hat on the end of the bed.

"There's running water out back," she said, "and I've freshly laundered the linens."

"That explains why they smell so lovely," quipped Drucker, leaning over and taking an exaggerated whiff. She blushed, and Drucker caught himself thinking she looked quite pretty again.

"Any questions?" asked Margaret, her cheeks scarlet as she handed Drucker the key.

He thought for a moment. "Will I be seeing you tomorrow?" he asked, with some surprise at his own courage.

Margaret was duly surprised. She blushed deeper yet and moved quickly toward the door without answering his question. "Good night, Mr. May," she said, without turning to him.

"Good night, Margaret," said Drucker, watching her as she moved through the little room's doorway. *There really is something quite appealing about her,* he thought. She was young and fresh-faced and slender, but she was also quite obviously the brains behind

Lucky Lyle's operation. *Did he tell you the password?* He smirked, recalling how confidently she had handled him at the front desk, how she had been the one busy doing the books while Walter ambled between mail slots.

"Oh, Mr. May," said Margaret, the door half-closed behind her, "I forgot to ask. How many nights will you be staying with us?"

Drucker pursed his lips in thought. "I'm honestly not sure yet," he replied.

Margaret gave a small smile and nodded politely. Quietly, she pulled the door shut behind her.

CHAPTER TWENTY

Drucker woke to repeated knocking on his door. Tarantula juice had spent the night working its way through his veins, and whatever was left of it rushed to his head as he took to his feet, his eyes still squinting from unfinished sleep, even as he opened the door.

"Letter for you, May." It was Walter. He had climbed the grand staircase to hand deliver the mail. Drucker wondered if, with those broomsticks for legs, Walter had taken the steps two at a time.

"Thank you," said Drucker, taking the envelope and opening it in the doorway.

"It's from your friend Hogg," said Walter, as Drucker shucked the letter from its envelope and read it quickly, which proved no real feat since it hardly contained more than a dozen words.

> Meet me for breakfast at Lucky Lyle's restaurant at 8:30 this morning.
>
> —J. S. Hogg

Drucker looked up at Walter. "He wants me to meet him for breakfast."

Walter nodded. "I know."

Drucker was taken aback. "You've read my mail then?"

"No," said Walter matter-of-factly. "He told me himself when I saw him downstairs." He pointed down to the floorboards as if to point out Jim Hogg's exact location below them. "How do you think I got the letter?"

Drucker conceded the point. "It says 8:30." He looked up at Walter. "Do you have the time?"

Walter reached into the pocket of his trousers and fished out a copper-colored timepiece. He flinched. "Uh-huh, and you don't have much of it."

"How long?" asked Drucker, sensing Jim Hogg was not a man who liked to be kept waiting.

"I'd say 'bout six minutes," said Walter before he turned to go, leaving Drucker all of six minutes to wash, dress, and begin to consider the question he had meant to ponder all night.

━┿ ┿━

When Drucker entered Lucky Lyle's restaurant just minutes after the invitation had been delivered by Walter, Jim Hogg waved him over to the table where he was already fully engaged with his breakfast.

"Take a seat," said the AG without getting up. "Hope you don't mind," he continued, pointing to his plate with both fork and knife. "I got started without you."

Drucker did as he was told. Once seated, he looked at his companion's plate and saw that AG had already made it halfway through a glistening strip of thickly cut bacon. "Of course not," he said. "I'm sorry to have kept you waiting." Under the table he sneaked a glance at his own timepiece. Eight minutes earlier he had been asleep.

"They find you a suitable room?" asked the AG.

"Yes, thanks to you, Ji—"

"Good," said the AG, cutting Drucker off. He set his down his utensils. "And did you have a chance to give my offer some thought?"

This man doesn't beat around the bush, thought Drucker. "Not as much as I'd like," he said. Having washed and dressed in three minutes, Drucker had only three left in which to consider whether he was ready to step in between the presumed next governor of Texas and his overprotective crony.

"Excuse me, gentlemen. I've got a fresh pot of Arbuckle's here. Care for any?"

Drucker looked up. It was Margaret.

"Thank you, darlin'," said the AG, holding up his mug.

"And you, Mr. May?"

"Yes, thank you, Margaret," said Drucker. She filled his cup, and the nutty aroma of steaming coffee wafted up from it.

"Something from the kitchen?" she asked him, smiling.

Drucker looked at the fatty remains of pork bacon strewn across the AG's plate. "Perhaps just a biscuit," he said.

"Of course," replied Margaret, and Drucker found it difficult to take his eyes off of her as she walked away. He was so distracted by her that the AG was halfway through his sentence by the time Drucker realized that the half-complete sentence was addressed to *him.*

"—which is why all I'm asking is that you stay on until Election Day."

"Ah, I see," murmured Drucker, trying to latch on to the conversation.

"And if it's compensation you're worried about, you should know—"

"No, it's not the compensation I care about," cut in Drucker, as his eyes followed Margaret whisking by, wordlessly placing a plated biscuit in front of Drucker.

"What is it, then?" asked the AG, without stopping to wait for an answer. "Tell me, Drucker, what's on your mind. If it's Horace, I can assure you—"

Drucker let the AG's voice fade into background noise. There was someone on Drucker's mind, but it wasn't Horace. Staying on until the election would mean eight more weeks in Austin, perhaps in that very hotel.

Drucker lifted and examined the golden ridges of his biscuit. "Would I be living here for the duration of the campaign?" he asked, hoping to appear impartial.

"Only so long as it's agreeable to you."

Margaret whisked by again, setting down a plate of eggs in front of a nearby patron without slowing her gait. She was at once girlish and competent, and Drucker found something very attractive at the intersection of the two.

"Fine," said Drucker, his casual tone belying his excitement at the prospect of better acquainting himself with Margaret in the weeks to come. "I'll do it."

"Very good," said the AG. His voice had the tone of confirmed expectation, but his face wore the look of hard-won relief.

"When do I start?" asked Drucker, setting down the still-intact biscuit.

The AG appeared thoughtful as he put down first his knife and then his fork, and then covered them both with his grease-stained napkin.

"Right now," he said, slapping both free hands down on the table.

Then the AG hoisted himself up out of his chair and motioned for Drucker to follow him as he led the way out of Lucky Lyle's fine hotel and restaurant establishment.

CHAPTER TWENTY-ONE

Horace should have shunned the news that Drucker would be joining the Hogg campaign. But instead, he surprised everyone by relishing it.

Perhaps it was because he, like Hogg, felt that a Democrat's campaign for governor in the state of Texas had all the trimmings of an effortless win. As such, it would require little in the way of campaign management and offer little in the way of recognition for a campaign manager.

Or maybe, instead, he lacked the candidate's confidence; perhaps with his deeper knowledge and understanding of the players and politics of the race, he worried that victory was *not* a foregone conclusion.

Either way, by the time he met Drucker, Horace had already spent several weeks desperately hunting for an idea that would not only lock in the win for the AG but also make himself appear the hero for thinking of it.

The day that Jim Hogg brought Drucker into his campaign office was the day that Horace finally thought of the idea that he'd been searching for, and it was Drucker's arrival that sparked it.

"Make yourselves decent, boys," announced Jim Hogg jovially as he burst through the doors of his campaign office. "We've got company!"

He tugged on Drucker's sleeve, dragging him into the center of the room, where Drucker found himself encircled by the same gangly crew that he had met at the card table plus a few unfamiliar faces. Just as he had a day earlier, Drucker caught a chill off their icy, scrutinizing stares.

Drucker raised a quiet hand in greeting, but no one spoke. The silence didn't surprise Jim Hogg, but it irked him nonetheless. When he next spoke, his tone was clipped.

"I've asked Drucker to join the campaign," he declared, and when there was no response, he added, "as a second campaign manager."

At that someone gasped, and all eyes snapped over to Horace, whose own eyes were cast down on the paper in front of him, on which he was scribbling something furiously.

"Campaign manager?" squeaked Brownie. "But what about Horace? Isn't he the—"

"He said *second*," said Horace with a growl that revealed that he had been listening despite his apparent distraction.

"That's right," said Hogg. "Drucker is part of this team now, and you'll treat him as such, y'hear me?" The men nodded gravely and hummed murmurs of assent.

"But what will he *do*?" asked one of men from the card table whose name Drucker had not caught.

"What do any of the rest of you do?" sniped Horace. Then he turned to Drucker. "How 'bout *this* for something to do? I've got an idea that'll blow this campaign wide open, but Jim don't like it. How 'bout *you* break the tie?"

Drucker looked nervously over at Jim Hogg, whose breathing was heavy, though whether it was due to anger or the flight of stairs to the second-story campaign office, Drucker couldn't quite tell.

"There's no tie to break," huffed Hogg. "It's my call to make. I'm the candidate."

"And I'm the candidate's manager," snapped Horace.

"You're the *campaign* manager," corrected Hogg. "You don't manage me."

Horace snorted and rolled his eyes, and for a minute neither man said anything. Hogg was the one to bring the long uncomfortable silence to an end. "Fine," he said finally, "we'll let Drucker decide."

"Fine," said Horace, crossing his arms in front of his chest indignantly.

"Well," said Drucker, breaking a second tense silence, "let's have it." But Horace wasn't done making him wait.

There was another moment of icy silence before, staring off into the distance, Horace said, "There's a man I met a few weeks back. Goes by the name a Cagney, I think. An older man. Bald up here"—he waved a hand over the top of his head—"white down here." He transferred the waving motion to a few inches below his chin. "You catch my drift?" His eyes suddenly came alive and darted up to meet Drucker's.

"I'm afraid I don't," said Drucker, shaking his head.

"'Course not." Horace rolled his eyes again. "Don't you see?" he demanded, growing animated. "The man looks just like Flanagan! Well, maybe not exactly like him, but that don't matter, all we need's close enough." Horace looked at Drucker expectantly, as if it were obviously now time to weigh in with his judgment.

"So you met a man who looks somewhat like Jim's opponent," summarized Drucker. "And the big idea is...?"

"Isn't it obvious?" cried Horace. "We've got to send that man on a campaign tour of the state. He'll impersonate Flanagan, shaking hands and making speeches at saloons. But, you see, he'll be working for us, so while he's out campaigning for Flanagan, he'll be doing so with…with…what did it I call it the other day?"

"'Terrific ineptitude,'" supplied a voice from across the room.

"That's right! Terrific ineptitude," continued Horace, picking right back up where he'd left off. "He'll shake those hands bone-crushingly hard, refuse to buy drinks for those that come to see him speak at the barrooms. By the time he's through, there won't be a soul left in the state a Texas that will be able to stomach even the thought of voting for such a horse's ass," concluded Horace excitedly. "Now d'you see?"

Yes, Drucker nodded, now he did see. He could also see the flashes of mania that animated Horace's eyes as he described his plan. Those flashes told Drucker to proceed with caution. "Not bad," said Drucker carefully. "But this Cagney, do you know him well? This man who you met just a few weeks ago. You said Cagney's his name, right? Cagney, you think?"

"Yes, Cagney, I think, but what difference does his name make? He'll be Flanagan to us," said Horace with a devilish grin.

"There," said Drucker, "you said it again. Cagney, *you think*. You aren't even sure of the man's name, so you can't possibly know this man very well at all." Drucker turned to address the rest of the group. "Do any of the rest of you know this Cagney fellow?"

The group collectively wagged their heads left and right.

"That's the only problem with your plan, Horace. It's the height of political cunning," Drucker assured him, "but it hinges on the character of a man none of us know from Adam. What if his fraud is discovered, and he rats us out? From what I understand, this election is Jim's to lose. The last thing we need to do is feed a scandal to the public. It's the one thing that could turn this race on its head."

Drucker was surprised to hear murmurs of agreement from the others.

"He has a point, Horace," said one man.

"We need someone we can trust," said a second.

Horace waved a dismissive hand. "Bah," he grumbled and re-turned to his scribbling.

"Why don't we make one of *us* up to look like Flanagan?" con-tinued the second man. "That way we'll know we can trust the impersonator."

"Forget the impersonator," said the first man, and all eyes shift-ed back over to him. "Why worry about campaigning when we can go straight for the votes? Why don't we bring some folks over the border from Louisiana to vote for Hogg on Election Day? At the very least they'll jam up the polling stations," he said, swelling with pride as the group cooed their collective interest.

"Or," said the second man, in an effort to swing the group's atten-tion and admiration back in his direction, "we could send Drucker to the *Austin Statesman* with a story about Flanagan. Since he's so new in town, they wouldn't know he's with us. We could cook up something nice'n juicy for the reporters to sink their claws into."

Horace lifted his head. "Or," he said, suddenly reengaging with the others, "Drucker could work for the campaign."

The men exchanged puzzled glances.

"But Horace, he already does," squeaked Brownie.

"Not ours," said Horace coolly. "Flanagan's."

There was quiet as the men shifted uncomfortably in their seats.

"Well, he's a detective isn't he? What's wrong with doing a little detective work from the inside?" he asked of no one in particular.

"A detective isn't the same thing as a spy," said Drucker, "and I'm not a spy. I've told you that."

"Who said spy?" asked Horace with feigned innocence. "You're the only one who said spy. All I'm suggesting is that you use your detective skills to find out if Flanagan's boys are planning any at-tacks on *us*. I'd imagine it would be an easier thing to do from the inside, but of course, you're the professional when it comes to this kind of work."

"That's quite the double cross," said Drucker, wrapping his mind around Horace's scheme. "I don't know how I could stand to look at myself in the mirror—or if I'd know which version of me I was looking at—if I had to be two different people at once."

Horace pouted with mock concern. "You wouldn't be two different people."

"That's exactly what I would have to be," said Drucker, "to make them think I work for Flanagan, when in truth I work for Hogg."

"Now, Drucker, you worry too much," said Horace, putting an arm around Drucker's shoulders. "Don't you see? This idea here, this is your ticket to greatness. We're not asking you to hurt anybody. Just a little innocuous detective work, that's all. You could be the one to clinch the win for our man Hogg here."

His overture, however, was met with skepticism. Drucker could sense that someone would emerge the hero from all of this, and it wouldn't be him if Horace had anything to do with it.

"I'm not so sure it's a good idea," Drucker said. When he had agreed to work for Hogg, he hadn't imagined doing so from inside the belly of the Flanagan campaign.

"Just promise me you'll consider it," said Horace.

"Careful, Drucker," the AG warned with a wink. "The last time I heard those words, I found myself agreeing to run this damn race in the first place."

Drucker looked from Horace to the AG and back again. "Fine," he said, "but I'll need some time to think on it."

"Congratulations, Horace," the AG said with another wink. "I've heard *that* before, too, and now Drucker is working with us."

"Good," said Horace, patting Drucker's back a little too hard for comfort. "Welcome to the campaign, Drucker. I'm envisioning where this could go," he said, smiling, his eyes closed, "and I must say—I like it very much."

CHAPTER TWENTY-TWO

Drucker knew that he owed Horace an answer, but he dragged his feet for three weeks before giving it. While it didn't take him long to make his decision, coming up with the courage to tell Horace about it took considerably longer.

As Drucker delayed, the relationship between the two men grew increasingly strained. The trouble was, the harder Horace pushed, the more Drucker recoiled. Nothing could frustrate Horace like not getting his way, and Drucker's refusal to act as his pawn irritated him to no end. And so, while Drucker's first days at the campaign were quite pleasant, Horace eventually lost patience with playing the game on Drucker's terms. It wasn't long before their relationship had returned to its original state of Horace despising Drucker and Drucker knowing it full well.

It didn't help matters any that as tensions between Drucker and Horace escalated, the affinity between Drucker and the AG quickly grew, forcing Horace to watch as day after day, the threat to his power built right before his eyes.

Horace's ill will toward Drucker reached a fever pitch on the day that Drucker finally found the courage to admit that he had reached the decision not to participate in Horace's deceitful ruse. Drucker's dissent made Horace so fuming mad that he had to leave the building in order to prevent himself from punching Drucker square in the jaw.

It wasn't just Drucker's defiance that infuriated Horace, it was the demise of his perfect plan. Could there have been a more fool-proof way to be rid of Drucker, regain uncompromised access to the AG, and look the hero all the while?

But the plan had no legs without Drucker's compliance. Horace couldn't *force* him to play the role of "Drucker, two-faced spy." Instead, all he could do was try to make Drucker's life at the Hogg campaign as uncomfortable as possible, a task he undertook with increasingly bitter spirits, thanks to his miserable lack of success at it. For several weeks, Drucker hardly even noticed Horace's attempts to make him suffer.

He was too busy enjoying his blossoming friendship with the AG. The two men found that they sincerely enjoyed each other's company, and for hours on end the AG would amuse Drucker with stories of his rascally boyhood in Cherokee County, Texas, and Drucker would return the favor with tales of own puckish youth, without mentioning exactly where he had spent his formative years. Many nights the two would take dinner together at Lucky Lyle's restaurant, which pleased Drucker, since it allowed him to exchange smiles and winks with Margaret as she served them dinner.

When they had finished with their supper, Drucker and Hogg would routinely cap off the night with a scotch and a smoke on the front porch of Lucky Lyle's, which is exactly where they were one evening five weeks before the election when the course of Drucker's life in Austin took an unexpected turn.

The night that changed everything for Drucker started out like so many other nights that he had spent in Austin. He and the AG had taken their evening meal at Lucky Lyle's, after which they had retreated to the front porch. There they smoked and laughed and enjoyed an evening that had all the markings of a perfectly ordinary one. That is, until a man emerged from the shadows with a message for Drucker.

When the man approached, Drucker was alone on the front porch. Moments earlier, the AG had gone around back to relieve himself, leaving Drucker alone with his thoughts and his cigar, blowing wisps of smoke into the warm October air and watching them shape shift until they disappeared.

As he tipped back on the chair's hind legs and inhaled, Drucker caught sight of a man emerging from the shadows of the street corner. The stranger scaled the steps of Lucky Lyle's porch in a single stride and sat down next to Drucker in the seat that the AG had left unoccupied.

"Sorry, friend," said Drucker as he tapped the ash off the end of his cigar. "Seat's taken."

"I know it is, Mr. May," said the stranger, making Drucker's heart skip a beat with the realization that the lack of familiarity wasn't mutual. Drucker studied the man's face, craggy with pockmarks and scars, searching for something that would jog his memory.

"I beg your pardon," said Drucker, finding nothing recognizable, "but do we know each other?"

The stranger gave a crooked smile, revealing that he had only three of his top teeth. "I certainly know who you are," he said as if reading some invisible dossier. He lowered his voice. "You're Drucker May. Been here in Austin just a couple a weeks. Friend a Jim Hogg. Sound 'bout right?"

"Particularly the last part," replied Drucker, trying to keep calm in spite of the unnerving exchange. "In fact, I'm expecting him to rejoin me here at any moment. Perhaps you'd like to talk to him directly."

"No, my business is with you, Mr. May," replied the stranger. "You see, I've been sent here by my employer with an offer for you."

Drucker craned his neck to see if the AG was in sight. "If it's an offer you don't want Jim Hogg to weigh in on, you'd better hurry." He hoped the imminent return of the AG might scare this unwanted visitor away, but the man didn't appear to be in a rush.

"Frankly, I don't give a rat's ass what Jim Hogg thinks about this or any other business in the state a Texas," hissed the man, "but because it will behoove you to keep that fat flapdragon in the dark about this, I'll cut to the chase. I work for a man by the name of Jay Gould." He paused and locked eyes with Drucker. "Ever heard of him?"

Drucker nodded solemnly. Besides the fact that anyone who had picked up a newspaper in the last twenty years could hardly avoid reading about the nefarious financial exploits of Jay Gould, his name also came up as a frequent topic of conversation at the Hogg campaign. Gould was a well-known anti-Hoggite who despised Hogg for his long-standing vow to fight railroad industry corruption. He had made it known that if Hogg were to be elected governor of Texas, Gould would spare no expense to make each day that Hogg spent in office a little more miserable than the last.

"Good," said the stranger. "Then you'll understand what I mean when I say that information from the inside of the Hogg campaign would be worth a great deal to my employer, Mr. Gould, and that he is prepared to pay whatever it costs to obtain that information. I've been sent here to make you an offer of six weeks in Mr. Gould's employment."

The man's grave expression took on a hint of confusion as he watched Drucker break into a grin.

"Oh, I see what's going on," said Drucker stifling his laughter. "Horace has sent you, hasn't he? This is some sort of practical joke. Or some test of my allegiance, perhaps?"

Drucker felt certain this man had not been sent by *the* Jay Gould, but if he had hit on the real origin of the proposition, Drucker's new companion gave no sign of it.

"This ain't no joke," said the roughneck. "I been sent here by Jay Gould and none other." He reached into his pocket and pulled out a stack of greenbacks that he placed onto Drucker's palm. "This's for you. From Mr. Gould. An advance for your work, should you choose to accept his offer. Does that clear things up?"

Drucker looked at the brick of bills that had been placed in his hand. The stack was so thick it would surely have to have been sent by someone the likes of Gould who could get his hands on a small fortune like it in the first place, much less stand to part with it.

"You're telling me you haven't been sent here by Horace? To get back at me for not agreeing to—" Drucker stopped himself short of divulging the details of the Flanagan campaign ploy on the off chance that the man was, as he claimed, not playing a joke and also not aware of the by-then-defunct plan to install Drucker as a spy in the opponent's campaign headquarters.

"I can assure you, Mr. May, this is no joke, and neither is the handsome fee Mr. Gould is willing to pay for your partnership. That there," he said, pointing to the bundle of bills in Drucker's hand, "is just to whet your appetite. Mr. Gould has given me strict instructions to let you name your price for your service to him."

Drucker looked away from the man and turned his gaze upward toward the night sky. He inhaled deeply, drawing out one last puff on his cigar, then dropped what was left of the stub and stamped it out, grinding it into the porch's floorboards until nothing was left but a mound of ash.

He thought of Hogg, the way his face lit up with joy when they laughed together. Was there anything in the world that could make him betray the affection that had grown so quickly and so naturally between the two of them? Drucker turned to the man with every intention of telling him to take his cash and get lost, but when he opened his mouth the words that came out were quite different.

Instead he asked, "What exactly does Gould want from me?"

"Information," answered the man without hesitation. "From inside the Hogg campaign."

"Delivered how?"

"Through me or one of my associates. You'll give me the answers Gould wants, and I'll give you the *dinero* in exchange."

"How often?" asked Drucker.

"Once a week."

For a moment Drucker was quiet, letting the offer drift and shape shift in his mind as the smoke from his cigar had done in the air.

"How much did you say was in it for me?"

"How much do you want?"

"How much is this?" Drucker had split the stack of bills into two and was shuffling it like a deck of cards.

"A thousand," said the man.

Drucker's eyes widened. Even for him it was a hefty sum. "I admit I've been caught off guard by your offer," said Drucker, shaking his head in bewilderment. "But nothing surprises me more than my response to it." He looked over his shoulder to make sure Hogg wasn't in sight. "I'll do it. For a thousand a week."

The man didn't mirror any of Drucker's amazement at the conclusion he had reached. "Fine," he said flatly, as if no other answer could possibly be given in response to a proposition like this.

"Fine," repeated Drucker, feeling the weight of the word that committed him to this unseemly stranger. "When shall we begin?"

"I'll find you right here next..." The words dissolved midsentence when Drucker coughed several times, and the man read his signal perfectly. Without looking over his shoulder, he smoothly launched himself from the chair and disappeared back into the shadowy night as quickly as he had emerged from it.

A moment later the AG retook his seat and picked up the stub of the cigar he had left smoldering. "Who was that?" asked Hogg.

"One of Gould's toughs," replied Drucker without pause, "in the market for an informant. Someone to feed Gould information from the inside of your campaign."

Hogg nodded without surprise, recognizing the tactic as quite fitting with Gould's notorious style. "And what's that?" he asked, pointing to the stack of bills Drucker made no effort to hide.

"The money he's going to pay me for being Gould's informant on the inside of your campaign," said Drucker, raising an eyebrow, his eyes sparkling with amusement.

One beat passed and then another. Then both men broke into wild grins.

"You didn't," said the AG, thoroughly entertained by the notion.

"Oh, but I did," said Drucker, sending both men into fits of face-flushing laughter.

The two laughed so long and so hard that when they finally were able to pull themselves together, they each wiped tears from their eyes.

"Oh, this is rich, boy, rich!" exclaimed Hogg when he finally regained composure. "We're gon' have some fun with this!"

"I was hoping you would think so," said Drucker, his lips still pulled tightly into a boyish grin.

The AG wiped from his forehead the sweat that he had worked up by laughing. Turning toward the dark streets of Austin, he gave one long looping whistle and then another. *Whoooooh-eee,* Jim Hogg let fly out into the night. *Whooooooh-eeeee.*

CHAPTER TWENTY-THREE

Lacking both a proper political operation to occupy their time as well as—with all signs looking favorable for Hogg—a pressing need to create one, Hogg's men spent most of the days leading up to the election holed up playing poker in the back of the saloon. When they tired of cards, Drucker and Hogg would head across the street to Lucky Lyle's, though not without incurring spiteful looks from Horace. Drucker and the AG hardly noticed them, though. They were too caught up in their new diversion: thinking up artfully twisted stories to feed to Gould through his henchmen.

Just as it had been agreed to, once a week someone or another from Gould's ruffian crew would meet Drucker on Lucky Lyle's porch after Hogg had taken his leave for the night. Some of the men were more menacing than others, and none were particularly genial. The game was a thrilling but risky one for Drucker, the penalty for being caught unstated but understood. Perhaps the most unnerving part of it all for him was knowing that the men who emerged from the shadows spent their evenings lurking in the dark, watching and waiting and, ultimately, appearing without warning.

As the days ticked by, Drucker delighted in not only his ever-tightening alliance with the AG, but also his slowly blossoming courtship of Margaret. Their relationship, which fell somewhere between the friendship that he had enjoyed with Anna and the passion that he had shared with Lucinda, could best be character-ized as being quite tender. In equal parts he admired her refined beauty and her shrewd mind, and spending time with her both relaxed and excited him. Over time, his nightly routine, which be-gan with supper and a smoke by Jim Hogg's side, began to feel incomplete if it didn't include time with Margaret.

And so after the cigars had burned down and the AG had re-tired for the night, Drucker had taken to heading inside to help Margaret tidy up after the dinner hour, the two of them talking and brushing elbows as they passed each other on their way to and from the kitchen. Several times she had even let him kiss her, but it was always quite chaste. Each time he had been left wanting more. Not more from her, but more of her. And not just more of her body, but more of her time, a few more moments in which to linger on her lips. Being around her felt so natural to Drucker that he found himself envisioning an entire lifetime with her.

Never before had any woman, any work, or anywhere made him feel quite like she did.

⋙⊹⊹⋘

One night, a week before the election, Drucker hadn't been able to contain his feelings for Margaret any longer. Together they had tidied the dining quarters and then walked side by side out to the porch, where Drucker had turned to her. Taking her hands, he had pulled her closer to him. "Margaret"—he moved a gentle hand to her cheek—"when are you going to be mine forever?"

Margaret had given him that pretty smile of hers in return. "Well, it can't be tonight," she protested with good humor, "because *forever* could take quite a while, and tonight I have to be getting home before it gets awful late."

"No you don't," countered Drucker, playfully wrapping his arms around her. "You don't, you won't, and you can't. Not if I have anything to do with it." He pulled her to him closer yet, bending to place his head next to hers, giving her neck a nuzzle.

Margaret giggled and chided, "Drucker, I have to go," but she leaned into him rather than away.

Drucker could tell that the subtle shifting of her weight, the fact that she allowed herself to relax into his arms, was Margaret's way of expressing her amorous feelings, and Drucker reciprocated by kissing his way up her neck to the soft skin just below her ear, before stepping back to admire her once again.

It was as he pulled his head away from hers that his eyes, by then well trained at spotting Gould's men before they emerged from their shadowy posts, caught the outline of a man lurking in the shadows. Drucker stiffened at the thought of just exactly whom Margaret might encounter during her long walk home.

"I can't let you go alone," he said, trying to mask his apprehension in chivalry.

"That's sweet of you to look after me, Drucker," she whispered, touching a gentle finger to the tip of his nose, "but I won't be going alone."

"You won't?" Drucker took a step back.

"No." Margaret shook her head, giving her blond ringlets a bounce. "My brother is coming to escort me."

At that moment, as if on cue, the man whom Drucker had been eyeing stepped out of the shadows, revealing himself. Drucker had assumed that the shadowy outline on the street belonged to one of Gould's henchmen, but as the man's face appeared in the moonlight, Drucker saw that it was even worse.

"Oh, there you are, Ace!" exclaimed Margaret, quickly extricating herself from Drucker's embrace.

"Hello, sweet Margie," replied Horace warmly. Then he turned to Drucker, their eyes meeting like cold clashing steel. "Good evening, Drucker," he added, his voice barely audible through his clenched teeth.

"I was just telling Drucker that you were coming to—"

"Wait a minute." Drucker found himself unable to stop from interrupting. "You're telling me *Horace* is your brother? Why didn't you tell me that before?"

"I thought you knew!" exclaimed Margaret. "I can't believe Jim Hogg never told you."

Drucker couldn't believe it either. He looked back and forth between Margaret and Horace in disbelief.

"Yes, surprises all around tonight," said Horace grimly. He beckoned to his sister, his expression turned hollow, cold. "Come now, Margie. Let's go."

Margaret hurried down off the porch, but when she reached her brother's side, she hesitated for a moment. Abruptly, she turned on her heel, lunged back up the stairs, and planted a kiss squarely on Drucker's lips.

It was the only circumstance under which Drucker could imagine wishing she hadn't done so.

Horace glared fiercely at Drucker, and this time Drucker couldn't help but notice. Margaret didn't seem to, though. She gave his hand a squeeze and wordlessly bounded down the steps again.

Drucker stood alone on the porch as he watched the two of them walk away, Margaret's arm looped through her brother's. As he watched them go he shook his head, wearily recalling the words that Horace had said to him on the day he had thought of the Flanagan campaign ploy.

"I'm envisioning where this could go," Drucker said aloud, mimicking Horace's statement but adding, "and I must say I don't like it one bit."

⟞⟝ ⟞⟝

With less than one week until Election Day, tensions at Hogg headquarters reached explosive levels. Long on boredom, short on patience, and trying as best they could to tamp down their nerves with liquor, the men could hardly contain their restlessness.

Horace channeled his angst through the onslaught of aggression toward Drucker that had begun in earnest weeks earlier. And though Horace's attacks had hardly registered in the beginning, ever since Drucker had learned of Horace and Margaret's relation, his sensitivity to the attacks had heightened dramatically. Whereas once Horace had been a menace whose offenses had been easy enough to shrug off, once he glimpsed how easily Horace could threaten his future with Margaret, Drucker had become acutely aware that he was being iced out by his would-be brother-in-law.

Four days before the election, Horace finally broke Drucker's resolve to take the high road. Drucker had kept his composure when Horace had slammed a door in his face in the morning, and he had held his tongue when Horace had spilled a drink on him in afternoon. But late in the day, when Horace had looked Drucker in the eye and told him that if he knew what was good for him he would stay the hell away from Horace's one and only little sister, those contentious words pushed Drucker over the edge.

He lunged at Horace and even managed to get his hands around Horace's neck before several of the others rushed over to pull the two away from each other. The men were able to restrain Drucker for only a few seconds, though, before he could shake himself free and charge at Horace once again. When he broke away from the

179

others, Drucker leaped toward Horace with great athleticism, his forward motion thwarted only by Horace's fist making crushing contact with his face.

Drucker staggered backward, both hands cupping his right eye while Horace looked down to admire his own right hand. It was practically glowing with the pride he felt at landing such a punch.

Then again, it was so much more than just one punch. It was the blow that Horace had wanted to land when Drucker had first sat between him and Jim Hogg at that card game weeks earlier; it was the cuff that he'd been itching to give since the day that Drucker had told him that he wouldn't join the Flanagan campaign, thereby foiling Horace's perfect plot; certainly, it was the punch that he had wanted to throw when he'd seen his sister plant that kiss on Drucker.

After landing such a perfect punch, Horace had been distracted by breathtaking pride, which may have been exactly what allowed Drucker to deliver, at just that moment, a counterpunch of his own, striking Horace squarely in the nose.

Though his right eye was rapidly swelling shut, through his left, Drucker saw that he had landed an excellent, blood-summoning blow. Unfortunately for Drucker, at the very instant that his tightly clenched fist met Horace's face, the AG entered the room.

"What in tarnation is going on in here?" boomed the AG from the doorway.

All the men turned to him, but none dared answer his question.

The AG looked from one man to next. When his eyes landed on Horace, they caught sight of a man doubled over in pain, his shirt and shoes covered in his own dripping blood.

"Drucker!" barked the AG. "Get over here." Without waiting for Drucker, he opened the door that he had just entered through and disappeared out of sight on the other side of it.

Drucker hesitated, knowing that he had no choice but to oblige, but having trouble taking that first step toward the door with his head spinning and his vision blurry at best in his throbbing right eye. By the time he finally joined the AG on the other side of the door, his entire body was shaking, but Hogg didn't seem to notice.

"What in the Sam Hill was that?" the AG demanded. Drucker opened his mouth, but Jim Hogg didn't wait for an answer. "I know you and Horace don't get on but, Drucker, I expected more of you. That's the way fools and lowlifes settle their problems, and I won't condone it from any of my men."

Drucker tried to interject, "You didn't see—"

The AG sighed. "Let me guess. He attacked you first?"

This made Drucker think for a moment. He watched the scene unfold in his mind's eye and was dismayed to realize that, in truth, he had been the one to lunge at Horace, not the other way around. "Well, no, but—"

"Jesus, Mary, and Joseph!" the AG wailed in exasperation. "You're telling me *you* started the damn thing? Well, it hardly matters any. I'm disgusted by you both."

The AG turned away from Drucker and began pacing in the narrow hall, sweat racing furiously from his brow. "How do you fancy that?" he muttered to himself. "Four days until the election, and I've got two bruised-up campaign managers, and I can't stand to look at either of 'em."

When he reached the end of the hall, he turned back to Drucker. "I need you to leave now," he said. "And I need you not to come back tomorrow."

"But there's only a few days left before—"

"All the more reason for you to stay away. Surely the election's already been won or lost by now. Whatever any of us do at this point can't possibly make much of a difference. The only thing you two are capable of affecting now is my temper. That's why I don't want to see you tomorrow. Either of you," he added, motioning toward the door that separated the two men in the hallway from Horace and the others.

Drucker felt the hot sting of tears welling up in his one remaining open eye. Over nearly eight weeks of shared stories and meals and cigars, he had come to view Jim Hogg as a dear friend and a father figure. Seeing the disappointment in his face hurt Drucker more than Horace's fist ever could.

The AG turned to Drucker. One look at his dejected, battered face was enough to prove that the feeling of a familial bond was mutual. He threw his meaty arm over Drucker's shoulder and pulled the younger man close to him.

With his tone softened he said, "Look, Drucker, I know I'm being harsh on you. Harsher than I should be, perhaps. Just take the day off tomorrow. Tend to that"—he gestured toward Drucker's swollen eye—"situation of yours. A day apart will give us all some time to settle down."

"So you *do* want me to come back then?" Drucker asked cautiously. "Just not tomorrow?"

The AG smirked. "C'mon now," he said, his tone warmer yet. "This ain't good-bye." He smiled as he pulled his arm off of Drucker's shoulders. "It's just now get the hell outta my sight," he said with a wink and a playful shove.

With that, the AG returned to the room where the rest of his men were waiting, and Drucker walked back to his tiny quarters at Lucky Lyle's. While it hurt to be sent away, there were certainly worse punishments than being furloughed for a day, Drucker told himself as he walked back to the inn. The more he thought about it, the more he realized that the AG's order hardly constituted much of a punishment at all. It was more of a much-needed reprieve, really. And though his face and his ego were undeniably bruised, the whole ordeal did seem to have a silver lining: a day away from the campaign meant a day that he could spend with Margaret.

The sentence that the AG had doled out was not a punishment at all, Drucker realized, but rather a gift.

CHAPTER TWENTY-FOUR

The next day, Drucker did as he'd been told and stayed away from Hogg headquarters as well as the saloon, where Hogg's men were sure to be whiling away the day. Instead, he spent the day with Margaret, who tended to his wounded eye with a gentle, healing touch.

At the breakfast hour he helped her serve and clean, and in return she shelved her bookkeeping work for the day, agreeing to take a walk with him so long as he promised that they would be back in time for her to serve dinner. He agreed.

And so Drucker and Margaret spent the afternoon walking and talking their way through the streets of Austin. As they meandered, their conversation flowed easily, unrestrained. They talked about their memories of the past and their wishes for the future, and at times both of them felt as if they needn't speak at all in order to know what the other was thinking. When Drucker groped for a word, Margaret readily supplied it. When she asked if he saw a future for himself in Austin, he confessed that recently he had been thinking quite a lot of it. And when she confided that she often wondered if there wasn't something *more* she was supposed to do with her life, he could hardly believe that she too had been haunted by the question that had caused him to abandon everything and leave the only home he'd ever known.

Talking with her as they walked side by side down the dusty, windswept streets of Austin, Drucker saw in her the kind of companion he could walk with for a lifetime. He pictured what their life together would be like, and for much of the day he felt certain that if he could spend every day like he had spent that one, he would indeed have everything.

At the dinner hour, however, he realized that wasn't quite true. Even though the day that he had spent with Margaret had been close to perfect, it had lacked one thing. He missed Jim Hogg terribly. After just twenty-four hours away from him, Drucker ached to have the AG back in his life. He wanted him to win that election, and he knew that, despite Hogg's continuous declarations to the contrary, in truth that's what *he* wanted, too.

Election Day meant something more to Drucker, though. It marked the day that his services as a second campaign manager, a human buffer between Horace and the candidate, would no longer be needed. Win or lose, it was the date on which his contract was up, which meant that it would be the day that he and his friend Hogg would finally part ways.

But bidding farewell to Jim Hogg was a good-bye that he wasn't ready to give, and a good-bye that he wouldn't have to give if he were to stay on and work for Jim in the statehouse, Drucker mused. In that moment, for the first time in his life, Drucker knew exactly what the life he wanted to lead looked like. He saw the completed picture: a life with Margaret and a job with Jim Hogg, no longer just the AG, but Jim Hogg the governor.

As the dinner hour approached, Drucker found himself wishing desperately that his friend would forgive him already so that they could pick up their tradition of supper and smoke right where they had left off. At their usual mealtime, Drucker moped out to the front porch, in part to sulk, and in part to get a better view of any approaching patrons, of whom he hoped Hogg would be one.

The better part of an hour had passed with no sign of Hogg when Drucker caught sight of a man whose face he didn't know, but whose approach he recognized well. The stranger took the seat next to Drucker, eyes facing straight ahead, fingers stroking his patchy whiskers.

It was a sight Drucker had seen often, once a week to be precise, ever since he had contracted with Gould's posse. Though he could never predict which lackey he would be dealing with on any given day, he could recognize all of them by the telltale wordless approach, the averting of the eyes, the scratching of the cheeks.

"So," said the man without looking at Drucker, "which one did you decide on?"

The question took Drucker by surprise. *Which one? Of what?* A week ago he had been asked whether Hogg intended to make the railroad corruption commission his first order of business if elected, and it was the only question he was prepared to answer. *Which one?* didn't fit. There must have been a mix-up among Gould's men.

"That isn't the question I was asked," said Drucker, careful not to look directly at his companion.

"Well, that's the answer I'm here to collect."

"Perhaps there's been a mistake then," Drucker said. "Some confusion among your crew."

"Ain't no confusion," the man retorted. "That's the question I done been told to ask."

Drucker was on the verge of insisting that a mistake had been made when he was suddenly struck by curiosity. He shifted his body toward the man and lowered his voice conspiratorially. "How did you know I would be out here at this time?" Drucker asked, his interest piqued.

"Not much to it," said the man, without matching the intrigue of Drucker's tone, "since this's the time you always meet up."

"No," replied Drucker quickly. "At this time every night I'm in *there,* eating. With Jim Hogg," he added bitterly.

"Look, buddy, alls I know's I was told to meet one a Mr. Gould's insiders here on-a porch a Lucky Lyle's during the dinner hour, which is when he always meets up. If it ain't you, then who is it?"

That's when it made sense to Drucker. He wasn't the only one. Someone else was on Gould's payroll.

But who? Who would have the audacity to rat on the AG and in plain sight just yards away from where he ate his supper?

Instantly, Drucker knew.

There was only one other man who had the kind of access to Hogg's inner workings that Gould was willing to pay for, one man power hungry enough to sell out his friend just for a taste of it. Yes, there was only one man capable of conducting such brazen treason right under Hogg's nose: the one man who didn't have to worry that someone might question what business he had on the porch of Lucky Lyle's, because if he was asked, he could simply say that he was there to escort his sister home.

CHAPTER TWENTY-FIVE

Though one day earlier Drucker had felt certain that he had found the life that he would feel right leading, just hours later Drucker couldn't help but feel as if that life was slipping through his grasp.

What he had learned about Horace made it impossible for him to go on living life in Austin as he had before.

As he saw it, the only way that Horace could be absolved from guilt was if he, too, was an informant in the way that Drucker was—that is, with the AG's support and participation. But if that was the case, surely Hogg would have said something about it, Drucker felt certain.

On the other hand, if the far more likely scenario were true, then Drucker had discovered a terrible truth about a man who was inextricably bound to his own future in Austin if he intended to marry Margaret and work for Hogg. He couldn't hold on to a secret like that one and be made an accomplice to Horace by doing so.

But how could he marry Margaret without telling her what he knew to be true about her brother? How could he go on working for Hogg with two-faced Horace right beside him, like a ghost only visible to Drucker?

He knew that he could do neither. Keeping what he had learned about Horace a secret from the two people he cared most deeply for would weigh too heavily on his heart—and for what, for whom? For the man who had done nothing but his very best to make Drucker's life miserable since the moment they had first met. No, there was no question in Drucker's mind that this secret was not worth keeping. He had to tell them both.

But how, he wondered as he returned to Lucky Lyle's after taking a long, doleful walk when, once again, Jim Hogg had declined to join him at the dinner hour. Drucker had left Lucky Lyle's to clear his head, but he returned with even more questions and self-pity than he had left with.

"What do I do?" Drucker pleaded aloud to the heavens. "What do I do?" He moaned.

"You tell the truth," answered an unexpected voice from somewhere behind him.

Startled, Drucker turned to see who was lurking in the shadows. When he saw who it was, Drucker found the suggestion much stranger than the encounter itself, which he had known he wouldn't be able to avoid for long.

"That's the last piece of advice I would ever expect from you, Horace."

"Why?" asked Horace without curiosity. "I love the truth. I love everything about it."

"Everything but telling it," retorted Drucker.

"Oh no, Drucker, unfortunately for you, I'm afraid I *do* love telling it."

"So you'll have no problem then, if I tell the truth to Jim Hogg and Margaret about who you really are?"

Horace gave a wicked smile. "Why don't we start with the truth about who *you* are? That way everyone in this goddamn town can finally get past this horseshit you've been feeding them about being some fancy detective from Boston and see you for who you really are—a lousy, lying, two-bit runaway from Atlanta."

Drucker turned away from Horace, hoping the darkness of the evening would obscure the redness he could feel filling his ears and cheeks. "Well, well, look who's the detective now," he said, unwilling to lie to hide the truth about his identity. After all, he hadn't lied about it in the first place. He had coughed and then not corrected.

"So you admit it's true, then?"

Drucker hesitated a moment, still averting his eyes. When he finally turned to Horace, he looked directly at him. "Yes," he said, "it's true. But how did you find out? What have you done—hired someone to investigate me?"

"No need for that," said Horace coolly. "Not that I didn't think of it, of course. I knew I smelled a rat from the second I laid eyes on you. But before I had to do much hunting for it, the *truth* found *me*." Horace held up a newspaper. "See for yourself," he said, extending it toward Drucker.

Drucker eyed Horace suspiciously. He took one cautious step forward, not sure what exactly Horace had up his sleeve but certain there was something.

"Go on, please—be my guest. After all," he said with mocking lightness, "it's public knowledge."

Drucker took another slow step toward Horace and then one more. He stood just close enough to take the paper from Horace without getting an inch closer than he needed to, lest he be up against some sort of trick to make it easy for Horace to attack him.

Horace didn't attack, though. He allowed Drucker to take the paper from him, even stepping backward graciously after the transfer, allowing Drucker a moment to examine what he held.

Drucker fingered the paper gingerly, wondering what could be written about him and who could have written it. He found that Horace had opened the paper to one particular article and folded back the pages with precise, crisp creases. When Drucker finally let his eyes lock in on the text, the headline hit him hard in the gut, harder than Horace had walloped him in the face. His stomach tightened, dense as a rock, and promptly sank to the bottom of his being as he read:

In Continuing Trend, Five More Southern Banks Fail

He knew what was coming then, but Drucker refused to believe it until he read it. He felt his body stiffen as he arrived at the last paragraph of the article. Atlanta Southern had gone under, it said, and its president, Samuel May, was dead of a heart attack at sixty-one, survived by wife, Helene, preceded in death by only son, Drucker May, missing since July and presumed dead.

Drucker felt as if his spine were being sucked out of him. The only thing that kept him from collapsing was the fact that Horace didn't give him time to feel sorry for himself.

As soon as Drucker finished reading, Horace began to gloat. To him, the article wasn't about a continuing trend of failing banks. It wasn't about Drucker or his father or their now defunct Atlanta Southern. For Horace, the article was about nothing more than his own power and how this late-breaking news was certain to increase it. The headline may as well have read, In Continuing Trend, Another Lucky Break for Horace. Drucker felt thankful for Horace's fanatical egotism at that moment, though; it was the only thing keeping him upright.

"What luck for me, wouldn't you say?" asked Horace, smugly. "To find the answer I've been looking for right under my very own nose. That one little article clears up quite a few dilemmas for me."

"Such as?" asked Drucker, Horace's arrogance allowing him to forget for a moment the crushing gravity of what he had just read.

"Well, Margaret, for one," said Horace, preening. "It turns my stomach to know how you two have been getting on. But this new revelation should unravel that whole mess. I'm sure she's told you that the one thing that she hates more than anything in the world is disloyalty."

Drucker swallowed. Of course she had.

"I don't suppose she'd want much to do with a common runaway, a deserter like you who leaves his family to presume him dead. Yes, in fact, I'm certain she won't want anything to do with you once she hears that her brother has found you out for the louse and the liar that you are."

"Yes, well, it takes one to know one," countered Drucker quickly, "and I don't think she'll be pleased to hear the truth that I've discovered about you either, Horace."

"And what might that be?" asked Horace, grinning despite Drucker's grave tone.

"That you're a two-faced traitor who's on the take from Gould."

Horace laughed, releasing what sounded like staccato coughs of amusement. "How very clever of you," said Horace, his laughter ceasing. "But the question is, can you prove it?"

"I don't have a newspaper article stating as much," said Drucker folding Horace's copy of the *Austin Statesman* and stashing it away in his coat pocket. "I've got Gould's men, though. The ones who meet you *here* at the dinner hour."

"And why on Earth would they tell *you* anything, some common slug they don't know from Adam?"

"That's where you're wrong," said Drucker, too quickly, letting the excitement of the moment carry him. "They know me as well as they know you. They think I work for them, too."

The second the words escaped, Drucker desperately wished that they hadn't. He gasped at his own folly, understanding immediately how foolish this last statement had been.

"Mmm," said Horace, biting his lip as if embarrassed by the good fortune of Drucker's slip of the lip. "A *double* lying louse," he mused. "Tell me, Drucker, is there *anyone* you won't lie to?"

"I'm not a liar," protested Drucker, "not when it comes to the things that really matter."

"That's a mighty strong assertion," purred Horace smugly. "I say we put it to a test. How about this? I'll show Hogg and Margaret that little article and see if they think you've been honest about the 'things that really matter' once they know who you really are. I'm sure they'll have plenty of questions for you about why you left Atlanta in such a hurry. Or maybe"—Horace's eyes glittered with pleasure—"they won't give a damn, because they'll want nothing to do with you once I tell them what I know."

"Do that," countered Drucker without hesitation, "and I'll tell them both that you've been selling out to Gould."

"Ah, yes, Gould," echoed Horace. "How do you suppose he'll take the news that you've been *pretending* to work for him?" Horace twisted his face into a pained grimace to illustrate the ugliness of Gould's anticipated reaction. "I don't suppose he'll take *that* news very lightly, and if I know one thing about that man, it's that he hates to be played for a fool. When he learns that you've been lying to him all this time I wouldn't be surprised if he sends one of his men to find you, and it very well may be the last time that anyone ever does."

Drucker shuddered. He knew Horace was right, but he couldn't stand for him to have the last word. "I hardly think Jim Hogg will take the news of your treason any more lightly. You know as well as anyone that a man like that also has resources to take care of finks like you, Horace."

With this they had reached a stalemate. The men stood quietly, eyeing each other, neither wanting to come to blows again, though to break such a standoff, it seemed inevitable. Drucker's right eye, still swollen and purple, had suffered a fate that he hoped would not befall his left one. At the same time, though, he knew that taking another punch in the eye from Horace would likely be the best-case scenario if they settled the matter by way of Texas tradition. If they did, Drucker knew he would be risking far more than just taking another punch, as Horace and his cronies surely had access to one thing Drucker hadn't left Atlanta with: a gun.

After a long uneasy moment Drucker broke the silence with the only thing that he could think to say to break the impasse.

"What do you say we settle this with a hand of poker?" he asked.

Horace stood quietly for a moment, considering the offer. In truth he was no impressive marksman, and his nose still throbbed, days later, from Drucker's skillful jab. His life would be on the line if Drucker revealed the nature his relationship with Gould, and Horace preferred not to risk it unnecessarily in the meantime. Besides, he'd been playing cards in Austin longer than Drucker had been alive, he told himself, a thought that boosted his confidence greatly.

"Fine," Horace said finally, "but if I win you have twenty-four hours to get your ass out of Texas."

Drucker did his best to keep a straight face as he weighed Horace's proposition. He hated the thought that he might bet away the life that he wanted to lead on a game of cards, but the alternative was a sure death at the hands of either Horace or whichever of Gould's henchmen could get to him first. After a moment, he nodded his agreement.

"But if I win, I stay here and marry Margaret. With your blessing. And I work for Hogg." He paused. "Without you."

Horace recoiled at the thought of what a win by Drucker would mean, but at the same time he felt confident that it wouldn't come to pass. He, too, nodded his approval of the terms.

"Tomorrow then," suggested Drucker.

"Yes—" Horace began, but stopped himself. "No, wait," he paused for a moment, "isn't tomorrow Sunday?"

"It is," said Drucker, trying to understand Horace's point. "What of it?"

Horace's face grew solemn. "Gambling on Sunday is a sin," he said in earnest, shaking his head. "I won't do it."

"Ah, yes, how ungentlemanly that would be," Drucker said, thinking back on all the things that each of them had done in the last two months alone that he felt were far more reprehensible than playing a hand of cards on Sunday, but he acquiesced nonetheless. "Monday then?"

"Monday," repeated Horace. "The backroom at high noon," he proposed and Drucker agreed.

Thus, the two men decided to meet one day before the election, in the saloon where they had met in the first place, this time to settle their long-standing discord like the gentlemen it turns out that they were, despite all evidence to the contrary.

⚒

On the day of the big game, Drucker woke feeling so weak that he could hardly get out of bed. He hadn't bothered to get up at all the day before, heartsick over the news that both his father and Atlanta Southern no longer existed. Considering the ill will he had harbored for so long toward the bank, he was surprised by how deeply saddened he was to learn that it was gone. And for the man to whom he had never felt he could relate, he was shaken to the core by a paralyzing mourner's guilt.

And so Drucker lay completely still in his narrow, iron-framed bed, exhausting guilt weakening both his mind and his body. He shouldn't have left Atlanta that way, he lamented. Shouldn't have run away as he had, from the bank and from his family, when both—apparently—had needed him.

The remorse that he felt over the way he had left things with his father was matched by the regret that he felt over the way that things had been between them before he left. He felt sorry for not having wanted the same things that his father had wanted for him. At the same time, though, he knew that in truth he had left Atlanta because he *did* want the same thing as his father.

His father had wanted Drucker to be someone special, someone admired, someone who accomplished something extraordinary with his life. And Drucker wanted that too. Except that he was certain that he could never be that person at his father's bank, and that's where they had differed.

Whereas his father saw that special, admired, accomplished Drucker as president of the bank, Drucker knew that he could never be any of those things if he were to live a life that didn't feel like his own. To shape his life to fit his father's designs for it would be to live a lie. A lie about an important thing, perhaps the most important thing: who he was at his core.

That's why Drucker had left. More than anything else he had wanted to be the person that his father hoped that he would be so that he could truly earn and deserve his father's pride in him, and Drucker knew that he could never do that at Atlanta Southern. Then again, maybe he had never been going to make his father genuinely proud, no matter what he did. Now he surely wasn't. Now it was too late.

At half past eleven, Drucker finally managed to drag himself out of bed. Despite the acute feeling of having lost everything, he reminded himself that the things that the newspaper told him he had lost were things to which he had already said good-bye. It was time for him to focus on what was at stake in the back room. He'd said good-bye to the past already; it was time to win the future.

Drucker packed his pockets full with the rolls of cash that he'd been paid by Gould—which seemed only fitting to gamble with—as well as a good portion of the money that he had brought with him from Atlanta. Certainly Horace would come prepared to play as if his life was on the line, but perhaps, if nothing else, Drucker could outspend him. To be safe, he set aside just enough to get by in case of the unthinkable: a loss in cards, which would mean the loss of everything. Everything, that is, except for the modest amount of savings that he reserved and tucked away in the pocket of another pair of pants, which he then folded and packed away in his valise.

When he arrived in the saloon's back room, Drucker found a small crowd of men assembled there. He recognized most of the faces. The usual campaign-and-cards crew, including Horace, plus a smattering of strangers who must have heard that the game was one not to be missed, the stakes being as high as they were.

One face was noticeably absent from the crowd, and that relieved Drucker to no end. For the first time in days, Drucker found himself hoping desperately *not* to see his friend the AG. His wish, it appeared, had been granted.

When the clock struck noon, Horace motioned toward the table, and six men took their seats. Drucker chose a chair directly across the table from Horace, two men separating them on either side.

"Five games," said Horace when the men were seated. "Brownie will deal."

Drucker nodded in agreement. Though he knew it was fully possible that Horace had Brownie under his thumb, a known entity in the dealer's seat was better than the alternative. At least Brownie could be read easily, and Drucker had seen him play enough over the course of the last eight weeks to be able to keep an eye out for obvious cheats between Brownie and Horace. With any other man dealing, even a stranger off the streets, Horace would be likely to have some connection to him, and Drucker would be less likely to be able to read him. So Drucker nodded and accepted that five games would determine his future in Austin, and that Brownie would deal all of them.

As luck would have it, Drucker was dealt three of a kind in the first game and made it a full house with his redraw, which beat the man to his right's flush in the showdown and allowed Drucker to rake in a handsome $1,000 from the pot.

The brute sitting to the left of Drucker took the second game. To his chagrin, Drucker had to fold in the first round of betting. He wasn't the only one who was dealt a luckless hand, though, and the pot, when the man next to him collected it, was hardly more than the sum of their opening antes.

The third game was more competitive than the first two, with only one man folding in the first round; four out of the five remaining men raised the bid that came before him. When the cards were revealed, it was Horace who came out on top, winking at Drucker as he raked in the bulging pot, which was worth five times what Drucker's early lead had earned him.

The fourth game went to Drucker when he called Brownie's unconvincing bluff and then beat out two men's straights with his flush. Despite Drucker's best attempts to stoke the fires of competition to build up the pot, though, he still lagged Horace by a significant margin.

By the time the fifth and final game began, Drucker was in sync with the rhythm of play. As soon as the cards were dealt, he watched the other men's eyes for so much as a glimmer of emotion or a subconscious tic. When he looked down at his own cards, which he was quite pleased by, he exaggerated his engineered tell, fingering the bills in front of him, massaging his money as if readying it to be bet. When one of the spectators announced that he needed a drink and made for the door, Drucker expertly shielded his hand. He had no doubt that the roving bystander was on Horace's payroll and intended to scope out the others' cards under the pretense of needing to refresh his beverage.

All of this served to make Drucker feel increasingly confident. Though he had only won half as much as Horace had, with his ample reserves to draw on, Drucker felt certain that with a little luck on his side he could outlast Horace, no matter the cost.

When it was his turn to place a wager in the first round, Drucker bet aggressively, but Horace appeared nonchalant, and when the betting made its way around the table to him, he placed three times what Drucker had into the pot.

Though Horace's sizable bet made Drucker nervous, when it came time for a discard, Horace relinquished three out of his five cards. *His hand couldn't have been very strong if he's willing to part with most of it,* thought Drucker, which gave him the boost in morale that he needed to make a bold move in the second round of betting.

When it was his turn again, Drucker looked Horace directly in the eyes and with one hand pushed his entire pile—thousands of dollars—to the center of the table. Everyone in the room gasped, and the two men who had placed their bets before Drucker looked relieved to have done so before Drucker upped the ante so.

Because the man to Drucker's immediate left had already folded in the first round, just Brownie and Horace were left to place their bets before the showdown that would crown the winner. Brownie, wide-eyed, looked at Drucker's bet. "How—how much is that?" he squeaked nervously, but before Drucker could answer, Brownie threw down his cards. "Not that it matters any. I couldn't match that kind of bet in a thousand years." He turned to Horace. "Can you?"

"Yes, Horace, can you?" taunted Drucker. They were the first words that he had said aloud since the game began.

Horace rearranged his own stack of money revealing he'd brought more cash with him than Drucker had originally been able to see.

"I can," said Horace flatly, "and I will." He pushed a matching bet to the middle of the table as Drucker felt a bead of cold sweat materialize on his brow. It was quite a sum for a man who had drawn three new cards. If not for the fact that his own hand had blossomed into a very fortuitous straight flush with the redraw, Drucker's confidence would have begun to flail. Given his near-perfect hand, though, plus everything he knew about Horace, Drucker felt fairly certain that this elaborate show was nothing more than a flagrant bluff.

"So," said Horace, looking unnervingly calm, "time for the showdown." He turned to the man to his left. "What d'ya got, Alvin?"

The man set down his cards, a full house of sevens and eights. Horace looked down at the cards and nodded solemnly. "And you, Luther?"

The man to Drucker's right threw down a pile of mismatched cards. "Ain't got shit," he growled, biting down hard on his cigar. "But at least I bet before he did," he added, nudging Drucker with his elbow.

Horace nodded. Without lifting his eyes he pointed a meaty, soot-stained finger toward Drucker. "And you?"

Trying to keep his expression restrained, Drucker laid his cards face up on the table. A straight flush of hearts numbered two through six. Whispers sprang up from the crowd of onlookers. There was no denying that his hand was strong.

Horace's face hardened. "Nice cards," he said grimly. "Hard to beat a hand like that."

Drucker held back a smile. With his five hearts laid out in front of him, his own heart was pounding like a drum beating out a song of celebration.

"Hard," Horace continued, "but not impossible. Let's see, what would I need in order to beat that? A royal flush, I suppose. Nothing else could beat that hand."

Drucker felt his heartbeat pick up in pace. Horace was talking too much for comfort.

"On the other hand, if I had a—"

"Oh, for the love of God, Horace! Shut your damn mouth already and show us what you've got," Drucker demanded. He was surprised when Horace, without excuse or argument, did as he was told. Immediately and with great gusto, Horace threw down his hand.

For an instant, Drucker simply felt relief that the game was finally over. A second later, though, the entire room watched his face fall as the damning realization crept across it: Horace held a royal flush, which meant that Drucker had just lost.

⭲⭰

Long after the others left, Drucker remained in the backroom of the saloon. The loss stunned him into silence and stillness, his body immobile in the seat that he had occupied all afternoon. While his body was motionless, his mind ran circles around the fact that in the course of forty-eight hours he had lost his past, his present, and his future.

"Good-bye, Drucker, and good riddance," Horace had hissed just after he'd thrown down the winning hand. Drucker had only nodded vaguely in Horace's direction, as if seeing him through a fog.

The fog didn't wear off. More than an hour after the last of the other players and patrons had ambled off, Drucker sat sulking, barely able to see his own fingers flipping through the deck. He squinted to see their outline, watching them move the cards but unable to feel the cards against his skin, as if his hands were detached from the rest of his body. What his hands were doing wasn't the real question on his mind, though. It was what he would tell Margaret.

At that moment he didn't know what he would tell her, but he knew one thing for certain: he wouldn't just abandon her. This time he wouldn't run away, disappearing like a shadow before the light of day revealed him. That didn't change the fact that he had to leave, though.

"Ain't gotta go home," Horace had called over his shoulder just before he'd left the room, "but you can't stay here." And Drucker knew that he couldn't.

If he tried to stay, Horace would undoubtedly make good on his promise to expose him. He very well might do it anyway the moment Drucker left town, but if Drucker tried to stay, Horace would surely and immediately take great joy in bending the ear of Margaret and Hogg and anyone else who would listen to him, leaving Drucker with a hell of a lot of explaining to do.

Of course, telling Margaret exactly why he had to leave town so quickly would also leave him with a lot of explaining to do, so instead Drucker told her that he could build a better life for them both if she would agree to leave Austin with him. Given the circumstances, it was the truth, if not the whole story.

She didn't have to go immediately, Drucker assured her when she protested. He would go to California, he told her, and find a place for them to live, perhaps near a little inn where they could work side by side, as they had while cleaning up after the dinner hour at Lucky Lyle's.

And then he would come back to get her, he swore to her as he kissed away her tears, barely able to hold back his own. As he tried to convince her that it was the best way for them to build a life together, he found himself realizing that it might very well be the only way.

Horace had taken him for every dollar that he had brought to the table and, afterward, when Drucker had counted up the bills that he'd set aside in case of the unthinkable, he found that he was a little shorter on cash than he ever thought that he would be. Truth be told, he realized that he needed to go on to California without her, to find work and to save a few dollars before bringing her to be with him. It wasn't just his promise to her; it was his plan, born from necessity. He couldn't afford to have it any other way.

But it wouldn't be long, he told her, before he would be back to collect her, to marry her and to bring her to their new home in California. She cried as he spoke, her fists clinging to his shirt, but she nodded her agreement. She loved him, this surprisingly gentle man who stood apart from any man she had known before, outshining the others like the North Star in the night. She couldn't understand his hurry to leave, but she saw no choice but to wait for him to make good on his promise to come back for her.

⟞⟝

Drucker didn't have a chance to cast his vote on Election Day, not that it mattered much. Hogg won by a margin as wide as his waistline. When the votes were tallied, it was evident that he had thoroughly cleaned Flanagan's clock and would need to begin gearing up for what would be a much more challenging fight: the years-long battle with Gould that was to follow.

Hours before Hogg learned that he would be the next governor of Texas, though, Drucker was already well on his way to California.

Margaret accompanied him to the station at dawn. He kissed her once, hard, before boarding the train, then had leaped down from the train to kiss her again harder still. He watched through the window as tears streamed down her face while she stood on the platform. She was the first woman, he realized, to whom he actually had said good-bye.

As he watched the tears wash down Margaret's cheeks, Drucker wondered if he hadn't done his mother, Anna, even Lucinda, a great favor by sparing them all from having to say good-bye. Had it been crueler or kinder to allow them to simply wake up without him one day? If there had been tears, at least they had been shed without the pain of being able to see, but not stop, the train as it stole him away, hurrying him out of their lives forever.

It had certainly been easier for him, there was no doubt about that. Saying good-bye was awfully painful etiquette, and watching Margaret disappear out of sight was pure torture for Drucker. He stared through the window, watching her become small and then smaller and then ultimately...gone.

When she was no longer even a tiny black dot in the distance, Drucker tore his eyes away from the window, and looked around him at the plush red interior of the westward-speeding train. He tipped his head back and stared at the arched ceiling, watching the last week unfold again in his mind's eye.

He recalled the confrontation with Horace, the exchange of the newspaper, his bed soaked through with his perspiration, his tiny room worse than a prison cell because he was allowed to leave but simply couldn't muster the energy to do so.

When he reached the scene in which Horace revealed his winning hand, Drucker could feel his body tremble with something new coursing through his veins: Anger. He shook as all of the guilt of the previous days gave way to it. He began to feel indignant at the thought that Atlanta Southern had crumbled into ruin and outraged that he would never see his father again, would never have the chance to make him proud.

More than anything, though, he felt enraged to have been cheated out of the life that he wanted. For the first time he had been able to envision a desirable future for himself, had been close enough to touch it, even. And then he'd been robbed of it.

Yes, robbed, there was no other word for it, Drucker decided. Horace had committed a crime, hustling Drucker out of the future that by all rights should have been his.

Drucker brooded over that thought, letting waves of anger wash over him until suddenly it dawned on him that he had pilfered some futures in his day, too. After all, hadn't he robbed his father of the future that he had dreamed of for his bank, his family name, his legacy?

And Mayor Newton, with his vision for his daughter's future, for Clayton's? Hadn't Drucker stolen that possibility away from him as well? Those men must have felt the same anguish at their own losses that Drucker felt now. He hated that he had caused them to feel such misery, and his torment was redoubled by its corollary: his father didn't feel anything now, nor would he ever again.

The razor-edged truth of that thought stabbed at him. The only thing more painful than the fact of his father's death was the question of whether he was blame for it. Had he inflicted a frustration so complete that it broke his father's heart beyond the ability to beat? The very thought of it triggered an ache in Drucker's head that echoed between his ears. For not living the life that his father had envisioned for him, did he bear responsibility for the demise of both the bank and its president?

Drucker found the prospect both possible and chilling. He watched his skin turn to gooseflesh despite the car's warm and stagnant air. He felt a desperate longing to see his father, but at the same time he felt profound relief that his father couldn't see him at that moment. Would he even recognize such a poor, worn-out, bitter version of his son? Even if he could, certainly he wouldn't approve of him. But then, would he have ever approved of any version of Drucker other than the one that existed in his own mind?

As Drucker wrestled with that question, the rhythmic hum of the train lulled him into a sleep too dark and deep for dreams.

IV. JEROME

CHAPTER TWENTY-SIX

When he woke, Drucker could feel Margaret hovering over him before he could see her. He could hear the timbre of her soothing voice and smell the feminine scent of soap wafting from her bosom. Then, through fluttering eyelids, he could begin to see her outline, the details of her face coming slowly into focus. Drucker wiped the fog from his eyes, letting them rest, with their restored vision, on the face of the woman who was craning over him.

"Margaret?"

"Well, look who decided to wake up!" exclaimed the woman. She released his wrist from her grasp, and his arm fell back to his side without her fingers to prop it up. "Good news is your pulse is strong as an ox." She laughed, causing her generous bosom to heave beneath her crisp white apron. "How d'ya feel?"

Drucker considered the question. His hands moved to his face, feeling his temples, cheeks, and chin. He found his skin unbroken but soaked with perspiration when his fingers reached his neck.

"I feel...fine, I think," answered Drucker. "Am I in California?"

"Didn't quite get that far I'm afraid," said the woman, busying herself with the cart she had rolled up to Drucker's bedside. "They say you lost consciousness on the train. Brought you in here runnin' a fever damn near 104. That was three days ago. Been in and out a fever dreams ever since."

"Then I'm in Texas still?" asked Drucker, suddenly hopeful that the real Margaret may be near.

The nurse turned her attention from the cart back to Drucker.

"No, sir. Town's called Jerome. In the Arizona territory." She raised an eyebrow at Drucker. "Ever heard of it?"

Drucker shook his head and realized that it still ached.

"Puts you in good company. Hardly anyone who comes through here ever has." She gave a little laugh. "Hadn't heard of it myself till I got here. Tongue up," she instructed and then swiftly inserted a thermometer between Drucker's lips. After a minute, she removed it and glanced at it. "Well, look at that!" she said, smiling as she gave the instrument a shake. "Fever's broke. You hungry?"

Drucker nodded.

"Good," she said. "Should be. You've hardly eaten a thing in days. I'll fetch you somethin'."

Drucker smiled weakly but gratefully. Now that he thought of it, his stomach was burning with the ache of emptiness. "Thank you," he said, and the nurse patted his shoulder affectionately. A warm smile settled itself between her fleshy cheeks.

When she had gone, Drucker took a moment to examine his surroundings. Concrete walls stretched to high ceilings, and tall windows marked the room's perimeter, which was lined with a dozen-some narrow beds just like his own, some occupied, some empty. From one of those beds, two down the line from where Drucker sat bolstered by a stiff pillow, came a sharp whisper.

"Psssst, hey."

Drucker turned toward the voice and saw that it came from a young man whose left leg was wrapped and suspended above the bed in a contraption that hung from the lofty ceiling.

"Hello," said Drucker, keeping his voice low so as not to wake the sleeping patients around them.

"Glad to see you finally woke up," whispered the young man. "I was beginnin' to wonder if you ever would. Got your color back, too. That's good."

Drucker nodded toward the man's bandaged leg and asked, "What's happened to you?"

The young man looked at his leg, and for a moment his face contorted as if he were feeling the pain that must have preceded his arrival there. "Got it stuck in the mine shaft," he said, reeling in his grimace. "Coulda been worse, though. Doc says there's a chance I won't lose it if I keep it elevated." He leaned his head back for a moment, clenching his teeth as he weathered a wave of pain. When it passed he turned back to Drucker. "How 'bout yourself? What landed you here?"

Drucker shrugged and shook his head. "The last I remember I was on a train headed to California. Now I hear I've just spent three days in this bed in...in...what's the name of this town again?"

"Jerome," supplied the young man, sounding disappointed to be reminded of it. Then he brightened as he asked, "California? What you got there?"

Drucker gave this some thought. "Not much," he said finally. "A fresh start, that's all. Going to build a life for me and my...my Margaret." He smiled at the thought of her.

The man nodded. "Fresh start, huh? You'd fit in good 'round here. Just 'bout every person you come 'cross in this town come here lookin' for that very thing. Come to the territory lookin' for a fresh start, and next thing you know, you're tucked up inside the United Verde hardly able to remember the last time you seen the light a day. Ain't much fresh 'bout that."

Drucker's wistful smile faded, and his new companion look pained to see it go.

"Awww, now look at me. I don't mean to dash your dreams none. I'm just saying a fresh start's an easy thing to chase and a

hard thing to find. That's all. Anyway, I'm sure you'll find yours"—
he lowered his voice—"or die trying, right?" He put a finger to his
lips and hushed himself. "Can't say *die* 'round this crowd. They
might take the advice."

The man laughed, and Drucker joined him, put at ease by the
mischievous spark he caught in the other man's eyes. When their
laughter subsided, Drucker turned to the man. "I don't believe I've
caught your name," he said.

The man held up his hand, too far from Drucker for a shake,
in greeting. "Name's William Wesley McCall Junior, but you can
call me Wes."

"Wes," repeated Drucker, "pleased to meet you." He lay a hand
on his chest, "Drucker May," he said. "I take it you came here chasing a fresh start, too."

Wes nodded. "Sure did. Everyone in Jerome's come from somewhere else. I, myself, come from the town a Wichita in the state a
Kansas. You ever been?"

Drucker shook his head. "I can't say that I have," he said, and
then felt himself compelled to ask, "Is that where William Wesley
McCall Senior is?"

"Was when last I saw him," Wes replied. "Ain't heard from him
since I lef', though. Could be dead, for all I know."

Drucker opened his mouth to reply, but at just that moment
the nurse returned with a bowl of steaming soup on a tray, which
she began arranging in front of Drucker.

"Mmmm mmmm, that smells nice," said Wes, inhaling theatrically from two beds away. "You got some a that for me, Ruth?"

"Oh, you hush now," chided the nurse, still fussing to arrange
Drucker's meal. "You go back to sleep and give this man some
peace and quiet while he eats his first meal in days."

Wes propped himself up on his elbows. "If I do, will you sneak
me some a that good smellin' stew there when I wake up?"

"Only one way to find out now, isn't there?" replied Nurse Ruth.
With her ample rear pointed toward Wes, she gave Drucker a wink.

"Yes, ma'am, that's right," said Wes, giving a mock military salute while her back was still turned to him. He slid off his elbows, laid his head back on his pillow, and shut one eye.

"Enjoy your lunch, Drucker," he said before snapping shut the other eyelid.

"Sleep tight, Wes," said Drucker.

"Looks like you done made a friend," said Ruth, taking a step backward, after finally arranging the tray of food comfortably and accessibly in front of Drucker.

"We seem to have some things in common," said Drucker, giving a sideways glance toward Wes, who had already fallen back asleep, his dirty-blond curls strewn messily across his forehead. "It's easy to like a man who's looking for the same thing as you. Makes a person feel a little less alone in the world."

It was true—Drucker did like Wes immediately. He thought perhaps he wouldn't even mind becoming friends with Wes if not for the fact that he had already made up his mind to turn around and go back to Austin as soon as he could get his strength up enough to get out of bed.

That thought prompted Drucker to turn his attention to his meal, and he tasted a spoonful, pleased by the salty, heavy ration of meat that had made it into the stew.

"Eat up," said Ruth, nodding in approval. "You get strong enough to be up and walkin' about, and you could be out of here tomorrow."

Drucker nodded eagerly as he spooned the hearty soup into his mouth. 'Tomorrow' sounded like as good a time as any to begin his trip back to Austin. He gulped down another spoonful and then another, his hunger building the more he ate.

"You eat that and then get some more sleep," said Ruth. "I'll wake you for dinner." Drucker nodded at her between frenzied bites, and Ruth moved on to attend to another patient, leaving Drucker to his frothing stew and his newly forming thoughts of how quickly he could get back to Austin.

CHAPTER TWENTY-SEVEN

True to her word, Ruth gently nudged Drucker awake. As soon he opened his eyes, Drucker was glad that she had. His stomach rumbled for more of what the stew had started in there hours earlier. At least he hoped it had been just hours, and not, as he had learned of his last slumber's duration, several days. He could tell that the world outside of the tall windows had gone dark with November's early nightfall, but exactly which night's fall he couldn't be certain.

Drucker felt great relief when Ruth asked, "You feelin' up for dinner?" when he had shaken free from the last bonds of sleep. He nodded, licking the salty remnants of lunch from his lips. He shifted in bed, readying himself for a tray to be placed on his lap, as it had been hours earlier, but Ruth just laughed.

"No, no," she said, "not this time." She shook a finger at him, and her lively jowls swung in time with it. "Supper's in the mess hall. You feel up for a walk?"

Drucker took a deep breath, summoning his strength. He realized that he hadn't used his legs in what was approaching four days. He hoped they would be up to the task that his stomach demanded of them.

Slowly, with the help of Ruth, Drucker removed the thin blanket that covered him. He swung his legs over to the side of the bed and tested the ground, slowly shifting his weight first on to one foot and then the other, surprised, though pleasantly, to find that his ankles could indeed bear the weight of everything that rose above them.

Nurse Ruth put an arm around Drucker's back and steadied him. Then she took a step back and watched as he stood on his own, weakly at first, but then gaining confidence with each step that he took as he followed her—and his nose—toward the wafting smell of food.

Just before they reached the corridor, Ruth stopped and turned to Drucker. "Think you'll be able to make it through supper on your own?"

Because the answer that immediately came to him was *no*, Drucker said nothing, concerned that answering so might compromise his chance at a hot meal in the near future. He turned back, remembering Wes, who was still dozing in his bed, his leg suspended awkwardly half a foot above the rest of him.

"What about him?" asked Drucker.

"Little hard to get to the mess with your leg attached to the ceiling," said Ruth without slowing her gait. "But don't worry about him, we'll get him what he needs."

Drucker nodded. "Of course," he said, glad that Ruth had misunderstood his question. It wasn't Wes being fed that worried Drucker so much as not being sure that he could make it to, through, and back from the dining hall on his own.

Luckily, Drucker didn't have reason to worry for long. A few steps later, Ruth slowed her gait when her eye caught another patient passing by them.

"Hiya, Ruth," said the patient, and both Drucker and his nurse turned their bodies toward the voice.

"Heya, Easton," replied Ruth. "Howya feelin' tonight?" The patient sidled up next to Drucker, a wiry waif of a woman, boyish from her frame to her close-cropped haircut and unmadeup face.

"Like a million bucks, Ruth," said Easton, looking at Drucker instead of the nurse. "Who's this?"

"Drucker May," said Drucker quickly, before Ruth could.

"Y'new here?" asked Easton.

Drucker nodded cautiously.

"C'mon then," said Easton, breezing toward the mess hall, beckoning for Drucker to follow.

Drucker looked at Ruth questioningly.

She nodded. "Go on. Easton'll take good care a you in there." Drucker took a few steps closer to Easton, who was poised on the threshold of the buzzing hall, waiting for him to catch up.

"Eat up," called Ruth, as she began walking in the other direction. "Got to get that strength back."

Drucker nodded and quickened his pace for a few strides until darkness crept up behind his eyes, forcing him to slow to a halt.

"Feelin' weak?" asked Easton. She squirmed her way under Drucker's armpit, supporting him like a crutch.

"Do I look it?" he asked. He hoped her answer would help him determine just how much longer his wobbling legs would be able to support him.

Easton shimmied around to look Drucker in the face. She took a moment to assess him head to toe before delivering her prognosis. "Nah," she declared. "You'll be fine. Nothin' a hot meal won't fix." She patted Drucker on the back. "C'mon, let's get you a seat."

Together Drucker and Easton moved into the mess hall, their bodies linked as one, Drucker willing himself to stay upright and Easton propelling them both forward, keeping Drucker upright when his will alone was not enough. As if built for heavy lifting, her compact body was sturdy and square, her legs squat and strong.

Drucker was grateful for her assistance, and even more so when, in the middle of the mess hall, Easton pointed to two empty chairs flanking the end of an otherwise crowded table and said, "You sit there. I'll get us some grub."

Drucker, doing as he was told, took a seat and watched Easton walk toward the supper queue. He had never met a woman like her before. A female built with a man's strength, and more of a boyish charm than a lady's grace, but with an impish, fresh face that even without the aid of cosmetics was curiously feminine.

When she returned, Easton brought with her two trays of piping-hot food. She placed one tray in front of Drucker and the other in front of the empty seat across the table from him, where a moment later she plunked herself down cheerfully and rubbed her palms together as she appraised the meal in front of her.

"Well," she said, picking up her fork and driving it into a lump of potato, "bon appeteet, as the Frenchies say." She raised her fork to toast with as if it were a flute of champagne and then took it eagerly into her mouth and chewed open-mouthed as she asked, "So whatcha in for?"

The smell of the still-steaming meat on his plate tickled Drucker's nose and further roused his stomach, but before he reached for his utensils, he answered, "Fever. From what I gather, I lost consciousness on the train, and they had to cart me off and bring me here." He paused to reach for his own fork and knife. He carved into the slab of gravy-covered meat. "And you?"

"Aww, nothin' big," said Easton, digging around in her pile of vegetables for a lone stub of carrot. She found it, speared it, and chewed it vigorously. "Only way to get the good painkillers is to check into this place, and I like the strong stuff, so I'm an old hand 'round here." She looked up from her plate, and her eyes glinted mischievously. "Come in 'bout once a month. Tell 'em my arthritis is actin' up real bad, but really it's just"—she rubbed her midsection—"lady troubles, y'know?"

"Mmm." Drucker nodded, feigning indifference but feeling jarred, not only because the topic was not one that he was accustomed to discussing, but also because at that moment he realized that he had forgotten that Easton was, in fact, a lady at all. Her demeanor was so puckish, her manners so crude, that Drucker had found himself feeling as though he were eating supper with another man.

"Anyway," Easton continued, "I'm feelin' much better now, so I'll be gettin' outta here in the mornin'. Usually don't spend more than a night or two. S'all it takes to get the good stuff." She gave a smile, and matching dimples sprang up on either side of it.

"I'm envious," admitted Drucker, feeling jealous of her impending release and also a little sad to know he wouldn't be seeing Easton again. Despite her lack of etiquette, she was warm and affable, and he was deeply grateful for her assistance in getting to the dining room, with each bite more so. "I'm hoping they'll release me tomorrow, too," he added.

"Sure," said Easton, scraping her fork around her nearly empty plate. "Tryin' to get back on that train soon's ya can, I'm sure. Can't blame ya for that." She nodded knowingly. "Which direction you headin'?"

"Opposite way as I came," said Drucker resolutely. "I *was* headed west to California, but this detour has made me realize I can't go on without what I left back in Austin."

Easton sighed. "Let me guess, you got a lady back home?"

Drucker stopped to consider this. Was Austin home? "Something like that," he said after a moment, allowing her words to become his truth.

When they had finished their meals, Easton offered Drucker her arm as a crutch but Drucker felt strong enough to limp along on his own. Though he could have moved faster leaning on her to support him, he knew he had better get used to walking without the help, since he wouldn't have it for even one more day. In the corridor outside the men's sleeping bay, the two stopped and turned to each other.

"Easton," said Drucker, "thank you so much for your help tonight."

"Don't mention it," said Easton, batting a hand bashfully. "Been nice knowin' ya. Good luck."

With that, they headed toward their own beds, Easton to spend her last night in the clinic, at least for a month, and Drucker to lie awake, hoping that it would be his last night there, too, so that in the morning he could get on with the business of getting back to Austin.

$$\Longrightarrow\!\!+\!\!+\!\!\Longleftarrow$$

The light of day blazing through the tall windows woke Drucker, and at the very instant that he opened his eyes, he heard a familiar sound.

"Psssst, hey!" whispered Wes. "Glad you're up."

Drucker shifted onto his right side to face Wes, one eye still clogged with unfinished sleep. "Morning, Wes," said Drucker groggily, bringing one hand to his brow to shade his fast-blinking eyes from the morning's harsh light. "What's new?"

"Oh, not much," said Wes, trying to sound casual. "How was supper?" He tried to turn his head away but his foolish grin was like a magnet pulling his face back toward Drucker.

"Fine," said Drucker. He shifted onto his back and sat up in bed. "It was good," he added, as the memory of it took clearer shape in his mind. "Why? What of it?"

"Oh, no reason," said Wes, still casual. Then quickly, "Heard you met Easton." He raised both eyebrows.

"You know her?"

Wes blinked twice, theatrically. "Know 'er? I get my ass to church on Sundays just to try to forget 'er." Wes gave a little laugh, but Drucker cringed, confused.

"Why? What's wrong with Easton?" asked Drucker. "She comes across as perfectly"—he thought for a moment—"nice."

"Might seem that way," said Wes, lowering his voice. "Betcha Beelzebub comes 'cross as pretty nice too, till he's gotcha in his clutches."

"That seems a little harsh," said Drucker, bristling at the insinuation that the woman who had helped him get a hot meal was some incognito devil incarnate.

"No, it's not," said Wes unwaveringly. "Trust me, Drucker. That woman is bad news." Wes turned his body toward Drucker as best he could, and whispered, "I heard she came to Jerome after she got chased outta Tombstone for killin' a man after he caught 'er stealin' from him and"—he paused for effect—"kissin' on his *wife*." His voice was soft but full with the tone of salacious gossip.

Drucker shook his head. "Do you know that for a fact?"

Wes ignored the question. "Just promise me you'll stay away from 'er," he insisted. He flattened his palms against each other and held them in front of his chest as if in prayer. "Only sayin' this 'cause I like you, Drucker, but you gotta stay away from that she-devil. Promise?"

Drucker wanted to protest but he held his tongue. He remembered that Easton was due to be released that morning and, unless Nurse Ruth kept him in bed for another month, he almost certainly would never be seeing her again anyway. Plus, he liked Wes, and though he didn't have much reason to believe his tall tale and wasn't inclined to make a judgment based on hearsay, it wasn't worth losing the friendship of the man two beds down in favor of upholding the reputation of a woman he would never see again. So Drucker made the promise that Wes asked of him.

And he probably would have made good on it, too, if not for a series of events that began with Nurse Ruth pronouncing him fit for release later that morning and ended with Drucker leaving the hospital a few hours later, only to see stars again just steps outside the infirmary's doors. He only narrowly escaped injury when Easton's arms caught his fall.

As expected, Easton had been released late that morning, but Drucker had been released first, by a matter of moments. She had been a dozen yards behind him when he left the clinic and—miraculously—underneath him just before he hit the ground.

"C'mon," she said, pulling Drucker to his feet and giving him a light slap on each cheek. "They see ya hit the dust, and they'll make ya go back in there." She lifted Drucker's hand up and forced a wave to the guard who stood watch at the hospital's door. "Wave at 'im," she whispered and then called, "He's all right! Jus' tripped a little." The guard nodded uninterestedly and waved them off.

"Thanks," said Drucker curtly. He brushed the dust from his shirt and sleeves. "Which way is the train station?"

"Train station? Ha!" laughed Easton. "You could barely make it five steps outta your hospital bed without eatin' dirt. Now you wanna catch a train right away? What're you plannin' to do, ride face down on the floor of it?"

Drucker looked at her suspiciously. "I've got to get back to Austin," he said quietly.

"I know, I know," she said, patting his back reassuringly. "And you'll get there. But all I'm wondering is why's it got to be today— the day ya almost bit it jus' one minute after they letcha outta there."

Drucker thought for a moment. "Well, for one, I've no place else to go."

Easton didn't hesitate. "That's not a problem, just come stay with me till ya get your strength up."

"Oh, no," said Drucker, a little more quickly and vehemently than he had intended. "I really couldn't."

Easton shrugged, looking hurt. "Suit yourself," she said. "Train station's 'bout three miles that way. That's jus' 'bout sixty-some times the length a what ya walked right there." She pointed, and Drucker's eyes followed her finger back toward the doors of the hospital and the mere yards he had walked before going dark.

"C'mon," she said. "My place ain't far from here. And it's nice!" She grinned and the dimples cropped up.

"Well," Drucker found himself saying, "maybe just for one night."

And so, with Easton as his crutch, Drucker limped back to her place, all the while wondering if Wes would ever be the wiser.

CHAPTER TWENTY-EIGHT

E aston's flat was so opulent, so richly lavish, that Drucker needed step no farther than the entry foyer in order to be convinced that what she had told him as they walked there had to be true. The apartment belonged to her husband, a mine owner of substantial means, she had told him as they limped along. She expected him to return home in a few days time, but until then, Drucker was welcome to stay, she had said.

While Drucker had been skeptical at first, the moment he stepped foot inside the generously proportioned home, there was no question that he had entered the property of someone with the means of a mining magnate. His eyes bounced from one piece of intricate artwork to the next, then down to the luxuriant rugs, imports from the Orient, Easton informed him as she led him through the corridor.

Together he and Easton walked down the hall, past a grandly appointed dining room to the equally plush parlor. Easton left Drucker momentarily alone while she darted into her chamber, and as Drucker stood wide-eyed, admiring the ornamental artistry of the décor, after a moment a different sort of beauty caught his eye. From the kitchen emerged a woman with sun-kissed brown skin, sparkling dark eyes, and a braid of long lustrous hair swinging behind her as she careened toward him, her arms open, her eyes wide, and her pouting lips pillowy.

"Thank heavens!" she cried, her arms outstretched and her eyes sparkling with desire as she moved toward him. "I've been waiting for you."

Drucker stood frozen, in equal parts confused and delighted to see such a beautiful woman display the elation that his arrival excited in her. But how could she have known to expect him?

He began to ask her as much but could hardly get out a single word before the attractive woman breezed right past him and flung herself into the arms of Easton who had emerged behind him from the bedroom chamber. Drucker's head swiveled around just in time to witness Easton dipping the woman back in a passionate embrace and kissing her on the mouth, one hand cupped firmly beneath the woman's backside.

Drucker stared at the two of them, his delight now faded, his confusion utter.

"Missed you," Easton whispered to the woman when they were standing upright again. She wiped her lips with the back of her sleeve. "Sorry 'bout that, Drucker," she said, turning to him. "Hope you don't mind." Her eyes drifted around the room as if to remind him that if he did mind, he could spend the night under someone else's—surely less intricately appointed—roof.

Lacking for any other roofs in Jerome under which to spend the night, Drucker simply said, "So is this your...*mining magnate?*"

Easton laughed. "Not exactly," she conceded, slipping her arm around the waist of the lovely dark-skinned woman.

Drucker began shaking his head, slowly at first. "Mining magnate, my foot," he muttered, suddenly feeling quite agitated. He shook his head faster still, recalling Wes's warning and growing angry with himself for not heeding it. "No, of course you're not married to some wealthy mine owner. It's all a lie." He took an angry step toward Easton. "Where are we?" he demanded. "And who is this?" he added, pointing to the woman leaning her weight languorously onto Easton.

"Calm down, Drucker," said Easton, taking a careful, measured step toward him. She held both hands in the air, exposing her open palms to show Drucker she would not harm him. "This is William A. Clark's place," said Easton. "May a heard a him. In addition to this little ol' place he owns the United Verde Copper Company, 'bout half a Montana, and more'n likely that iron horse they carted you off of. And no, I'm not married to him, but that was a joke, not a lie." She smiled sheepishly and roughed her hand through her short-cropped hair. "Believe it or not, Drucker, girls who look like me don't tend to rake in the marriage proposals from the fat cats."

Drucker stared at Easton through squinting eyes. "If this is William A. Clark's home, why are you in it?" he asked after a moment.

"Easy now, Drucker, no need to get upset. I'm a guest a hers." With her thumb she pointed to the other woman, who nodded in earnest.

"It's my home too, after all, seeing as how I'm his—"

"Wait," interrupted Drucker, recalling Wes's yarn of lurid gossip. "Let me guess. You're his wife?"

The woman gave a short, shrill laugh. "I'm not his *wife*," she snorted. "I'm his maid."

⇌ ⇌

A warning voice in his head told him to run, but because he still felt weak in the knees, Drucker stayed put long enough to allow Easton to explain. They were indeed in the apartment of the railroad and mining tycoon William A. Clark, a fact she could verify by retrieving a few of his personal documents from a desk drawer in the study.

When Clark was elsewhere which, given the other properties that he owned, was more often than not, Easton stayed as the guest of his maid, Yumi, an Indian girl whose preference for being paid wages only a white man could afford, and paid attention to like only a sapphic woman could dream, had caused her to shirk life on the reservation. Yumi chimed in to explain that Clark was not expected back for several more days, and as long as he was away, both Easton, as a guest of Yumi, and Drucker, as a guest of Easton, were welcome to stay. The apartment had plenty of room to accommodate them all, Yumi assured him with pride in her voice. Drucker could have his own handsome bedchamber with adjoining indoor water closet.

This last piece of information was of particular interest to Drucker as it was delivered just when he was beginning to feel quite exhausted. Despite the echoing of Wes's warnings, he allowed Easton to show him to the chamber and Yumi to prepare the bed for him. The room was fit for royalty, the bed a far cry from the stiff, narrow mattresses to which he was accustomed. As he sank into it, Drucker caught himself thinking for a moment that a man could be tempted to stay longer than he meant to with accommodations like this. Given his financial standing, with hardly enough money to survive a week on his own, the price was certainly right. Yet as he drifted off to sleep, Drucker made himself a promise that he would leave for the train station first thing in the morning.

And that is what he did.

CHAPTER TWENTY-NINE

The next morning, Drucker snuck out of the apartment at dawn. He tiptoed gingerly down the hall, careful not to wake Easton or Yumi, hoping to avoid any interaction that might delay his departure. He worried that if either of them saw him trying to leave, they would somehow convince him not to, and so he left without ceremony.

Instead, he left only a brief note thanking them both for their hospitality and for the two biscuits that he found in the kitchen and pocketed before he left.

The three-mile walk to the train station didn't exhaust Drucker as he had expected that it would. With his strength mostly returned, he was able to walk quite easily without assistance, and at a steady clip. In less than an hour he arrived at the train station and headed directly to the clerk, who informed Drucker that while trains left for Austin only twice per day, the next one would be leaving in just thirty minutes. Drucker nodded intently and held up one finger to the clerk, who in turn passed one ticket back to Drucker.

"That'll be fifteen dollars," said the Clerk.

"Sure thing," said Drucker as he fished into his pocket. Though money was tight after his unthinkable loss to Horace, he was pleased to learn that a ticket to Austin was within his budget.

Or at least it would have been if when he opened his billfold there had been so much as a single dollar there. Drucker's eyes went wide at the sight of the bare bottom of the billfold.

Not wanting to show the clerk his panic, Drucker turned his back to the man and, doing his best to maintain the appearance of calm, patted down every pocket, digging his fingers into the depths of them, scrounging fruitlessly. When he had checked every pocket twice and rifled through his valise, Drucker turned the search inward. Mentally, he retraced his steps. He had left Austin with money—not much, but some—of that he could be certain. He could clearly remember buying the train ticket to California. In fact, it was one of the last clear memories he had before waking up in the hospital.

Then, of course, there had been the dark period of fever dreams, days that he could not remember at all until he had woken to Nurse Ruth hovering about his bedside.

Where had his billfold been while he had slept, when he had adjourned to the mess hall? Any number of strangers—on the train, in the hospital—could have had access to it in the time since he'd bought that ticket to California. While he couldn't be certain of who had done it, one thing was clear: somewhere between the train that had sped him away from Austin and the train that he hoped would rush him back there, Drucker had been robbed penniless.

Despairingly, he turned back to the stoic clerk. "I'm sorry," he said, stepping up close to the booth. "I seem to have misplaced my cash." The clerk stared at him blankly and shrugged. Wordlessly, he held out his hand, motioning for Drucker to hand over his ticket, but Drucker held it close to his body as he considered the choice in front of him: he could run for it, hiding out until he could hop the train, hoping word would never make it to the conductor that his ticket was a stolen one. Or he could relinquish it, delaying his return to Austin—perhaps indefinitely.

Drucker eyed the clerk as he weighed the risk of stealing the ticket with the reward of making it back to Austin in a day's time. He cringed at the thought of staying in Jerome, with its bleak sky and air tinged with the black dust of mining soot. Plus, something didn't feel right about staying another night with Easton and Yumi as the uninvited houseguest of the copper magnate Clark. When he even considered it, he could hear Wes's voice in his head, pleading with him not to do it. Suddenly, he realized what he needed to do.

Drucker looked the clerk in the eye as he handed back the ticket to Austin and set out to find Easton to demand that she give him back his money.

The three-mile walk back from the train station felt much longer than its reverse, in part because Drucker kept stopping and turning back toward the depot. He didn't *want* to believe that Easton had robbed him. She had given him shelter and a place to sleep when he had nowhere else to go, she had lent him a shoulder to lean on when he had been too weak to walk. But she was also the one person Wes had warned him about, and though Drucker hated to go on hearsay alone, all that he actually knew about Easton suggested that Wes might just be right.

As he walked, Drucker took stock of the facts. He had met Easton at the hospital—fact. By her own admission, Easton was there in the fraudulent pursuit narcotics. And yes, Easton had shown great generosity, helping him to supper and offering him a place to stay; this too was a fact. But he had only accepted the offer of shelter because he had believed her when she told him the apartment was her own. This was a lie—fact. She was not the owner of the apartment, nor was she married to a millionaire mine owner, though she was quite contentedly ripping one off, making great use of his apartment and his maid, unbeknownst to him. The nature of her relationship with Yumi only stood to make Wes's story more plausible.

And so, while Drucker was grateful for what she had done for him, he couldn't tamp down the nagging suspicion that Easton was to blame for his every last cent going missing.

More than an exhausting hour later, Drucker succeeded in storming back to the Clark property. He had every intention of laying into Easton the moment he saw her, but he didn't have a chance to because it was *she* who saw *him* first, hissing his name when he was just steps away from the ground-floor entrance that led up to the second-story flat.

When Drucker heard her voice, he stopped short and looked around with alarm, trying to determine from which direction it had come. He turned in a full circle, looking up, down, and sideways before he finally saw her, crouching down behind a rangy bush beside the building.

"Easton?" Drucker took a few steps closer to the bush and saw that it was indeed she. He summoned his sternest voice. "What the devil are you—"

"Shhhhh! Get down," instructed Easton with such concern on her face that Drucker instinctively ducked and looked over his shoulder.

"What is it?" From his crouched position the sternness in his voice melted into worry.

Easton shifted her weight to look past Drucker, keeping a watchful eye out for anyone who might approach. "Keep your voice down. Old man Clark's back early," she whispered. "Weren't expectin' him for another couple a days, but Yumi just got word that he was on the 10:03 to Jerome Junction. Could be back any second now."

"Ah," said Drucker, understanding perfectly. "The owner of 'your' place is back, so naturally you're hiding in a bush."

"Didn't have a choice," said Easton without acknowledging his sarcasm. "We just found out not five minutes ago. Didn't have time to get much farther than, well, here." She looked around her at the dusty makeshift-hiding place.

Drucker stood upright, straightening his back. He cleared his throat to begin his censure, but there was something so pathetic about Easton as she huddled in the dirt that he decided to spare her the lecture.

"Look, I'm here for my money, Easton." He extended an open palm. "I know you took it, and I need it to get out of here, so if you just give me the money you stole, I'll leave you to your lady friend and—"

"There he is!" Easton interrupted in an excited whisper. "Get down!"

Drucker turned to see a slim, bewhiskered gentleman stepping down from his stately carriage. As he watched the coachman step down off his driver's seat to retrieve Clark's bags from the boot under the wagon, Drucker felt Easton's hand latch onto the back of his coat and yank him back and down so that the two of them were sitting side by side, their backs against the wall of the building, the straggly bush just barely obscuring them from the approaching pair's view.

"Stay back, like this," instructed Easton, pressing her back against the wall and keeping her head low. She peered through the gaps between the bush's low branches, watching Clark and his driver as they approached and then disappeared out of sight around the sharp corner of the building.

"Easton," said Drucker, keeping his voice to a harsh whisper. "I'm not here to cause trouble. Give me back my money, and you can take my word for it that I'll be on the first train out of this place and neither you nor"—he paused for effect—"*Clark*, will ever hear from me. Just give me my money back."

Easton wrenched her eyes away from the bush and looked Drucker squarely in the face. After a long moment she asked, "What money?"

"What money?" repeated Drucker mockingly, scrutinizing her face, hunting for a twitch that would give her away. He continued slowly, not blinking an eye lest he miss her liar's tell. "The money that you stole from me."

Easton didn't so much as flinch. "Look, Drucker," she said, reaching out and gently brushing some of the dirt from his shoulder, "I didn't take your money. If it's gone missin', I'm sorry to hear it, but I don't got it, and I don't know what else to tell ya, 'cept for if you're worried about money, maybe we can find ya some work down the shaft."

From around the corner they could hear the clanking of keys jiggling in a lock, and both Drucker and Easton felt a wave of relief when they heard the sounds of the door giving way and then Clark and his luggage thumping up the stairs to the apartment. The pair sat in silence, listening for the fading sound of Clark's homecoming until it had disappeared altogether, at which point Drucker turned back to Easton. "Down the what?"

"Shaft. Mine shaft. They always got room for one more over in the United Verde copper mine. I go on over and sign up for a couple a days' work if I need the cash when I can't stay with Yumi."

"A mine?" repeated Drucker quietly. "No, I don't think I could—"

"Look, I'm not sayin' it's a party down there er nothin', but ya wanna make money, don't ya?"

Drucker nodded solemnly.

"Not a whole heck of a lot else to do in a place like this if you're trying to scrape some dough together," continued Easton matter-of-factly.

Drucker could feel his face starting to droop. He didn't want to accept the idea that he might actually be stuck in Jerome for another day, much less have to go looking for work down the shaft of a mine, but if Easton really didn't have his money, it could be the surest way to make it back to Austin.

Easton stood up and patted the dust off her backside. "Aww, c'mon now, Drucker, don't look so down in the mouth. You pick up a couple a shifts in the UV, and it probably won't take much more than a week 'fore you've saved up enough to get back to your delicate Texas rose."

Drucker considered this along with its short list of alternatives.

"Well, you coming?" Easton asked, looking back at Drucker who was still sitting in the dirt with his back against the wall, just as she'd positioned him.

With no money and no other leads as to who had taken his money, Drucker didn't see that he had much of a choice. He stood up, dusted himself off, and took a few steps toward her.

"Yes," he said sullenly, "I'll come."

Easton swung an arm up and over Drucker's shoulders as if she were his kid brother consoling him after a fray in the schoolyard. "I can see money's got ya worried, buddy, butcha ain't the only one. When Yumi's place ain't available, money's tight, but ya don't see me mopin' around lookin' like a lost dog. C'mon now, buck up." She pulled her arm off his shoulders and gave him a playful punch in the side. "We'll get work before you know it, Drucker. Don't worry, we're in this together now."

Despite Easton's encouragement, though, Drucker couldn't help but worry. How he would pay for food and shelter worried him and what it would be like to work in a mine shaft worried him even more. At that moment, though, as they walked side by side toward the United Verde copper mine in search of work, it was the "being in it together" with Easton that worried Drucker most of all.

CHAPTER THIRTY

True to Easton's word, both she and Drucker found work in the mine without trouble but, unlike she had predicted, Drucker didn't accumulate enough savings to make it back to Austin in just a mere matter of days. Despite his attempts to squirrel away whatever he had left over after food and rent expenses, when he counted his kitty in mid-December, a full month after he had taken up work in the damp, dark United Verde, he found that he had managed to save up no more than a handful of coins. This time, though, he knew he had no one to blame but himself, because in truth his wages hadn't been dedicated solely to the procurement of food and shelter.

In the four weeks he had spent mining the United Verde, Drucker had picked up the costly habit of capping off his day of backbreaking work with a few hours at the saloon. Though he had never been much of a drinking man, the reality of his drafty, sooty little miner's flat was too lonely to bear with a clear mind, especially as winter's approach sent through a chill on the increasingly frequent blustery nights.

So rather than go home when his shift was through, Drucker had taken to joining the other miners as they leaned up against the rail and wrapped their calloused hands around sloshing copper mugs. Occasionally, as the fog of inebriation rolled in, Drucker would find himself thinking of how his father would turn over in his grave if he could see his son now: a thousand miles away from the life that his father had tried to bestow upon him, covered in soot, nursing a drink among the working men who couldn't even have opened an account at Atlanta Southern, much less ever dreamed of running the place.

For whatever else could be said of them, though, the men of Jerome were the type who put in a hard day's work, and Drucker spent many a blurry-eyed hour at the saloon trying to decide if he was one of them. He had proven that he could wield a pickaxe with the best of them, his body strong enough to sustain the burden of physical labor. But his will to endure it was weak. He may not have been cut out for life behind a desk at Atlanta Southern, but neither was his constitution designed for life at other end of the spectrum.

While the others seemed resigned to accept that the rest of their days would be spent in the mine, with each day that passed Drucker grew increasingly exhausted and frustrated. He would have abandoned the mining life in a heartbeat if only he had the means.

Easton, for her part, had put in a few days' work in the mine alongside Drucker before moving herself back into the hospital on the pretense of debilitating joint pain. Drucker hadn't seen her for more than three weeks when she strolled into the saloon one evening, so covered in the streaking black scars of mining residue that Drucker hardly recognized her. When she sidled up to him and nudged him softly in the ribs, it took him several beats to realize whose elbow it was that met with his midsection.

"Well, well, look who's had her fill of ether," teased Drucker, hearing more bitterness in his own voice than he expected. He lifted his eyes and looked around the saloon self-consciously, noting a few sideways glances being thrown in Easton's direction. He could feel his body shifting away from hers instinctively.

Easton didn't seem to notice either the bitterness or the shifting. "How you holdin' up?" she asked as she caught the barkeep's eye and, without a word, he sent her usual pick of poison sliding down the bar toward her.

"Poorly," answered Drucker. "It's even more miserable than I could have imagined down there."

Easton nodded knowingly. "Tell me about it," she said, wiping a slick of grime from her forehead and examining it briefly before wiping it off on her overcoat. "But, hey, it ain't like you're the only one 'round here gettin' your hands dirty." She shrugged, and her nonchalance made the low burn of anger that Drucker had been feeling for weeks ignite into a flame in the pit of his stomach.

"At least you knew what you were getting into," he snapped, and then the words he spoke next took them both by surprise. "I'm only here because I'm flat broke, thanks to *someone* stealing every last cent I had. And *you* said that if I picked up work in the mine, it would just be a few days before I could get the hell out of here, but it's been a month, and I've been working day in and day out, and I still can't afford one lousy ticket to Austin—"

Drucker stopped when he noticed Easton looking at him with amusement. "Well, pardon me for sayin' this, Drucker, but it don't look like you're tryin' particularly hard to get out a this place," she said, gesturing toward the crowd of regulars that now included Drucker. "Maybe ya don't actually wanna leave."

"Oh believe me," scoffed Drucker, "the minute I can scrape together enough money to go get Margaret so we can start our life together in California, that's what I'll be doing." Drucker had had one drink too many to be able to hold back his emotion, but Easton remained calm in the face of it.

"Look, Drucker, I know you're hard up," she said, pausing to take a long gulp that drained her mug. "That's actually what I'm here to talk to y'about. I've got a little proposition—"

"No thank you," said Drucker before she could finish. "Whatever it is you're peddling, I'm not buying."

"Now hear me out, Drucker. I know you're tired, you're frustrated, and ya wanna get the hell outta here as fast as ya can. So, what wouldja say if I told ya I had a plan that's guaranteed to make both of us rich in short order?"

"I'd say 'not interested,'" replied Drucker quickly, forcing himself looking away.

"All right, fine by me," said Easton, her tone deliberately casual. "Suit yourself." She paused for a few beats then added, "But you're the one who's got yourself into a lather over how *miserable* it is workin' in the mine, sayin' how all ya want to do is to scrape together enough dough to get the hell outta here."

"I just want to get back to Margaret," said Drucker, hearing his own exhausted desperation.

"So maybe ya oughta hear me out, then," Easton reasoned. "I'm tellin' ya, Drucker, with this plan I got, forget the damned ticket, you'll be rich enough to buy the whole stinkin' car. Why, you'll show up on your miss Margaret's doorstep with diamonds and pearls."

Drucker could feel the first nagging tugs of an interest to which he didn't want to admit. Without looking at Easton, he asked cautiously, "And if this plan of yours fails? Then what? They'll send us to the gallows?"

Easton shook her head. "Nah, they won't hang ya for anythin' less than murder 'round these parts. Worst that'll happen is they'll run us outta town." She paused, and then as if she could read his thoughts, she added, "Which might be better'n what ya got goin' on here."

Drucker considered this, wondering if one could choose in which direction to be run out of town. After a moment he finally turned to look Easton in the eye. "So you're saying murder isn't involved in this grand plan of yours?"

Easton pouted her slightly sooty lips. "Drucker, I don't know what you've heard about me, but I ain't no murderer."

"Right," said Drucker, "and you didn't take my money."

"No," said Easton, "I didn't take your money, but y'know what, Drucker? Who cares who took your damned money? 'Cause all that matters is the fact that ya ain't got any now, so the way I see it, ya got two choices. Either ya keep splittin' rock and drinkin' away any chance ya got at getting' back to your lady before ya both go gray, or ya consider a quicker way to get the money ya need."

"And your plan is that quicker way to get it."

"That's right," said Easton. "So ya wanna hear it or not?"

Maybe his misery in the mine was to blame, or maybe it was the image of his arrival on Margaret's doorstep bearing gifts that the reality of his current livelihood meant he would likely never again be able to afford. Or maybe it was simply that one drink too many made the words coming out of his mouth heavy with emotion and the words coming out of Easton's mouth make sense. Whatever the reason, when Easton asked again if he wanted to hear her plan, Drucker said, "I suppose it can't hurt just to hear it."

"Absolutely right," said Easton, beaming. "How 'bout I buy us each one more, and we talk this through over there?" She motioned to an empty area toward the back of the saloon.

Drucker nodded, and Easton held up two fingers in the direction of the bartender. "Never hurt a man to just open himself up to possibilities," she said, and with that sentiment Drucker had to agree.

CHAPTER THIRTY-ONE

I t took Easton about twenty minutes to lay the plan out for Drucker, forty more for him to fully understand it, and another hour before she convinced him to agree to it, but before the night was over, Easton had herself a partner in crime. Though how much actual *crime* her plan entailed wasn't clear, which is why, in the end, Drucker agreed to participate.

The scheme called for no murder or physical harm to be inflicted, no hold-up or forcible robbery to be conducted. What intrigued Drucker about Easton's plan was the psychological nature of it. The success of the deed she described did not call for brute force or weaponry. Instead, the ruse would rely on his acting skills, once honed so finely at Atlanta Southern, in his days of pretending to be engaged in a life that, in reality, he lived only on the surface.

To carry out their caper required diligence in the way of preparation, which Drucker and Easton devoted themselves to religiously over the course of the next two weeks, holing themselves up in her grungy miner's flat in the dark and chilly hours after their shifts ended.

At first, Drucker found it difficult to break the habit of lubricating himself into numbness at the saloon each night, but the prospect of regaining at least some of his lost wealth drew him to Easton's planning sessions. Plus, Drucker was pleased to realize, by forgoing his nightly ritual at the saloon he was finally able to start saving a bit. Though the small amount he accumulated couldn't buy him much, it meant that he could afford to abandon Easton and head back to Austin if he should so choose.

For each moment that leaving felt like the obvious choice, though, there was one in which he felt compelled to stay on long enough to take a shot at the real money. Easton, sensing his uncertainty, talked increasingly of the reward that was sure to greet them on the other end of their operation. The prospect of arriving in Austin with more than just the spare change that he would have left over after buying the ticket to get there appealed to Drucker, and they both knew that in order for that to happen, he would need to accumulate a good deal more than he was on pace to earn anytime soon by working in the mine.

The more time that he spent on the planning, and the more that Easton talked about their imminent payday, the more Drucker became convinced that they could and would pull off their pursuit and both emerge a good deal richer for their efforts. Then he could return to Margaret with enough money for them to live comfortably together in California or wherever else they should choose to go.

—=≺┼ ┼≻=—

One night in their second week of planning, with their heist just days away, Drucker found himself deep in daydreams. As usual, they had convened in Easton's snug and dingy flat, and Easton was flopped down on her bed, arms crooked and looking like wings with her hands beneath her head, cradling it as she gazed at the ceiling.

"...so that's why I'm sayin' it's got to be Thursday," concluded Easton after a lengthy monologue. A beat passed after she finished, then another without any response from Drucker. Easton raised herself up onto her elbows. "Hey, you awake over there?"

Drucker murmured from his usual seated position on the floor. Slumped against the wall was his preferred position, despite Easton's repeated offer of a chair. He insisted it was the only way to give his aching back muscles a modicum relief after a long day in the mine.

"You're awfully quiet tonight," said Easton pointedly. When Drucker didn't respond, she shifted onto her stomach, with her head at the foot of the bed close to where Drucker sat. Her tone softened. "Penny for your thoughts?" she asked gently.

"Oh," said Drucker, pulling sharply away from the glowing haze of his imagination, "I was just thinking about what life is going to be like after we pull this damn thing off."

"And," asked Easton, "what'd ya come up with?"

Drucker opened his mouth to start talking about Margaret when it struck him how mundane and repetitive he sounded when he talked about his future with her. He looked away from Easton. "You know, just..." his voice trailed off.

"Oh, c'mon, Drucker, don't get bashful now. What'll your first move be once we've got the money?"

Drucker turned back to Easton and locked eyes with her, examining her for signs that she would laugh at his simple wish. But where he expected to see a glint of mocking he saw only curiosity. So he answered her, speaking slowly at first.

"Well, I'll go back to Austin, of course. I'll go to Margaret and ask her to marry me. I'd like to buy her a gift, something nice, a brooch or a pendant maybe, and with the rest of it, we'll buy a house, I suppose. Just big enough for a family. Or maybe something bigger, if that's what she wants. Someplace near an inn. Or maybe I'll buy her an inn of her own if it will make her happy."

Easton listened patiently. "That'd sure be nice," she agreed in earnest. "Maybe even get yourself a little garden and a couple a chick'ns," she added, fueling the fire of Drucker's daydream. "Always wanted to get myself a couple a chick'ns. Freshest eggs I ever had were plucked right out from 'neath a layin' hen. Shells were still warm from bein' jus' laid and all."

Drucker smiled to himself as he conjured the image, the taste. "Yes, maybe we'll do that," he said. After a moment he asked, "What about you? What's the first thing you'll do with the money?"

"Me? I..." she hesitated, turning scarlet and suddenly shy.

Drucker grinned. "Look who's bashful now," he teased, but gently. "What could it be that has Easton tongue-tied? Something special for Yumi, perhaps?"

"No...it's just that I, well..." She pushed herself up into a seated position at the foot of the bed. When she spoke, it was with frustration. "Look, it's not worth talkin' 'bout, all right? Let's just say I got an ideer 'bout what I'd like to do with it, but I don't think I can do it."

"Oh come now," coaxed Drucker. "Just tell me. I told you."

Now it was Easton's turn to size up Drucker. She looked into his eyes, searching for a hint of judgment. When she found none, she answered him.

"I want to invest it."

"Invest it?" repeated back Drucker with surprise. "In what?"

"Aw, what's the difference? Can't happen anyway," said Easton, her voice thin and childlike.

"Maybe it can't," said Drucker evenly, "but what good does it do you to keep it a secret?"

Easton nodded along with this reasoning, and after a moment she inhaled deeply. "Listen," she said, lowering her voice, "there's this fella that's been in town the past couple a weeks. A salesman. Goes by the name a Horton, I think. James or John or J-somethin'-er-other Horton. Anyway"—she paused—"you seen 'im?"

"No," said Drucker after thinking for a moment. "I don't think so. What does he sell?"

"Bonds," said Easton. "For a new bank they're startin' down in Phoenix."

"Bank bonds?" squeaked Drucker. "That's what you want to invest in?"

Easton nodded. "It's a solid investment, Drucker," she said. "Ya see, ya buy 'em for one price, and then ya cash 'em in later on for more than you paid for 'em. They guarantee ya that ya can."

"Yes," said Drucker, feeling impatient, "I know how bank bonds work."

"Sure, sure sorry," said Easton, preparing to hurry back to the point, but suddenly stopping when curiosity struck her. "Wait—you do?" she asked. "How? Y'got some?"

"No," said Drucker sharply, "not anymore. I did. In the past. Please continue with your story."

Easton eyed him warily. Drucker could tell she wanted to know more about the bank bonds of his past, but Drucker felt in no mood to go into it. He gave her a stern look that prompted Easton to continue her story, though with added caution in her voice.

"Look, normally I wouldn't a given a thing like this much thought, ya see, but these are different. These are for a bank that hasn't opened yet. 'Stead a havin' to wait years to cash out, ya don't need to wait but for the New Year when they open. Soon's they start gettin' accounts y'can cash out for triple your money. Maybe more."

Drucker raised a skeptical eyebrow.

"I know," said Easton, understanding his wordless response perfectly, "but Yumi says she's heard Clark talkin' 'bout them bonds like they're gold nuggets. He's buyin' up whole bunches of 'em. If a fat cat like that is buyin' 'em, you know they got to be good. Gotta know what you're doin' to get rich, stay rich, and keep on gettin' richer." She turned her wide eyes toward Drucker as she tried to tamp down her excitement.

Drucker nodded without mirroring Easton's enthusiasm. "All right, so you want to buy some bank bonds. What's to stop you?" he asked, feeling that something was missing from his understanding of Easton's sob story.

"Oh, just the little fact that that Horton character says he don't sell to women," replied Easton as her face fell.

"Ah, yes, of course," said Drucker realizing that the salient point that he had failed to account for was not that a bond salesman wouldn't sell to a woman, but rather that he was currently in the company of one.

"Don't matter that I'm breakin' my back in there with all the other fellas, or that I'm one a the only people in this town that's managed to save enough to buy his damn bonds anyway," whispered Easton, her eyes glistening. "Hell, he's probably the only person in spittin' distance a Jerome that even thinks a me as a woman." She sighed. "Anyway, that's why I didn't wanta say nothin'. No point. That horse's ass ain't goin' to sell his bonds to a woman."

Drucker gave this a moment of thought. "That doesn't seem like an insurmountable obstacle," he said finally, hoping that it would indeed prove not to be. After all, buying some bank bonds seemed to be a perfectly admirable ambition. It was yet another unexpected turn by Easton, who seemed to always be surprising him just when he thought he had her figured out.

"Drucker, the man flat out tol' me he wouldn't sell to no woman, no way, no how."

"What if I bought them for you?" offered Drucker. "You could give me the amount you want to invest, and I could buy the bonds from Horton and then sign them over to you."

Easton looked up, and her wet eyes met Drucker's clear ones. "You'd do that for me?" she asked, wiping her sniffling nose with her sleeve.

"I'd sure try," said Drucker warmly. "But hey, we've got to make the money first. So let's both buckle down and focus on getting this thing done right so I can get back to Margaret, and you can get yourself a whole bunch of bank bonds."

Easton smiled and wiped a lone last teardrop from the corner of her eye.

"I think I had you figured wrong, Drucker," she said. "You're a real good guy. Better'n I took you for at first."

"Thank you, Easton," said Drucker, smiling at the irony.

CHAPTER THIRTY-TWO

D rucker and Easton agreed that Thursday would be the best
day to conduct their operation.

It would be best, they decided, for reasons not limited to, but
hinging on, the fact that Thursday would be the twenty-fifth of
December, otherwise known as Christmas Day. This meant that
they wouldn't be missed at the mine on Thursday, thanks to the
resolutely capitalist but also devoutly Christian shift captain an-
nouncing that the mine would close at noon on Christmas Eve and
operations not resume until the day after Christmas.

The fortuitous holiday closure would afford Drucker and
Easton the time to take a train to the neighboring town of
Flagstaff, just far enough away for them to be strangers, but close
enough to allow them to make it back in time for their December
26 shifts.

Not that either of them planned on working many more shifts
if they could successfully pull off their gamble. Still, it felt wise to
plan on sliding back into their usual routines for a day or two, at
least for the sake of an alibi, should they need it.

Drucker agreed to meet Easton at the train station at two in the afternoon on the day before Christmas, and so shortly after one o'clock he hurried out onto Jerome's unusually quiet Main Street. Most of Jerome's predominantly male population had adjourned down into the neighboring residential valley to mark the holiday in homes with wives and families, leaving the streets of Jerome much quieter than usual.

Drucker was grateful to not see a soul he recognized as he began making his way toward the train station. When he heard his name called, his first instinct was to ignore the voice and keep walking, hoping that whoever had spotted him would assume he'd been mistaken. When he heard his name a second time, though, Drucker couldn't help but turn around, especially because suddenly he recognized the voice.

"Wes?" Drucker stopped and turned to see Wes hobbling toward him with the help of a cane.

"None other," said Wes, beaming at Drucker as they neared each other.

"Why, I hardly recognize you at this angle," said Drucker. He cocked his head to the side to remind Wes that he had only ever seen him lying horizontal. "Upright looks good on you."

Wes smiled and rubbed his leg. "Took me a couple a weeks, but I finally got sprung. Doc says I should only need the cane for another month or so."

"That's wonderful, Wes," said Drucker with all sincerity. "I'm happy to hear that you're on the mend."

"Thank you kindly," said Wes, but then his smile dimmed. "Actually, Drucker, it's funny I should run into you. Heard somethin' 'bout you just the other day that's got me worried."

Drucker felt his pulse pick up in pace. "Oh, no reason to worry about me. I'm getting along just fine," said Drucker, trying to sound relaxed. He tried to quickly change the subject. "But you, with your leg—"

"I been hopin' to heck this is just a rumor, Drucker," said Wes, and Drucker cringed as he waited for Wes's next words to drop on him like a ton of bricks. "But word's gettin' around that you been keepin' company with Easton."

"Easton?" repeated Drucker. He gulped.

Wes nodded. "That witch I warned you about. You ain't been cavortin' with her, have you?"

Drucker couldn't bring himself to lie to Wes. He did everything he could to keep his pitch even as he asked, "Who told you that they saw me with her?"

Wes shook his head, ignoring the question. "I'm tellin' you, Drucker, she's bad news. Plus"—he lowered his voice and leaned in toward Drucker—"I got it on good authority that she don't even like men, so if that's what you're after, you're barkin' up the wrong tree."

"Oh, no, no," stuttered Drucker. "I would never—" He stopped when he could tell that Wes had mentally moved on.

"So where might you be off to on this Christmas Eve?" asked Wes.

"Oh," started Drucker. Admitting that he was on his way to meet Easton was out of the question. Either he had to lie or change the subject, and since he couldn't bring himself to lie to Wes, he said, "I'm looking for someone, actually. A bond salesman by the name of Horton," he quickly added when he saw that he had captured Wes's attention. "You haven't crossed paths with him, have you, Wes?"

Wes's eyes popped open a little wider. "You mean Jesse?"

"Could be," said Drucker, nodding eagerly. "J. Horton, yes. You know him, then?"

"Sure do," said Wes. "Bought me some a his bonds in that new United Trust of Phoenix they're openin'."

Drucker nodded. "That's him. I'm looking to buy a few of those myself."

"Are you?" asked Wes, looking hopeful. He leaned in close to Drucker. "You think they're a good investment, then?" He lowered his voice. "I been nervous 'bout the whole thing since I bought them bonds. Puttin' money in another man's hands is risky business." He paused briefly to look at Drucker to see if he agreed. "I wouldn't a done it 'cept for I sure could use a payday. I been fallin' behind on account a bein' laid up for weeks. Not sure I'll ever get back to workin' as many shifts like I was," said Wes, giving his bum leg a tap with the tip of his cane. "Jesse says when the bank opens in January the bonds can be cashed in for five times whatcha paid for 'em."

"That certainly sounds promising," said Drucker, wondering if perhaps this was an investment he himself should get in on. "Do you know where I can find him? J. Horton—Jesse, that is."

"You won't find him here," said Wes, shaking his head slowly. "He left town last week. Probably won't be back until they open the bank sometime next month, I suppose. I can give him your name when he comes back. Could be a little late to get in on the bonds, though."

Drucker suddenly thought of the time. Wes's use of the word *late* reminded him that he would be exactly that if he didn't start moving toward the train station in short order.

"I understand," said Drucker. He felt a rush of excitement course through his veins as he remembered what it was that he couldn't be late for. "Look, Wes, I have to go now—Christmas Eve and all—but it was a pleasure running into you. Please do give Jesse my name if you see him."

"Will do," called Wes as he watched Drucker hurry off. "Merry Christmas!"

"Merry Christmas, Wes," Drucker called over his shoulder without slowing his ambitious stride.

"And don't forget what I said 'bout stayin' away from that harpy," shouted Wes. "She's a wolf in sheep's clothing. Drucker, do you hear me?"

There was no response from Drucker, though. He was either too faraway or too excited about the mission he was about to embark on with Easton to hear the words coming out of Wes's mouth.

CHAPTER THIRTY-THREE

Later that night, Drucker and Easton found the streets of Flagstaff as deserted as the ones in Jerome had been. Lighted candles peered out through their windowpanes, keeping flickering watch over the empty streets, quiet save for the strains of organ music wafting felicitously out of the lone steepled church sitting high atop its hilly perch.

The next morning, as they had hoped and expected, Drucker was the first and only customer of the Hare's Head Hitching Post & Saloon when he entered a little before noon on Christmas morning, carrying the article that had been at the center of nearly every conversation that he and Easton had had for the previous two weeks: a vigorously shined-up, yet nevertheless very worn-down violin, packed tightly into its black leather carrying case.

Drucker's role was simple by design. He was to walk into the saloon, order a drink—maybe two, but no more—and then he was to ask the barkeep if he could leave his violin with him for a matter of hours. All of this Drucker executed flawlessly, operating exactly to plan, though taking his time to enjoy the two-drink option. Then, exactly as they had rehearsed, when the barkeep had agreed to watch the violin, Drucker left the saloon on the pretenses of attending the late-morning services at the hilltop parish.

Every move, every word, Drucker delivered with the poise and confidence of a seasoned professional. He walked out of the saloon like an actor exiting stage right. Then came Easton's turn.

When Drucker walked back into the Hare's Head a number of hours later, it was all that he could do to keep the barman from begging him to sell the greased up old instrument that Drucker had left in his care. Whatever Easton had done, she had done it to perfection, inspiring the barkeep to offer Drucker the contents of both the cash register and a discreetly located wall safe in order to offer a higher bid when Drucker showed reluctance to sell.

As his well-rehearsed role called for, Drucker put up a protest at the man's first several attempts to buy the violin. He feigned alarm at the very thought of selling his "beloved" instrument. The more Drucker demurred, though, the more money the saloon's proprietor came up with. The two went back and forth for half an hour until Drucker finally accepted the barman's offer.

Though inwardly he was pleased at how well the plan was working, Drucker maintained an appearance of concern, even grief, at the transaction, and whether this was only a matter of acting, even he could not tell. His customer, on the other hand, could hardly contain the foolish grin of a man who had succeeded in convincing the unknowing owner of a Stradivarius to sell him what he had on good authority was a near priceless relic. When it was all said and done, Drucker left the saloon with $10,000, and the barkeep was left with a perfectly worthless violin.

⊷⊶

On the train ride back to Jerome that night, Drucker and Easton drank rye from a flask until their eyes were blurry, congratulating themselves on a mission accomplished. They counted their newly acquired greenbacks over and over again and giggled deliriously at the amount that they had gotten as well as Easton's account of what it had been like to play the role of an East Coast auctioneer, visiting Flagstaff to see her brother for the holiday.

Just as Drucker had been earlier in the day, Easton had been the only customer at the Hare's Head when she had stopped in during the early afternoon. When she had caught a glimpse of the instrument resting in its case behind the bar, Easton had offered to appraise it at no cost, an offer that the bored bartender had accepted, if only to pass the time.

After meticulously and methodically examining it, Easton had declared the instrument to be damn near priceless, and the barkeep's eyes had gone round as saucers. When she had then told him that she just so happened to know a very wealthy frequent guest of her auction house back East who collected such relics and would surely pay just about any price for one like this, the barman's eyes had nearly rolled back in his head. And when Easton had told the poor fool that she simply *needed* to buy this violin from him, telling him that he could choose his price as she was certain to make it back the moment that her collector friend saw this piece, well, his eyes had nearly popped out of his head, Easton recounted. Both Drucker and Easton howled with laughter as they imagined what the poor dope's eyes must have done when Easton, much more willing than Drucker to tell a bald-faced lie, never reappeared to buy the instrument as she had promised.

After Drucker and Easton had exhausted themselves with the counting of their money and the recounting of the day's events, in a quiet moment Easton turned to Drucker and asked him if he was still willing to make good on his promise to buy her the bonds that she had mentioned to him. Drucker turned to her, feeling both quite proud of himself and warm toward Easton at that moment.

"I've already looked into it," he announced, slurring only slightly, despite his tongue being made heavy by the half-dozen visits it had paid to Easton's flask.

"No kiddin'," said Easton, making another visit to the flask herself before asking, looking hopeful, "so ya found Horton then?"

"Not exactly," said Drucker. "I found out that he's recently left town, but I spoke with someone who bought some of his bonds." He paused, remembering what Wes had told him about the expected five-times returns and then found himself adding, "He thinks it may be a shaky investment, though."

"Well, *I* don't," Easton quickly retorted, "and whoever does is a shit for brains that don't deserve to own them bonds or get rich off a 'em. I'm tellin' ya, Drucker, Yumi's been listenin' to ol' man Clark talkin' 'bout these bonds for months now. She says he's stockpilin' the things like they'd save him in a sandstorm."

"So why don't you just *borrow* some of his then?" asked Drucker, too quickly. His words, meant in jest, didn't carry much humor with them as they slipped out from between his well-lubricated lips. He immediately regretted them.

Easton turned to Drucker, looking genuinely hurt. "You really do think of me as a common thief, don't you?" she asked after a moment, holding his gaze as her lip began to quiver.

Drucker defiantly nodded his head toward the $5,000 that Easton had tucked away in the breast pocket of her men's overcoat. "Are you not?"

"Are *you* not?" she shot back immediately, nodding at his matching stack that had been similarly stowed away.

Drucker bristled at this. "Look, Easton," he said, feeling uncomfortable with the suddenly mounting hostility between himself and the woman for whom just moments earlier he had been feeling affection. "Forget I said anything, all right? It was only a joke, albeit a bad one. I'm sorry."

"Yeah, yeah," said Easton, looking uninterested and sounding impatient.

"Yeah, yeah?" repeated Drucker. "What might you mean by 'yeah, yeah'?"

Easton answered him without hesitation, as if she had been waiting to do exactly that for weeks.

"Yeah, yeah means you can take your apologies and shove 'em, Drucker. Ya spend all your time runnin' around lookin' down on everyone, thinkin' you're too fancy-pants for minin', what with your big dreams a gettin' outta Jerome and your snooty way a talkin' and all. As if those things make ya some kind a royalty that's too good to get your hands dirty with the rest of us. And you jus' love callin' *other people* liars and thieves, but in case ya ain't taken a good look at yourself in a mirror lately, I'll save ya the trouble and tell ya right now. You're just as much of a thief as I am, Drucker. And on top a that you had me thinkin' you were a real gentleman and all, tellin' me you'd be a hero and buy me those bonds so I could invest my money like any a the men in this town can. But now, if I had to guess, I'd say you're 'bout to start tryin' hard as heck to get out of it, so guess what, Drucker? That makes *you* the liar. Not me."

The biting accuracy of Easton's rant knocked the breath out of Drucker. She was right. The whole time that he had been in Jerome he had been so busy feeling sorry for himself, wondering if his father would even recognize the man that he had become, he hadn't stopped to realize that even *he* could barely recognize the man that he had turned into.

"Easton…" He paused. "You're right," was all that he could think to say.

Easton played at ignoring him, training her eyes on the back of the seat in front of her, giving Drucker no response.

"Easton," he said again, "you're absolutely right. I told you that I would buy those bonds for you, and I'll make good on my word.

Or at least I'll try. Very hard," he added in response to her suspicious sideways glance in his direction.

"You mean it?" asked Easton quietly, still staring straight ahead.

"Yes," replied Drucker solemnly. "How much do you want me to get you?"

Easton turned to him. "As much as ya can," she answered, her expression suddenly alive. She reached into her pocket, pulled out the bills and extended the entire stack toward Drucker.

Drucker looked at the bills. For a fleeting moment he thought of how taking her money and skipping town could mean easily doubling his money, but he caught himself and killed the shameful thought.

"No," he said shaking his head. "You hold on to it until I find out how much I can get you."

Easton nodded and tucked the bills away again, and Drucker felt relief when the stack disappeared back into her coat pocket. It didn't feel right to take her money just yet, perhaps because he didn't trust himself with it. Or maybe because he didn't trust her too-ready offer of it. Either way, Drucker could sense that an exchange of money at that moment would signal that someone was up to no good. He just couldn't be sure exactly which one of them it was.

CHAPTER THIRTY-FOUR

B ack in Jerome, Drucker couldn't bring himself to slip back into the life of a miner for even one more day, despite his plans to do so. Instead, when he returned to his tiny flat on Christmas night, Drucker tucked his thick stack of bills beneath his pillow and then allowed his fatigued body and adrenaline-addled mind to rest well past the time when his shift began the next morning, and even long past when it ended.

When he finally woke, night had fallen on the day that he had slept through. Before his eyes had even fully opened, Drucker shoved his hand under his pillow to make sure that the bills were still there. They were, which prompted him to rejoice in the thought that returning to Austin could finally become a reality. That thought, in turn, put a spring in his step as he once again repacked everything that he owned into his valise before crawling back into bed and waiting restlessly for morning.

When morning finally did arrive, Drucker was anxious to get back to Austin, but after wrestling with his conscience all night he couldn't bring himself to leave Jerome without at least speaking to Wes about the bonds for Easton. Though he hated to delay his trip back to Austin in order to do Easton a favor, every time he told himself that he didn't owe her anything, he couldn't help but wonder if that was really true.

He did have her to thank, after all, for the $5,000 that he had tucked securely beneath his pillow. Without her, he wouldn't have that, although perhaps he wouldn't have been desperate enough to get it in the dirty way that they had if not for her convincing him to take work in that awful mine. And he wouldn't have needed to take that horrible job in the first place if she hadn't robbed him of his every last cent, as Drucker remained fairly certain was the case.

But then again, if she *had* robbed him, she had done it while simultaneously providing him with shelter when he desperately needed it, which he wouldn't have accepted if not for her also having helped him to a warm meal when he was famished and weak and vulnerable. This brought him back to the beginning of his circling thoughts, which was also their conclusion: he owed Easton nothing, but also everything. She was either a very bad person or a misunderstood, fairly decent one. Drucker couldn't quite be sure which one it was, but he felt certain that if he left town without even trying to get her those bonds, he would have to think of himself as the former.

And so Drucker decided to stay for in Jerome for one more day which, as fate would have it, was all that it took to find Wes posted up at the saloon, three drinks deep and eager to tell Drucker what he had just learned about his recent investment.

CHAPTER THIRTY-FIVE

Wes was so happy to see Drucker walk into the saloon on Saturday night that he lifted his newly filled mug into the air with glee, sending a sloshing surge of dark liquid up over the lip of it.

"Drucker," he roared with intoxicated excitement, "get on over here!"

As Drucker neared, Wes extended his mug-holding arm around Drucker's shoulders, pulling him closer, drawing him into his armpit.

"Hello, Wes," greeted Drucker, smiling at his good fortune. He shifted his body to dodge the sticky drops still falling from Wes's cup. "I was so hoping that I would see you here."

Wes lifted his arm off Drucker's shoulders and raised it high in the air, signaling to the bartender. "Whatcha drinkin'?" he asked Drucker. "We got to get you in on this celebration!"

"Mule Skinner," said Drucker, naming the whiskey concoction that had come to be his drink of choice in Jerome. "What are we celebrating?"

Wes grinned. "Remember those bonds you were askin' me about the other day?"

"Why, yes, of course," said Drucker. "You said you thought they could be quite a risky investment," he quickly reminded Wes, hoping to shake his confidence enough that he might be willing to offload a few shares to Easton.

"Richie, we'll need a mule skinner over here," Wes said to the approaching bartender. He turned back to Drucker. "That's right, I did," he said, "but not anymore!" Wes grinned even wider and slapped Drucker jovially, but nevertheless too hard, on the back. "Horton sent a telegram up from Phoenix today. Says the bank's already startin' to open some accounts ahead a schedule, and the bonds are oversold. Got a whole list a men waitin' on 'em, he says. That means we can cash 'em in early, soon as next week, and get real strong returns for 'em, too." Wes looked at Drucker through bleary eyes. "Drucker," he said, "I think I might a done a real good thing when I bought them bonds."

Drucker's drink arrived at the exact moment that he was beginning to feel entirely too sober. "Wes, that's wonderful," he said as he realized that the job of buying a few of Wes's shares had just become a great deal harder. Still, he was determined to try.

"I can't hardly believe it," Wes sputtered. "I might never have to get work in the UV again."

Drucker paused for a moment while he chose his next words carefully. When he delivered them, in contrast to Wes's blubbering they sounded even more slow and serious.

"Wes," said Drucker, "I want you to listen to me. If you really want to capitalize on your good fortune, you're going to need to sell those bonds right away." He looked deep into Wes's eyes and saw the hint of fear that he was hoping for. "Not back to Horton. To someone else."

Wes began to mirror the look of concern on Drucker's face, though the cause for Drucker's concern was entirely different from what Wes understood it to be.

"Sell 'em?" asked Wes. "Why would I want to go and do a thing like that?"

This prompted Drucker to tell Wes the last thing one might have expected him to at that moment: the truth.

Drucker told Wes that he had spent years working at a bank and that the bank had been in Atlanta, and that he'd damn near become the president of it, too. He told him that he'd been around a bond or two in his time and that he'd certainly known plenty of investors, good ones and bad. The smart ones, Drucker told Wes, understood the need to *diversify risk*. When Wes admitted that he didn't understand what Drucker meant by diversify risk, Drucker slowed down and explained it to him evenly.

"It means that you can keep some of the bonds, but you should sell off a few *now*, just in case the whole thing goes south before you can sell them all back to Horton. That way you won't be risking everything, you see?"

Wes listened intently to his friend, riveted by what Drucker divulged about his past. He agreed to consider selling him a few of the bonds, just to be on the safe side. By the time the night was over, the two men had decided that they would meet at Drucker's place the next day at noon. Wes was instructed to bring the bonds. He didn't *have* to sell them, Drucker assured. They could just discuss it further, and privately. Without the crowd, without the mule skinners.

When they parted, Drucker went directly to Easton's apartment to tell her the news, but he found no one home. The same was true the next morning when he tried again. He was distressed to find that once again her door was locked, and there was no response to his repeated knocking, though at one point he could have sworn that he'd heard a rustling on the other side of the door.

When Drucker returned to his own apartment after his second attempt to find Easton, Wes was already there, waiting outside his door, looking like an unkempt sheepdog, with his curtain of wavy blond locks shading his eyes.

Though Drucker hadn't been able to find Easton to inform her of the recent turn of events or to collect her money, he didn't want to lose the opportunity to buy the bonds off Wes, especially—if he was honest with himself—given what he'd learned the previous evening about the increasing value of those bonds. After all, why should Wes be the only one to benefit from the good fortune of the Phoenix Trust now that there would be so much of it to go around? Easton should have her chance at profit, too. Or at least someone should.

Drucker led Wes in out of the bitterly cold late December wind and up the single flight of stairs to the door of his apartment, where he stooped low to lift the corner of a loose floorboard to unearth his key.

"Wes, you now know every secret I have," said Drucker as he slipped the key into the lock. "I ran away from life at a bank, and I keep my key under that floorboard." He rotated the key to the right and then, when it had done its job, stooped low again to place it back in its home underneath the floor. "I don't think there's another man in the world that I would trust to know so much about me."

Wes nodded at this but his expression was fixed, his eyes narrow behind their shaggy blond veil. He looked at the board that Drucker had maneuvered back into place. "Pleased to have earned your trust, Drucker," he replied quietly, tapping the floorboard with the tip of his cane.

Drucker and Wes spent the next hour hunched over the small square table that, along with a pair of rickety chairs, happened to be the only furniture in the apartment other than Drucker's bed. Their conversation proceeded in fits and starts; Drucker did his best to make it seem as if he was not bargaining with Wes so much as advising him. An experienced banker helping out a novice investor.

Buoyed by the recent dispatch from Horton, Wes was reluctant to part with the bonds, so to keep the sale from stalling, Drucker was forced to keep increasing the amount that he offered Wes on Easton's behalf. Though it worried Drucker that he hadn't had the chance to discuss with Easton exactly how much she was willing to pay for the bonds, he had her instruction to buy as many as he could, and so Drucker continued to chip away at Wes's resolve not to sell.

With each new offer, Drucker wondered more bitterly if Easton would even appreciate the great lengths that he was going to for her. Buying lucrative bonds away from the only man in Jerome, perhaps the only man in the world whom he felt he could trust, was quite a generous favor to her. Drucker found himself wondering why exactly he was willing to fight quite so hard on her behalf, until finally it dawned on him that he was no longer bargaining on Easton's behalf at all. Somewhere between the news that Wes had shared on Saturday and the rebuffs that he gave on Sunday, Drucker had glimpsed the opportunity to return to Austin as an even richer man.

Though Drucker may have been trying to convince Wes to sell, it was *he* who had become convinced that if he could succeed at the arduous task of getting Wes to sell him the bonds, he would have earned the right to keep them and cash them in on his own behalf, not Easton's. And since Horton had told Wes that the bonds could be redeemed right after the first of the year, he would only need to wait in Jerome for a mere matter of a few more days before Horton was sure to return for them.

If Easton were to resurface during that time, Drucker could simply tell her how Wes had refused to sell—which he had, in the beginning—and she would never be the wiser. With Wes's hatred for Easton as strong as it was, she wouldn't be able to get close enough to him to ask him directly about the bonds, and if she somehow did, surely he would never give her a straight answer. Wes had no interest in getting within spitting distance of Easton. Certainly he wouldn't just open himself up to a battery of personal questions from her about his recent investment.

Thus, Drucker became determined to buy the bonds—but for himself, not Easton—no matter the cost, and it was his desperate offer of $5,000 that became his final one. Wes accepted Drucker's entire haul from the Flagstaff violin swindle, a sum that far exceeded the face value of the bonds, in exchange for half of the bonds that Wes owned. It was a drastic move but, based on what Wes kept repeating about the expected returns, by Drucker's calculations it was sure to be a profitable one. So he paid the princely sum proudly, and though he had just traded away nearly all of his cash, Drucker felt that he had never been richer.

When Wes left the apartment, Drucker tucked the bonds under his pillow where he had kept his stack of bills before he had bartered them. Every time that he slipped his hand under the pillow to check on them, every time that he lifted it just to make sure that his bounty was still accounted for, the feel and sight of bonds, rather than the bills, caught him by surprise. Though he knew full well what he had done, was aware of what he owned and what he no longer did, Drucker was still taken aback by what had transpired between himself and Wes. It surprised him how quickly and how violently he had swerved off course from his original intention to buy the bonds for Easton and get out of town right away.

But despite his bewilderment at the sudden change in his plan to leave Jerome as quickly as possible, he also felt excited by the late breaking amendment to it. After all, the New Year was just four days away. A few extra days in Jerome could mean doubling or even tripling his money when he cashed in the bonds. Then he would finally be able to attend to the overdue task of getting back to Austin.

The wait would be well worth it, he told himself, if it would mean returning to Austin that much richer than when he left it.

⇥⇤

Not wanting to risk running into Easton and having to explain himself if he could avoid it, Drucker waited out the rest of Sunday, all of Monday and first half of Tuesday in his apartment. He didn't bother unpacking his valise or stepping out for a drink at the saloon or even so much as cracking a window, in case Easton were to drop by and see the sure sign that he was home.

It wasn't until Tuesday afternoon that he finally succumbed to a case of the fidgets and decided to venture out to get a breath of fresh air, a phrase that he never thought he would utter under Jerome's smoggy cloud cover. As he approached the seventy-two-hour mark in his tiny flat, though, Drucker felt certain that he was better off stepping out, even if it meant a run-in with Easton, than to remain cooped up in his apartment any longer, breathing and rebreathing his own overused oxygen.

So on Tuesday afternoon Drucker left his apartment, tucking the bonds securely in his pocket and the key snugly in its hiding place under the floorboard. He took lunch at a nearby canteen, placing only a light order of red beans and johnnycakes to conserve the meager budget he had left after cutting the deal with Wes. When he had finished, Drucker ducked into the saloon, but not even a generously poured mule skinner could save him from feeling uneasy, and after just one drink, he left.

He hardly made it ten steps past the doors of the saloon, though, before he was stopped cold in his tracks by the sight of Yumi running toward him, her face streaming with tears. Though his first instinct was to turn away, by the time he thought of it, it was

263

already too late. Before Drucker could so much as turn his head in the other direction, Yumi had run right up to him, panting and pulling on his coat sleeves when she was within arm's reach.

"Drucker!" She bent forward at the waist to catch her breath. "I've been looking all over for you."

"Yumi, what's wrong?" he asked, placing one hand on each of her shoulders to calm her shaking. "What's happened?"

"It's Easton," huffed Yumi breathlessly. "She's leaving town."

"Leaving town?"

"Yes!" cried Yumi miserably. "Tonight!" She let loose a single violent sob but quickly contained it and looked at Drucker with urgency in her eyes. "She told me that I had to find you. She needs to tell you something before she goes."

"Tell me something?" repeated Drucker. "Tell me what?"

"She wouldn't say what. Only that it was urgent, and that she might never see you again."

Drucker's mind darted between the best and worst scenarios. "Where is she now?" he asked.

"At the train station!" wailed Yumi.

Drucker felt a wave of relief wash over him. It would certainly be easier to wait out Horton's return to Jerome without having to worry about running into Easton at every turn. He didn't want to lie to her about the bonds. He didn't want to talk about them at all, in fact, which would be significantly easier to pull off if he never had to see Easton again. With her gone he could quit skulking around Jerome for the remainder of his days there. Even if it didn't clear his conscience, at least her departure would relieve him of the worry that he might run into her.

Meeting her at the train station would do exactly the opposite. It would mean questions and answers and a cruddy, cluttered conscience, and Drucker didn't want that. He didn't want to see Easton at the train station, or anywhere else for that matter, and he opened his mouth to tell Yumi as much when he was suddenly struck by a different thought: *why would Easton be leaving town so suddenly?*

Before Drucker could venture a guess, a different thought, like another cross-body blow, landed a jab. *What was it that she had to tell him?* There would be no way to know unless he went to the train station.

Despite everything he knew about Easton, Drucker couldn't help but think that if she had sent Yumi running all over Jerome to find him, it must be with good reason. Maybe she wanted to give him her half of the violin loot to thank him for trying to buy her the bonds. Of course he hadn't actually tried very hard to buy them for her, but she didn't know that. At that very moment she could be feeling both generous and indebted toward him, and unless he went to the train station to find her, he would never know—or benefit from—just how generous and indebted she was feeling.

So instead of telling Yumi that he had no interest in finding Easton, Drucker thanked her for the just-in-the-knick-of-time tip and handed her his handkerchief to dry her tears.

"You keep it," he said gently when she tried to hand it back to him when she was through.

Yumi smiled sheepishly at his chivalry, but in truth he couldn't have taken it back at that moment if he'd wanted to. He didn't have a free hand, what with one busy patting the bonds in his breast pocket to make sure that they were still safely stowed there and the other fingering the change he had left over from lunch to make sure that he had enough for a carriage to take him to the train station to find Easton for what he very much hoped was one last time.

CHAPTER THIRTY-SIX

Drucker arrived at the train station just as the sun was setting. He darted through the depot, glancing briefly at the clerk to whom seven weeks earlier he had handed back the ticket that he hadn't been able to afford without the contents of his wallet. Drucker felt a flash of embarrassment as he passed by the man in his booth, but the clerk took no notice of Drucker as he breezed through the building to the platform on the other side it. When he got there he saw Easton, looking forlorn, her jacket draped over the bag that she held in one hand, a flat white ticket in the grip of the other.

"Easton!" Drucker called, picking up his pace as he jogged toward her. Easton looked up at the sound of her name, and her wrinkles of worry seemed to dissolve when she saw who it was calling her name.

"Drucker!" She looked relieved to see him approaching. "You're just in time."

From behind her, the whistle of the approaching train shrieked the news of its arrival, and Drucker and Easton both turned toward the round nose of the steam engine as it nuzzled into the station.

"Yumi said you had something important to tell me," said Drucker as the trickle of passengers with any reason to disembark in Jerome did so.

"Yes, that's right," said Easton, inching toward the train. "I wanted to tell you...to tell you good-bye."

Drucker could feel a flame of irritation at her, but also at himself, ignite in his chest. "That's all? Good-bye?"

Of course she hadn't wanted to give him her half of the loot. He chided himself for being half-witted enough to rush out to her. For making such a foolhardy decision, he deserved it to be for nothing.

"Yes," said Easton. "I'm awful glad for the chance to say it, too."

"All aboard! All aboard!" called the conductor.

"You mean to say you sent Yumi on a mad dash through Jerome just so you could say good-bye to me?" demanded Drucker.

Easton nodded wordlessly, and Drucker fought the ungentlemanly urge to sock her. He stood very still, trying to marshal control over his nerves and muscles, unclenching his fists lest they act out on their own. *Good-bye, Easton,* he thought in the silence. *Good-bye and good riddance.*

A moment passed then, he nodding at her, gritting his teeth, she nodding back, an odd sparkle in her eye that piqued Drucker's curiosity and compelled him to finally ask, "So where are you off to?"

"Oh, I'm not goin' anywhere," said Easton, inching closer still to the train.

Drucker stared at her. "I don't understand. You just said you wanted to say good-bye to me. We're at the train station. Now you're *not* going anywhere?"

Easton nodded stoically. "I *do* want to say good-bye to ya, Drucker," she replied evenly, "but, ya see, it ain't me who's doin' the leaving." She lifted her chin and looked him straight in the eye. "It's you."

Drucker looked her up and down as if examining her for protruding signs of insanity. It was at that moment that he noticed that the bag under which her coat was draped wasn't her valise. It was his.

"This is for you," she said, extending the ticket toward him, placing it between his flexed fingers and nudging them until they wrapped around it.

Drucker continued to stare at her. "Surely you must be joking."

"'Fraid not," said Easton. She shook her head as she lunged toward the train and flung his bag up onto it through an open passenger door, giving him the choice to either follow it or stay and hash things out with her on the platform at the risk of losing his every last possession.

Drucker looked frantically toward the train and then back at Easton.

"Easton, what in hell—"

The train grunted and lurched and the conductor cried out "La-ast ca-all! A-all a-board!"

"It's been nice knowin' ya, Drucker, but it's time we parted ways," said Easton with a little wave.

At that moment, the last railroad official left on the platform stepped up on to the train, entering through the same door through which Drucker's luggage had. Drucker lunged for the train just as the wheels completed one full revolution. By the time they'd completed a second, Drucker had both feet up on the train, but his bag was still out of reach. Taking the time to retrieve it would mean losing the chance to jump off the train before it was too late, leaving Drucker with the choice to part ways permanently with Easton or his bag, and only seconds to decide which it would be.

Drucker lunged for the bag and as he did he could hear Easton's voice calling out from the platform, "This is what you wanted, isn't it, Drucker? To leave Jerome?"

Drucker clenched his teeth. On any of his days in Jerome save for the last three she would have been right. It was only since he'd begun counting down until the day that he could meet Horton that his wish to leave Jerome had become less urgent. Drucker instinctively reached for his breast pocket and pulled out the bonds. He waved them at Easton as the train pulled him farther away from her.

"Easton, I've got the bonds!" he shouted back, as if revealing this piece of information could possibly have any impact on the train's increasing velocity.

That very acceleration had already caused the train to travel too far for Drucker to be able to tell if there was any response from Easton, and so he quickly turned back to the task of collecting his valise. By the time Drucker could retrieve his bag and ready himself to jump off, though, the train was moving entirely too quickly over the rocky, mountainous terrain for him to land safely on the ground. A hasty assessment led him to believe that he could make the leap, but he would have only a coin flip's chance of surviving it. So instead of jumping off the train, Drucker scuttled to the nearest open seat, lifted the window and stuck his head out of it to watch Easton's form fade away. It wasn't just Easton's diminishing outline that he spotted in the distance, though.

Drucker's heart jumped into his throat as he realized that there was a man standing next to her—a man who, from that distance, would have been unrecognizable if not for his unmistakable combination of shaggy blond curls and a cane.

CHAPTER THIRTY-SEVEN

As the pieces of what had happened to him in Jerome floated and migrated together like pieces of a jigsaw puzzle in his mind, Drucker realized that, just as when he had left Austin, he was once again alone, nearly broke, and miserable on a train. This time, though, he had Easton to blame for it.

All indications suggested that she had robbed him twice: first she had taken all of the cash in his wallet, and then she had tricked him into handing over the far more significant sum of $5,000, to be precise.

Thinking of how Easton had wronged him time and again in the weeks that he had known her infuriated him. What incensed him most of all, though—more than the trickery, the thievery, the manipulation—was what he learned when the ticket taker passed through his car.

Despite the fact that Drucker had worn his heart on his sleeve with Easton for as long as he had known her, and in spite of the fact that he could not have been clearer in stating that his inten-
ion was not just to leave Jerome but to leave Jerome in order to

reunite with Margaret in Austin, when the ticket taker collected the flat white ticket that Easton had placed in Drucker's hand, he informed Drucker that the ticket was good exclusively for that train, which was bound not for points east toward Austin, but rather for points west. Toward California.

V. LOS ANGELES

CHAPTER THIRTY-EIGHT

When the train pulled into the final station stop of its westward journey, all passengers were ushered off, including Drucker, who stumbled off of the train and into Los Angeles, feeling bleak, looking haggard, and intermittently raising the back of his hand to his forehead to check for signs of fever.

Though his temperature never veered from normal, Drucker nonetheless spent the next several hours wandering around the depot as if in a fever dream, feeling little connection to the physical world. He floated aimlessly from one corner of the station to the next until finally being shooed from the premises by a uniformed guard. Drucker had briefly tried to convince the man that he was not actually a vagrant, despite the signs to contrary, until Drucker realized that it was he, not the guard, who was mistaken.

What else could one be called, after all, who is penniless, homeless, jobless, and who is drifting off a train whose destination means nothing to him? Forget what one could be called. What else could one actually *be* in such a state?

Drucker eventually obeyed the guard and wandered out of the station just as aimlessly as he had wandered around inside of it. He walked for one hour and then another, vaguely aware that he was walking toward the sun and that if he was indeed in California, then walking toward the sun at such an hour of the day would lead him to the ocean sooner or later.

It did, late that afternoon.

Reaching the ocean restored in him—if just for a moment—his faith in the laws of the physical world, and the sight of the Pacific, its blue waves recasting themselves as white foam as they crawled up over the sand, restored in him—if just for a moment—his belief in the beauty of it.

Drucker walked for another half an hour, this time heading north up the length of the beach, his heavy shoes digging into the sand with each step. The air was warm like he had not felt in months. The sun had a relationship with the beach quite unlike the one that it had with the desert in December. As his pale cheeks warmed and darkened like hotcakes on a griddle, Drucker could hardly believe that he was just one day removed from the biting winds that lashed the arid Arizona territory. How could a single day's journey transport him from the bone-dry, sooty-aired world of Jerome to this glittering seascape? *Could it have been more than just one day?* he wondered.

Maybe a whole lifetime had passed between the moment that Easton had tricked him into getting on the train and the one in which he trudged up the beach of Los Angeles.

When his legs could no longer carry his weight over the uneven sand, Drucker settled himself on a dune overlooking a pier that was growing crowded with people who, Drucker realized after a time, were making their pilgrimage to the sea to mark the last day of the year with revelry.

Observing the party-goers from a distance instilled in Drucker a dramatic kind of loneliness. He felt embarrassed by the spectacle of his solitude, though none of the revelers seemed to notice it. They paid him no mind as he watched act after act of their enjoyment unfold like theater before him. Scene 1: children buzzing with excitement, clustered into hives. Scene 2: gentlemen parading down the pier, each with an attractive lady on his arm, though none of them, of course, quite so charming as Margaret. *How nice it would be to ring in the New Year with her on my arm*, Drucker thought. An image of her innocently beautiful face sprang up in his mind. When her sweet pink lips parted, they asked him if he shouldn't have stayed in Austin, despite the risks. Immediately he regretted his original answer.

But then a different thought struck him.

Maybe he shouldn't have gone to Austin at all. He wouldn't be heartsick if he had never met Margaret in the first place. Perhaps he should have just stayed in Clayton. He could have been mayor of a very nice little town. But hell, if he had wanted to be crowned king just to sit on somebody else's ill-fitting throne, he should have just stayed in Atlanta in the first place. Being president of a bank might not have been his life's dream, but surely it would beat the backbreaking work that went on down in the mine. If he hadn't left Atlanta Southern, he might be unfulfilled, but he wouldn't be an entire continent away from home, alone and broke with nothing to show for his efforts to find...to find...

Drucker caught himself trying to remember what it was exactly that he had set out to find. If it was his long-lost governess Lucy, he had failed at that. In fact, he was twice as far from her as he had been when he set out from Atlanta to find her. He had reached the exact opposite end of the country from Boston: the beach of Southern California. He could get no farther away from her without taking a swim.

The thought of that failure pained Drucker, and his next thought was no gentler. He hadn't found what he was meant to do with his life, either. Or, if he had, he had gambled away his chance at it on a hand of cards.

Perhaps he really should have just stayed at Atlanta Southern after all, Drucker found himself concluding. But then he remembered: Atlanta Southern didn't exist anymore. *Would that have been the case if I had stayed, though?* he wondered.

The sun crept lower in the sky as the New Year's Eve revelers continued gathering on the pier. Drucker continued sitting on the dune, watching them. His thoughts on what to do next roared forward and then rolled back like the waves in front of him. He didn't want to stay in Los Angeles, but without the money that he had used to buy the bonds from Wes, he didn't have the luxury to go anywhere he wanted. He lacked even enough fare to go from Los Angeles to Austin, or even back to Jerome, for that matter.

The sun made cautious contact with the horizon as Drucker sat on the dune watching the waves rolling, the party-goers rejoicing. *Where can I go*, he wondered, *if I can't go back to where I've just been?*

At that moment he realized he had no idea where he *wanted* to go. For so long he had focused on getting away—running away from Atlanta, slipping out of Clayton, being forced to leave Austin in a hurry, trying to break away from the vicious cycle that Jerome had him in—that he hadn't stopped to think about where it was that he really wanted to go.

But then suddenly, with the next beat of his heart, he felt it. He knew where he wanted to go, and it tugged in his gut, like a hunger. The yearning to go home, to take off his shoes and slip back into his childhood bed so that everything that had happened since he had left Atlanta could just fade away like a dream at morning's light.

Yes, Drucker thought as another type of hunger began to set in; *I would so very much like to be at my mother's table once again.* He closed his eyes and conjured the smell of succulent sugar-cured pork wafting from the kitchen, and with it he could hear the familiar sounds that were as integral to mealtime as the meal itself. The whoosh of the door opening out from the kitchen, the tittering of Mary Alice as soon as she was safely back on the other side of it, the screeching of his mother's fork as it scraped against her fine bone china, as it had on the last night that he had seen her. Could he even remember the last words that he had said to her? That she had said to him?

Drucker strained, trying to remember, and the image of the long formal dining table came back to him first. A moment later, first his mother and then his father populated the memory, springing up one after another, seated at opposite ends of the grand dining room. Then Mary Alice joined too, dressed in her black-and white-servant's uniform, crisp somehow, despite the oppressive heat of a kitchen in an Atlanta July. There she came, and there she went, flitting in and out of their dining room, the bearer of cold cucumber soup. It was salty, that soup. Drucker could taste the piquant but creamy liquid pooling on his tongue. And then he could hear it: his mother's voice. *Too salty*, she had said, *too salty for me to stand.* Had those been her last words to him? Could they be?

No, thought Drucker, burying his head in his hands as he hunkered down deeper into the memory, covering his eyes but unable to block out the sights and sounds of that last night that were flooding toward him. It was his father's voice that he was hearing then, the fire rising up in his father's cheeks that he was seeing. *Get out*, he had roared.

Yes, Drucker could be certain, those were the last words that his father had said to him: *get out of my sight.* And Drucker had done exactly that. Gotten out of his sight, of his dining room, his house, his bank, his town. His life. And those words, *Get out*, those were the last that he would ever hear from his father. *They were also,* Drucker thought sadly, *my last memory of home.*

That is, his last memory, save for one. One that, when he remembered it, caused Drucker to turn suddenly to his valise and pounce on it like a feral cat launching itself onto prey.

The envelope. The envelope that had been lying outside his door on the morning that he'd left Atlanta. The one with the tall, swooping D on the face of it, in his father's looping longhand, his swirling black ink. Drucker had forgotten about it for months after tucking it away both physically and mentally, not wanting to accept another handout from his father, especially one born from the assumption—albeit a seemingly correct one—that Drucker couldn't make it on his own.

There was no room left in Drucker's heart for that foolish pride, though. Poorness and loneliness crowded it out. In the pit of his stomach, where just months earlier the satiety of hubris had him feeling full, the ache of desperation hollowed him out. He no longer felt too proud to accept his father's handouts. On the contrary, at that moment, Drucker felt eager to welcome them, impatient to find them, prepared to hunt for them.

And so, every last item in his bag found itself in the sand in the moments that followed. Drucker exhumed them all in short order to free up access to an interior pocket, nestled just above the floor of the valise. His fingers moved clumsily, trembling as they yanked at the zipper and plunged into the silk lined pocket where they scrounged frantically until finally latching on to what might as well have been a gold nugget.

Drucker brought the envelope close to his eyes to see it clearly in the evening's diminishing light. He was pleased to find it as he remembered it, marked with the **D** inscribed in his father's gentlemanly hand. Feeling the weight of it, the bulk between his fingertips gave him the frenzied, disbelieving relief of a desert wanderer stumbling up to an oasis. He looked up toward the darkening heavens and shook the yet unopened envelope, tears rushing to his eyes. *Thank you,* he whispered, *thank you, Father, for being right about me. I couldn't make it on my own, and I didn't know it. But you did.*

With those words, Drucker felt himself starting to weep. The tears clouded his vision so that the pier and the people on it and the lapping ocean and the sun that it had half-swallowed all blurred together. Relief and agony mingled behind his eyes, the combination of the two fueling his tears. He wept not just with but also *because of* his relief at finding the money that he needed so desperately at that moment, and he braced against his agony over what it meant to need it. Reaching the point of needing his father's money and utterly failing at becoming his own man felt not like two separate defeats but a single, devastating one. If there was a difference between them, he couldn't see it. The line there too, had blurred.

After a moment, Drucker wiped his eyes, steadying himself as he prepared to tear into his little white treasure chest. As his finger swiftly slid under the months old adhesive, he wondered not *if* he would find money, for of this he was certain, but rather just how much of it he would find. His father had been known to be a generous man when the spirit moved him, and though he had not been one to part easily with his money, Drucker felt confident that if his father had gone to the trouble of leaving him money at all, the sum would be significant. A gift like that, from a man like that, would be to the patron as much a reflection of his own ability to bestow wealth as his wish for his beneficiary to receive it.

So how much would it be? Drucker eagerly speculated. Enough to travel wherever he wanted? Most likely. Enough to live comfortably for years? Perhaps. Unable to withstand the suspense a moment longer, Drucker vigorously upended and shook the envelope, letting its contents cascade down and out from their bone white sheath.

When he looked down at his lap a moment later, the question of how much his father had given him was answered. An even more bewildering question sprung up in its place, however, as Drucker realized that the pile of paper that had toppled from the envelope was not at all the type that he had expected to find.

CHAPTER THIRTY-NINE

Drucker stared with disbelief at what had fallen into his lap. His fingers would not have moved more gingerly were they touching a ghost.

Where was the money he had been expecting to find, the money he desperately needed? He shook the envelope, searching it and shredding it before finally accepting that his father hadn't filled that envelope with money. He'd packed it full of photographs.

But why? Drucker puzzled. He picked them up one by one, examining each with cautious curiosity. One showed his mother, seated formally in a high-necked collar, the muscles of her face pulled with characteristic tightness, looking not much different than he remembered her. One was a portrait of him as a child, his eyes bright as they stared off into the diagonal distance. Next came one that must have been taken on the same day, with Drucker in his same small clothes, posed dutifully at his younger-looking mother's knee. Then one with Drucker in the same getup yet again, but this time posing beside Lucy. Though it was evident that the two had done their best to keep their faces straight, the tiny creases beside their mouths gave away their smirking.

Further down the stack, Drucker found a few photographs of the house and its grounds, which just moments earlier he had so longed for. He found a few of the office, including one of the front exterior of Atlanta Southern, and one of his father seated in his high-backed chair, his pose still, his countenance earnest, his gaze thoughtful.

The last of the Atlanta Southern set surprised Drucker as much for his reaction to it as for the image itself. It was a photograph of the desk that used to be his, standing solitary in his former office. When Drucker turned the photo over, he found that it had been marked with an inscription on the back of it, noting the location and date that the scene had been captured. As he read those words, he smiled to himself. For all the grief that desk had given him, it brought Drucker comfort to see it once again. He smiled and nodded at the photograph, as if glimpsing an old friend across a crowded room, feeling deeply grateful that his father had given him this gift of memories. But why had he?

Drucker's question was answered when he reached the bottom of the stack and found a single white square of his father's monogrammed stationery with two lines of text positioned squarely in the middle of it.

I wish I had done the same damn thing.
In case you ever miss us...

Drucker read the words over and over and over again. Each time they led him to the same conclusion: his father hadn't sent him off with a life raft of cash, nor had he intended to. He hadn't, as Drucker had assumed, given his son money because he was convinced that he couldn't make it on his own. On the contrary, he'd sent him off with portable, little bits of home because he was convinced that he would.

Drucker mulled over that thought, and it briefly boosted his confidence before sending him shooting back toward the thought immediately preceding it: his father hadn't given him money.

Strangely, though, Drucker felt unexpected relief. Perhaps because not being given money meant not having to know that he had accepted the money, which he eagerly would have done at this desperate juncture. That soothed the ache of half of his momentous failure. If nothing else, at least he wouldn't have to live with the shame of knowing that his attempt at becoming his own man had culminated in accepting his father's charity.

Even if he hadn't accomplished much else in the last six months, even if he hadn't been able to hold on to his wealth or keep the company of the good woman that he'd found, at least he would not have raised the white flag, not yet at least. If nothing else, he wouldn't have that cross to bear, even if he *had* utterly failed at finding whatever it was that he was looking for.

Drucker shuffled the photographs between his hands, letting them glide between each other like cards in a deck, the little white paper with his father's handwriting eventually rising to the top of the stack. Drucker looked down at the tiny black characters. They sat on the page as still and as earnest and as full of thought as his father looked in the photograph that he had sent of himself perched in his high-backed chair in the president's office of Atlanta Southern.

Drucker read his father's words once more and as he did, he felt a wave of contentment wash over him as he realized suddenly that the very thing that he had been looking for had been with him all along.

He'd been carrying it with him.

CHAPTER FORTY

Slowly, carefully, Drucker tucked each photograph, save for one, back into the pocket at the bottom of his valise, feeding them one by one into the pocket's silk-lined cheeks. When he finished, he pushed himself up from the sand and began striding toward the edge of the gently lapping water.

The one photograph he didn't pack away was the one in which that lonely desk of his stared back at him. Something about that one snap touched him. He was mesmerized by the way that it could simultaneously serve as a reminder of everything that he had left behind in Atlanta as well as all the reasons that he had chosen to leave. He gripped it tightly between his fingers as he walked toward the water.

When he reached the swath of sand made smooth by the tide, Drucker stopped and shifted his gaze from the photograph in his hand to the expansive, dark water. He looked out at mile after mile of ocean, vaguely aware that below its surface there was an entire other, hidden world, kept safely out of sight from the human eye. The fact that there was no way to see below the rippled, opaque surface made Drucker itch even more furiously with curiosity. He squinted in the day's last dying light, but the topmost water hid all that lived beneath it. If he wanted to know what lay below, he would need to feel it for himself.

So, gently, Drucker placed the photograph and the two-line letter from his father into his inside coat pocket, letting them rest lightly against his chest. He reached down and took off one heavy, black shoe and then the other. He removed his stockings, tucking each neatly inside its customary companion.

When his toes were bare, he wiggled them on the cool sand, pressing them down, leaving an imprint that was washed away moments later with the next lapping of the tide. Again he pressed his toes down onto the smooth patch of sand, leaving his mark, and again the water washed away any sign that his toes had lingered there.

The water was uncomfortably cold as it rushed up and over the top of his feet. Instinct told him to remove himself from the ice-cold flow, to dry and warm his feet, to run back to the relative warmth of the dune. Something stopped him from listening to those whispers inside his head, though. He recognized the feeling that the winter water inspired in him. And so he took a step forward.

Drucker was ankles deep in the Pacific when the last sliver of sun disappeared over the horizon. A wash of pink filled the sky when the sun finally set on the last day of the year that had seen him spiral out into the world on his own.

When the sun descended out of sight, it took with it the year that he had left Atlanta as a would-be boy king, escaping his own coronation as president of the bank as if it were his scheduled execution. Gone then was the year that he had dodged the opportunity to be the mayor of a town that worshipped him, wed to a woman whose adoration he couldn't match. Gone was the year when he had met Margaret and the AG, surely by then known as the Gov to his cronies, including the conniving Horace who had managed to run Drucker out of town in the year that the sun had just set on.

Gone, too, then, was the year in which Drucker had gained a windfall and lost it all just as quickly and foolishly, blinded by his misery in the mines. Or was it purely greed that had obscured his vision? Either way, the sun had set on the year in which he had fallen prey to Easton and his own naiveté time and again, only to let her get the best of him in the end.

Now it was time, Drucker thought as he watched the ocean growing more peaceful under the darkening sky, to put all of that behind him. Practicality would dictate that he give up and go home, that he follow those instincts to extricate himself from the uncomfortably cold currents into which he had managed to submerge himself. And for a moment Drucker wondered if he wouldn't be a fool to do anything but exactly that. A smarter man than he might say that he had explored quite enough for one lifetime. Or that it was one thing to dream of finding out what he really wanted to do with his life, but that morning would bring the new light of the new year, and it was time for Drucker to wake up.

Yes, he thought, *a wiser man than I might say any of those things.*

Drucker knew in his heart, though, that insofar as the journey to become his own man was concerned, he had just begun to get his feet wet.

ACKNOWLEDGEMENTS

I t took seven years to write *A Northern Gentleman*. I am endlessly thankful for both those forces in my life that inspired me to keep writing, as well as those interruptions that slowed the pace of forward progress (i.e. my wedding, graduate school, a full time job and the dozens of books that I wanted to read that stole time away from the one that I wanted to write).

For me, the fun of (reading) historical fiction has been largely tied to watching imagined characters interact with real historical figures, in the tradition of some of my favorite authors of the genre, Gore Vidal, Caleb Carr and Selden Edwards, to name a few. To that end, I also find it important to demarcate, as these other authors have, where the line between fact and fiction is drawn.

Mining magnate-cum-railroad tycoon-cum Montana Senator William A. Clark, for example, is a real character from history. His maid and her lover, on the other hand, to my knowledge are not – at least not as depicted in this book. Jim Hogg, the Attorney General and Governor of Texas was real, as was his campaign manager Horace. While Hogg's interactions with Drucker May were a work of fiction, his adverse relationship with 19th century robber baron Jay Gould was real. As Attorney General, Hogg won a lawsuit that he initiated against the Texas Traffic Association, forcing Gould – who controlled several rail lines in the region– to refine his railroad related business practices in the state. Gould worried that if Hogg became Governor he would threaten Gould's profits further by pursuing the creation of a railroad commission to regulate the industry. As history reveals, Gould had reason to worry. It turns out he was right.

The rest of the characters in *A Northern Gentleman* were imagined, but like most characters that make it onto the page, they were all based in small or large part on real individuals from my own life. Maybe you are one of them, and if so, I thank you for your inspiring traits.

There are quite a few people who have meant a lot to me before, during and after the writing of *A Northern Gentleman*. There are too many to name, certainly. Still, I need to thank a special few who have really helped to shape this story and its author. With that I say a heartfelt thank you to...

... Everyone who asked me how my writing was going, and also to everyone who didn't ask but listened when I droned on about it anyway.

...My dear friend Lindsay who made me promise that I would pick back up those first fifty pages I hadn't touched in four years and not put them down again until I had finished.

...Author Alison Pace in whose MediaBistro novel writing class I developed and wrote the first chapters of this book.

...My editor, Victoria, who caught over 4,500 errors after I was fairly certain I'd caught them all.

...All of the wonderful teachers I've been so fortunate to learn from, especially my English and History teachers at Breck School. Your classes gave me a deep appreciation for the written word. You gave me confidence.

...Leslie Schweitzer, whose listening ear and instructive insight has helped me to breathe easier and gain some perspective when my will to do so was not enough.

...Anna and Sasha, who made me feel loved and at home even when home felt like it was a continent away.

...My brother Ross, a fantastic listener and songwriter, and my sounding board for every crazy and/or creative idea I've ever had.

...My parents, especially my mother, who has done me about fifty thousand great favors, one of which was letting me read my draft aloud to her. And to my Father who, over the years, has sent me hundreds of pictures and momentos of home and family, in case I ever miss them.

...Nana and Claire, to whom I sent the first chapters and who encouraged me to keep up the story telling. And to Babulya in whose apartment I did many, many hours of my best reading (and also napping). This book is dedicated to the three of you and the others who are no longer with us, in addition to those whose arrival we (anxiously) await.

...Google, in more ways than one. How were books written before Google existed? *This book*, certainly, simply could not have been.

...My best friend Alex and all of the wonderfully brave iconoclasts I've had the good fortune of coming across. Thank you for fascinating me, inspiring me and lending little parts of yourself to Drucker, who found in himself the courage that I saw in you to live life on your own terms.

And finally, to B, thank you for your bottomless supply of love, support, encouragement and plot twists. Drucker was only able to find the courage to walk away from his depressing day job and go seek the life he wanted to lead because you did. You're everything to me. Thank you.

Made in the USA
Middletown, DE
16 September 2015